JUN

RAG AND BONE

Also by Joe Clifford

The Jay Porter Novels
Lamentation
December Boys
Give Up the Dead
Broken Ground

Nonseries
Wake the Undertaker
The One That Got Away

Memoir
Junkie Love

Anthologies
Choice Cuts
Trouble in the Heartland (editor)
Just to Watch Them Die (editor)
Hard Sentences (co-editor)

RAG AND BONE

A JAY PORTER NOVEL

JOE CLIFFORD

OCEANVIEW PUBLISHING
SARASOTA, FLORIDA

Frank Turner "Song for Josh" reprinted by permission.

ISBN 978-1-60809-326-7

Cover Design by Christian Fuenfhausen

Published in the United States of America by Oceanview Publishing

Sarasota, Florida

www.oceanviewpub.com

10 9 8 7 6 5 4 3 2 1

PRINTED IN THE UNITED STATES OF AMERICA

You can measure the mark of a man on the day that he died

In the mixture of memory and wreckage that he leaves behind

*And I know you were carrying too much weight on the evening
when you slipped away*

But I loved you like a brother . . .

—Frank Turner, "Song for Josh"

In memory of my brother, Josh.

In the words of our favorite singer, Frank Turner,
I'll remember that you were better than your end.

I love you, little brother.

ACKNOWLEDGMENTS

As always, first and foremost, thank you to my lovely wife, Justine. Writing the Porter books is hard on me; it's harder on you. Jay's journey wasn't an easy one. Thanks for taking the ride with me.

To Holden: now that you can read, I want you to know that every day I look at you and your brother Jackson's perfect faces, you guys remind me all over again why I worked so hard to get off the streets and make a better life. I hope to give you boys everything I never had.

And in no particular order: thanks to Rich, Tom, Celeste, my baby sister, Melissa, the crime writing community, Liz Kracht, David Ivester, and the Oceanview Publishing team.

Last, a big shout-out to you, the fans. Anytime I was mired in rewrites, freezing my butt off in the frigid New Hampshire mountains, suffering anxiety attacks by proxy, wondering why I did this, I'd remind myself of your commitment. So many of you got behind these books. You believed in Jay. You believed in me. We've netted a couple Anthony Award nominations and hit the top of the charts more than once. In some small way, I hope we've shone a light on the marginalized and helped put a face on the addicted; and maybe in the process we made a few folks feel a little less alone. These accomplishments are owed to your enthusiasm, dedication, and support. Thank you.

RAG AND BONE

CHAPTER ONE

WHEN I STEPPED in from the snow and cold and pushed open the precinct doors, the first thing I saw was my face on the wall. A composite sketch that didn't look anything like me, faxed and faded, copied too many times, likeness unintelligible. Should've asked my ex-wife for a picture. No wonder they hadn't caught me.

Heads glanced up from desks, bodies twisting from the vending machine and water cooler, gazes frozen, locked on the eyes of a stranger. Their confusion was understandable. I had been gone a while. My beard was heavier and, for whatever reason, it had grown out much darker than the sandy mop up top. With my ragged, padded layers, hobo hat, and gloves, Ashton PD probably thought I was just another bum wandering in from the Turnpike seeking shelter from the storm.

One by one, they came around and the faces dropped. I thought Claire, the receptionist who used to go around with my dead brother, might collapse from an aneurysm. Another cop, a recruit who must've joined while I was away, reached for his gun, until Sheriff Rob Turley came beside him and eased his itchy trigger finger. Kid couldn't have been more than twenty-five, fresh from the academy, all jitters and methy, hopped-up pupils. Must've been champing at the bit over the chance to nab a real fugitive. Ashton,

New Hampshire, population two cows short of a graze, didn't see a lot of America's Most Wanted. At least before the drugs started coming in.

"Jay," Turley said, calm and authoritative, taking control of the situation and his tiny team. "A lot of people have been looking for you."

"Yeah," I replied, disinterested. "Heard. Came in to clear that up." I scratched giant ice chunks loose from my bushy beard.

Out the long windows, fat snowflakes lazed like balls of eiderdown through the haze of streetlamps. Patrol cars sat idle in the parking lot, buried beneath the snows of November. Blizzards could hit as early as October up here, folks digging their way out long into April. Life on the Mountain.

Turley asked if I wanted some coffee, and I said sure, swatting the snow and sludge off my knit cap, clumps plopping to join the puddles by my boots. Turley motioned for Claire to bring me a cup. No handcuffs came out, no rights were read; I wasn't brought into a cell. Turley acted like he was extending a courtesy. Of course, I knew they'd caught the real killers or I wouldn't be here.

The town sheriff escorted me to the interrogation room, a communal space that doubled as a place to chow down on hump day. An empty Dunkin' Donuts box lay ravaged in the middle of the table, a trail of powder and sprinkles, fat gobs of jelly squirted out the blow hole, evidence of carnage left behind at the scene.

Turley took a seat, squeezing his big belly between the chair and countertop. I peeled off my winter coat and placed my damp cap on the table, facing him on the other side. I offered my best country boy smile.

"Where you been, Jay?"

"Around."

"Around?" Turley leaned back, adjusting the belt around his gut. The weight he'd shed last time I saw him, he'd put back on, another fifteen added for good measure. "Doing what?"

"The usual. Working."

"Working? Any particular outfit? Town?"

"I moved around."

"Moved around?"

"Are you going to repeat everything I say, Turley?"

"You're telling me you didn't know New England's had an all-points bulletin out for you? A BOLO. Be on the lookout. From Maine to Connecticut."

"I just learned the authorities wanted to talk to me. Which is why I came in. Sorry for the misunderstanding."

"Misunderstanding?"

"Will you stop fucking doing that?"

"Sorry, Jay. It's just that you've been *wanted . . . in connection to a murder . . .* for the better part of the past year."

"Murder?" I tried my best not to laugh. I'm not sure my mouth was visible beneath my wooly bum beard anyway.

"Someone killed Owen Eaton. Proprietor of the Clearing House in Lake Winnipesaukee. Same day you disappeared."

"I know who Owen Eaton is."

"Of course you do. He was your competition. And everyone knows how much you hated the guy. Oh, and your truck was left behind at the crime scene. Where Eaton's head was bashed in. In his office. Where you'd just visited him. So, yeah, 'questioning.'" He did that air quotes thing with his fingers I hated.

I kicked out my boots and settled in. "I'm here now. Ask away."

Turley didn't have anything. I knew he didn't. If I'd stayed disappeared this long, I wasn't waltzing into the Ashton Police Department and handing my ass over. Unless I confessed to knowingly evading arrest, he had nothing.

"We found out who really killed Owen Eaton," Turley admitted when I didn't take the bait. "Two men. Andre and Dmitry Volkov. Seems they'd been hiding out at Gillette Gorge. One of the blinds up there. Their shack caught fire. Tried driving away. Couldn't see in the smoke and fog. Drove over a cliff." Whistling softly, Turley smacked one hand against the other. He paused, trying to look cool, avoiding direct eye contact, an interrogation technique. No big thing. Try and catch me off guard. Turley dragged a nonchalant finger through the donut aftermath. "Last year? Didn't you claim you had a run-in with a couple hunters out by the Gorge?"

I shook my head. "Different guys."

"I'm sure." Turley turned to face me. "When moose season started in October, a hunter found their truck on a glacial shelf. Took a few weeks but forensics retrieved the remains, DNA linked them to the Eaton murder." He caught my eye. "You don't seem too surprised by any of this."

"Should I be? Who were they?"

"A couple troublemakers. Brothers, cousins. Unclear. Did time though. Assorted criminal activity. In Russia. State Department got involved. It's a mess."

I swatted my hat and stood to go. "Glad it all worked out."

Turley hopped up, or as much as a man that size could hop, hand on cuffs. "Where do you think you're going?"

"You said you found the guys who killed Owen Eaton?"

"We did. But that doesn't explain where you have been for the past ten months. There's an APB out for your capture."

"Was."

"Was what?"

"There *was* an APB. There's not now. I'm not wanted for anything, am I?"

"I've got some questions. Grab some pine, bub."

"Did you just call me 'bub'?"

"Ten months, Jay. Ten months. Vanished. Gone. Without a trace. No contact with anyone. Including your son." He knew that would hurt. And it did. Not talking to Aiden for almost a year was the hardest thing I'd ever done. He held up both hands, showcasing all ten of his porky links, mouthing the word "ten" to hammer the point home.

"I can count without using fingers, Turley. What do you want me to say? Sorry I didn't know you were looking for me? I was out of state, man. You got the real killers. Where's the crime? Being a bad dad? Yeah, I'm guilty. But you can't arrest me for that."

"For not paying your child support, I can."

"My ex and I have a verbal agreement. And I doubt Jenny would pursue it."

"You must be real proud of that."

I bit the inside of my cheek. Losing my temper wouldn't help. My lack of contact with Jenny and my boy shamed me to the core. I'd always stayed up to date on my child support payments. No matter how bad finances got, no matter how well off my ex now was—I'd always pay for my child.

"Did you call to congratulate her on their new baby? A girl. In case you were wondering."

"I wasn't."

"Cut the shit, Porter. Jenny told us. Same day she told you she and Stephen were expecting, you informed her that you'd be going away for a while."

"I did." I gave him a second to make the connection himself. But Turley had never been the sharpest tool. "And that conversation took place *before* Owen Eaton was killed. So unless you're saying his bashed-in head was premeditated . . ."

"No one is accusing you of killing Owen Eaton."

"Then what are you accusing me of? Taking an extended vacation? Not leaving a forwarding address? This is America, man. People don't have to register with the state every time they take a piss." I double-tapped the table, then was out the door. I did not look back.

I made it as far as the blustery parking lot before Turley came huffing behind me. He looked so pissed, red, puffy face chapped in the stinging cold. For a second, I thought he might try to jam me up on some bullshit charge. My disappearing act had to have been a humiliating pain in his ass.

"You're right," Turley said, shoulders slagging. "Technically, you didn't break any laws. But let me give you a heads-up. You running when you did—"

"I didn't run."

"Fine. You leaving the region when you did, okay? You made this bigger than our little mountain town." He forced a chuckle. "Someday maybe we can sit down and you can buy me a beer and tell me how you managed to stay hidden all those months, with every state trooper looking for you."

"Sure, Turley, we can have a beer together."

"The Feds got involved. There was a statewide manhunt. You made folks look stupid. My advice: lawyer up."

"Lawyer? I didn't do anything except leave. No one told me I had to stay."

Now it was Turley's turn to shrug, ineffectual and smug.

"The case against Owen Eaton is closed?" I asked but I already had the answer. I'd been assured. My inside man had told me the case was closed.

"They know you didn't kill anyone, but the case is far from over."

"What the fuck, Turley? Is this about Adam and Michael?" I'd long railed against the Lombardi Brothers, who ran this place, blaming them for what happened to my brother, but I'd been out of the state so long, out of their hair for almost a year; I hadn't caused them any grief.

"Adam and Michael Lombardi don't like you any more than you don't like them. With their connections in the state senate, having the ear of local—and federal—law enforcement? They can cause you a lot of aggravation."

I pulled my Marlboros, fighting to light one against the icy gusts that never relented, doing my best to keep my hands steady. I looked out over the expanse of this small mountain town I'd never be able to escape. What made me think I could outrun my name?

"You might not believe this," Turley said, "but I'm glad you're okay." Before I could paint-by-numbers another response, he stopped me. "Where you staying? And, no, it's not so I can tell the Feds where to find you. They want to talk to you, they'll get in touch no matter what I say."

"Planned on crashing in a roadside motel for the night. Shower, sleep. Figure the rest out tomorrow."

"I was filling up at Hank Miller's gas station the other day. Know for a fact he hasn't rented out your old room above the garage." Turley checked a make-believe watch. "If you hurry, might be able to catch the old guy before he goes to sleep."

"Thanks, Turley."

"Don't thank me. You're gonna need all your money for a lawyer. Nothing I can do to get you outta this mess."

I ducked down into my winter coat, turning to face the next storm.

CHAPTER TWO

DRIVING OVER TO Hank Miller's place, I checked the clock to make sure I wouldn't be waking the old guy up. Almost ten o'clock, I was pushing it. Like most that age, Hank set his clock to the Early Bird Special. I was glad to hear he hadn't rented out my apartment. I couldn't risk coming sooner. No matter what story I was spinning back at the station, I returned after dark for a reason. I hadn't expected a hero's welcome. But I didn't anticipate having to deal with the Feds either. Maybe Turley was blowing smoke. Wouldn't be the first time he tried to scare me straight. You don't stay alive underground for as long as I had without having a direct pipeline to reliable information.

I was there the day Andre and Dmitry Volkov killed Owen Eaton. I knew they were guilty before they dragged me up to the blinds, where they would've killed me, too, if I hadn't been able to set fire to that shack and make a run for it. So high up the mountain, the elements vicious, I couldn't see two feet in front of my face. Neither could they. And the edge was a lot closer than any of us believed. I didn't think those bodies could be exhumed. Gillette Gorge's gully runs a mile deep.

Not sure I would've come back sooner, regardless. I had a job to do, people to find. There was a hard drive with irrefutable proof

Adam and Michael Lombardi had sent workers to die in toxic pits, their passion project the Coos County rehab built atop the blood of the betrayed. But I never found that hard drive, and everyone I needed to talk to was dead. *Welcome home, little brother.*

Hank Miller's house lights flicked on.

"Haven't changed the locks," Hank said, bundled up, slouching to the porch.

I didn't get the chance to offer excuses or promise to pay back monies owed before my old landlord slipped a key in my hand.

"In case you lost yours in your travels." His old eyes crinkled with a sad smile. "Replaced the thermostat, switched the electricity and heat over to my name. Couldn't risk having the pipes freeze."

"Thanks, Hank. I'll make this right."

Hank waved me off, and then turned and trudged back inside.

The second-floor apartment above the garage looked the way I'd left it. Which didn't reassure as much as it creeped me out. Like time had stood still and I was entering a museum harboring the artifacts of a dead man, everyday objects frozen, surrendered to wherever they'd last been used. The oven-baked ruins of Pompeii. An algae-covered tea set on the Titanic.

I lit a cigarette off the stove and cranked the heat. Then I cracked open one of the beers from the six-pack I'd bought.

Huddled on the dusty couch with a scratchy old blanket, I watched plumes of smoke rise.

* * *

Soon as I woke, I headed down to the Desmond Turnpike to find an Internet café. I appreciated Hank's leaving the power and heat on— November on Lamentation Mountain, I wouldn't have survived the night—but expecting access to the World Wide Web was asking too much.

I found a café near the Olympic Diner, the twenty-four-hour restaurant where I used to hang with friends back in the day, back when I had time to hang, back when I had friends. The girl behind the counter at the café wasn't entirely unattractive. But she looked so angry. A tattooed dragon crawled out her tee shirt, which read "Don't Make Me Say It Again." She recoiled in horror when I asked for a regular coffee. Maybe she was expecting something fancier, whipped froth or candied syrup.

I searched the web for a lawyer. Didn't take me long to find the name and number I wanted. I scribbled down the address and dropped an extra dollar in the tip jar on the way out. She still didn't smile.

Robert "Mickey" Asal was an Ashton High alum with a rinky-dink law practice down the Turnpike, a run-down strip mall before you got to Pittsfield, the kind of place where hoodrats got stoned in the summer.

Mickey and my brother, Chris, wrestled together in high school. Different weight classes. Mickey was tiny—not that my brother had been big—but in wrestling, where you are paired up by weight, being tiny isn't a disadvantage. Except when I saw him at his law office, Mickey wasn't so tiny. He was still short, but older now, portly and balding. When Mickey was paying his respects at my brother's wake, Adam Lombardi showed up. Mickey called him a douchenozzle, which ingratiated him into my good graces. Making small talk, I learned he was a lawyer and filed his name away for later. You never know when you might need a lawyer.

Like Chris, Mickey was ten years older than me. I prayed I held up better by the time I made it to forty-seven. At my going rate, I wasn't sure I'd last that long. I hadn't bothered to phone ahead.

He'd been my brother's friend, not mine. And I'd tossed my last burner phone in the Berkshires. I needed to pick up a new one.

The squat brick building that housed his practice used to be a Blockbuster Video, back when people left their houses to rent movies. There was no receptionist, no lounge. There were cracks in the drywall and the overheads clung to life like a radio station dying in the heartland. Best I could tell, Mickey's business relied on reducing speeding fines and contesting DUIs. Tacked-up posters showcased Mickey in mirrored shades, arms folded in tough-guy posture, superimposed in front of sobriety field tests, with quips and phrases like "Blow on this!" and "Who can say the alphabet backwards sober?" Then underneath: "Mickey Asal will get you back behind the wheel. Fast!"

Maybe I should've called ahead. Because he had no idea who I was.

"Jesus. Jay Porter," he finally said after I introduced myself. "What's up the with the lumberjack beard? You been hanging out with Francis Phelan?"

"I don't know who that is."

"You look like fat Elvis."

"Elvis didn't have a beard when he was fat."

"I meant Costello."

"I'm not fat."

"Well, you're bigger than I remember, and that beard . . ."

"I plan on shaving it. You have a minute?"

"For the little brother of an old friend? I'll make the time." There was no one else in the place. A hollow wind rattled weaker joists. He reached up to pat my shoulder but being so much shorter he ended up awkwardly slapping my flank. "Can I get you anything, Porter?" He motioned at an abandoned desk, one step removed from a folding card table. "Sorry. My secretary has the day off. You want coffee?"

The empty waiting area played like the inside of a Jiffy Lube, down to the pot of coffee that hadn't been descaled since the Bronze Age. Two vinyl chairs leaked stuffing.

"I'm good."

"Please then," he said, guiding me into an office not much bigger than my bathroom. "What can I do for you? Let me guess. DUI? Those fucking Ashton cops—"

"No. Nothing like that. No, I... I mean, and... um..." I scratched the chin buried beneath my beard, running through the various places to start. They all sounded ridiculous. Hired Russian guns? International assassination plot? I was just a guy who cleared junk from dead people's houses. "I don't know where to start."

Mickey checked the clock on the wall, one of those big round ones with the plexiglass protector you find in middle school. "How about you start at the beginning?"

So I told him about the day I stumbled on Owen Eaton's murder, how I knew I'd be blamed, forcing me to leave town and live like a nomad while evading capture. With each word, Mickey's expression contorted more, a man fighting the sudden onset of gas, betraying the clusterfuck I'd stepped into.

"How much trouble am I in?" I asked.

Mickey plucked an Altoid from the tin, popping it in his mouth, snapping the lid shut without offering me one. "Depends," he said. "Got five bucks?"

I could see Mickey wasn't crushing it in the Friends Don't Let Friends racket, but I hadn't expected being hit up for money this fast. Whatever. I'd given that angry girl at the coffee shop a dollar for little more than snarling at me. I fished one of the few remaining bills from my pocket.

Mickey snatched it from me, a squirrel on an apple core. "That's my retainer. Which makes me your legal counsel."

"Might want to raise your rates."

Mickey laughed. A high, squeaky laugh, which evoked memories of my parents' kitchen, Mickey, Chris, Adam Lombardi, and the rest of the wrestling team hanging out after matches, my mother making fried dough, their girlfriends giggling, me scowling in the corner, jealous.

"Don't worry," he said. "If you need more than a consult, we can renegotiate. This transaction ensures that anything you say in this office will remain confidential. But if you want me to answer your question, I need to know the *whole* story."

He asked for it. I went back to where it all began and the stolen hard drive seven years ago, how my brother and I, along with my best friend, Charlie Finn, and that little runt Fisher discovered Gerry Lombardi was a pedophile, how later, after Chris died, we found out Gerry's sons Adam and Michael were bribing judges to lock up teens in order to win public support for their rehab, the Coos County Center. A townwide conspiracy. I skipped over the third part, my finding the missing Crowder boy, because it wasn't pertinent to my current predicament, and no one seemed to give a shit about that one. I told him about the toxic soil; how when I was searching for my then-girlfriend Amy's baby sister, Emily, I learned that the CCC had been built atop a mound of poisonous dirt—and the Lombardis had known all about it. It was all connected, and no one seemed willing to do a thing about it except me.

I was pretty riled when Mickey interrupted the backstory. "They really make that fat fuck Turley sheriff up there in Ashton?"

"Yeah. And then when I tried talking to the Coos County worker widows—"

"Man, I remember that tub of lard high on 'shrooms at Silver Lake and having to drag his fat ass from the freezing-tits water." Mickey pulled a pack of cigarettes from a drawer. Didn't offer one of those either. "Well, good on him. We're all getting older. Can use a little job security." Mickey smoothed a hand through the lingering strands on his pate. "This is all very interesting stuff. But I need to know *particulars*—where you went. After Owen Eaton was killed. Specifics. Save that 'needed a break' BS for Turley. Who did you talk to?"

"What difference does it make? They got Eaton's killers."

"Then why are you here?"

"Because Turley said I should talk to a lawyer and that the Feds were involved."

Mickey Asal finger-pointed a gun at me. "Listen, Porter. Being an attorney, I've gotten good at cutting to the chase. You were on the run because you knew too much. I get it." I didn't get a chance to object to the terminology. "Your beef with the Lombardi Brothers made you serious enemies. Forget about Adam, that douchenozzle. His brother Michael? He's in the state senate. Got eyes on governor. *That's* the real hurdle. And if he wants to pay you back for being a pain in their ass, yeah, there are a few charges they can level. Obstruction, evading, etcetera. They'd have to get creative. They'd be reaching. But it's possible. So I need you to be *one hundred percent* honest with me. Or I can't help you."

"I went down to Boston looking for a man named Bowman."

"What's so special about this Bowman character?"

"His real name's Erik Fingaard. Used to be the head of Adam Lombardi's security. That hard drive I was telling you about proves everything. I had reason to believe Bowman might have the hard drive. Or know where I could find it. At first, we thought the hard drive only contained dirty pictures of Gerry Lombardi with little boys—"

"Still can't swallow that one. Coach Lombardi? Molesting little boys? Gerry was a helluva wrestling coach, and I gotta tell you, his sons may be entitled pricks, but I spent a lot of time with the old man, in and out of the showers. A lot of other boys did, too. I didn't see anything that would suggest—"

"There's pictures. *Were* pictures. Doesn't matter now. Gerry's dead. Chris is dead. My best friend, Charlie—dead."

"Heard about Finn. Sorry."

"Thanks. But it's more than the pictures. There's something else on that hard drive."

"And this is the proof Lombardi Construction knew the soil where they built the Coos County Center was tainted?"

"Poisoned to the core. Killed the workers who'd helped build it. Paid off the widows and survivors. No one will talk."

Mickey Asal's eyes widened. "Another goddamn Erin Brockovich," he whispered to himself, and I could sense his attitude toward me changing, switching from placating a baby brother to growing giddy over the inevitable Hollywood treatment and billion-dollar payday.

"You talk to this Bowman character?" Mickey was so excited, eyes flashing dollar signs. Telling him felt like ratting out Santa Claus.

I shook my head. "Erik Bowman was stabbed in a prison fight. Dead."

"Jesus." He said it as contrition. Except I knew he meant it the other way. Took him a moment to recover. "What did you do with the rest of your time on the run?"

"Moved around New England, staying out of sight, staying alive."

"With every police force on the lookout?"

"Under-the-table day labor. Didn't call anyone I knew or loved." Meaning my ex-wife and son. "Then I read in the news that they found those bodies." I omitted a minor detail Mickey didn't need to know. What did it matter where I learned about Andre and Dmitry Volkov?

"When you get back?"

"Last night."

"Talk to your ex-wife?"

"Not yet. That's going to be a whole new shit show."

"Understood. Got a couple exes myself. Take my advice. Don't call her yet. I know you miss your boy, but we don't want the Division of Children, Youth and Families getting involved. Once they stick their noses into your business, we're looking at scheduled, supervised visits. Bureaucratic nightmare. Trust me—you want to avoid that at all costs. You have a phone?"

I shook my head. "I'm going to pick one up today."

"When you get a number, call me. I'll check out a few things, see how hot these boys are to make an example of you. I wouldn't worry too much. If no warrant was issued, any action runs the risk of your suing for false arrest. No one wants that. Then again, if their goal is to gum up your works? You've given them the ammo to cause grief, and if you need a lawyer to fight that? I'll give you the brother-of-an-old-teammate discount for a consult. But trial costs add up fast. Get your ducks in a row. Having a job helps if we go before a judge."

I thanked him for his time and stood to go.

"There's a Supercuts down the road on your right," he said, pointing at my beard. "Do yourself a favor and shave that thing off your face. Looks like a raccoon took a dump on your chin. You don't need a vagrancy charge on top of everything else."

CHAPTER THREE

SOON AS I walked out of Supercuts, I regretted taking Mickey's advice. Never mind that Supercuts is basically the Denny's of hairdressers; catching my reflection in the rearview, free of brush and cover, I longed for a rock to hide under. How had I let it come to this? How did I get so old? I once asked Hank Miller, who was now in his seventies, what he saw when he looked in the mirror. I wasn't trying to be mean; I wanted to know, because no matter how old I got, I still thought of myself as a sixteen-year-old boy.

"Truth be told," Hank said, "I see that same young buck I always have." He stooped over to pick up the snow shovel, creaking and wincing, hand bracing vertebrae with each arthritic roll. "But every once in a while, Jay, I'll see the years. Every wrinkle, every wrong turn, every heartache. And it scares the holy hell out of me."

The thing that stared back from the glass scared the holy hell out of me.

I'd packed on some pounds. Stress of life on the run, a fugitive's diet, the fast-food shits draining color from my complexion. My skin tone was pallid, a sickly mix of anemia and Casper the Friendly Ghost, like I was fighting off a perpetual infection, white blood cells working overtime.

Fuck this. I slapped the visor shut and headed home. I didn't bother getting that new phone I'd planned on. The only thing left for me here was my boy. If I couldn't see Aiden, what was the point?

Leaving Ashton, I'd had one objective: find that hard drive and prove Lombardi knew that soil was toxic. Once I learned Bowman had been shivved in the shower, existence became a game of survival. Stay one step ahead of the police, live to fight another day.

Spending a lifetime in estate sales, rummaging junkyards, mining castoffs, I'd gotten to know the day-labor racket well, which street corners yielded the best opportunities, how to manipulate the Home Depot hot spots for pole position. Most important, I had a line on the underground, the shadier outfits where they paid under the table. Cut out the taxman and there's no need for a pesky driver's license or social security number. This wasn't advertised, of course. Knowledge came via insider trading and a significant chunk of your pay to keep secrets safe.

In addition to fugitives wanted for murder, the day-labor scene attracted plenty of garden-variety scum. Deadbeat dads, junkies with failures to appear, domestic-abusing assholes, and run-of-the-mill drunks—there's no shortage of people wishing to remain anonymous.

Outside Worcester, I signed on with Labor Force, a shifty day labor agency where, for an added "service fee," you could get paid without an ID. The wages were already as low as legally allowed, but that didn't stop Labor Force's bloodsuckers from bleeding you drier. If you were stuck working for Labor Force, they had you by the short ones. The sad sacks who showed up at five a.m. weren't complaining to the Office of Consumer Affairs and Business Regulation. Which left contracted employees with fewer rights than illegal immigrants, and a take-home pay less than a truck stop waitress minus the tips.

Town to town, shacking up at assorted transient motels, I kept a low profile—and my mouth shut. The work was grueling, back-breaking, laying pipe or cable, sent down into sewers to fish out the crap clogging the line. They worked you till you dropped. Because someone else was always waiting to take your place.

Most of the men were addicted to something, evidenced by their blood-sapped faces if not palsied hands, but Labor Force paid at the end of every shift, which for a man feeding a daily habit is worth its weight in gold, even if the exchange rate was far from minted standard. After Labor Force siphoned their cut, convenience fees layered upon trumped-up charges, you'd be lucky to clear forty-six bucks. Which spelled a pack of smokes, six-pack of beer, and another night at a crummy motel with bedbugs feasting on your flesh.

Not everyone I worked with was a piece of shit. Sometimes I'd meet someone I could trust. I wouldn't tell them my real name, but we'd talk. I stopped worrying about who was hooked on which drug or how much they drank. As long as they were only harming themselves, what concern of it was mine? And pecking order doesn't matter when everybody's neck deep in the mud.

Sometimes these people offered places to crash, had rooms at their mother's house, apartments with beds, couches, cushions on the floor. Any night I didn't have to pay for a motel was money earned. You want to know the most generous people in the world? The poor. Because they know how much it sucks to go without. They'll rip the shirt off their backs, give you half so nobody has to freeze to death alone.

Crooked and sketchy as it was, Labor Force was the good times. At least I knew I'd be getting *some* money. But Labor Force had a limited number of assignments and, depending on the town, sometimes the work dried up. There was one rough stretch in the spring where, out of cash and out of options, I was forced to sleep at a shelter in Boston. Worst experience of my life, showering with strangers, looking at the emaciated shells of what men used to be, subsisting on the soft foods slipped from cans, boiled and bland, tap water that tasted like feet.

It wasn't long afterward that I landed in a Salvation Army, remaining there for the bulk of a rain-soaked April and May. Nothing in life is free, and at the Salvation Army you had to work to earn your keep. Fair, well, and fine. The proselytizing was tougher to take. I have no problem with God, even if we don't always see eye to eye. But I'd never been a fan of organized religion, and being forced to pray for shelter can rankle the most ardent believer.

The Salvation Army had different departments where you could work, some better than others. Hanging clothes. Sorting the shit that got donated. Kitchen duty. The Army took all comers. As long as you were willing to bow before their god, you didn't need identification. You also didn't get days off, overtime mandatory. The higher-ups had no problem using the free labor for personal gains. I spent three weeks constructing a deck on a Back Bay penthouse. Home was practically dipped in bronze. The executive who owned the place wouldn't let us use the toilet. We had to piss in a Gatorade bottle.

My time on the run gave me a lot of time to think. Living hand-to-mouth made me appreciate my junkie brother. All the years Chris was using, I acted like he was an inconvenience, on my best days. On my worst, I'd demean his being, demanding he be something he couldn't. Because it's easy to identify someone else's problems, point out how they should step when you aren't walking that mile. Drug problem? Stop doing drugs. No home? Stop being such a fuckup and get your shit together. When my parents died, I blamed my brother for not picking up the slack, for not carrying some of that load. It was his burden, too. Except he couldn't shoulder that stone. He wasn't capable. I expected my brother to have the same inner resolve I did. He did not.

My ten transient months on the open road offered a long, sobering look.

I stopped off at the Price Chopper for a six-pack and cold cuts, coffee, milk, sugar, the essentials. Maybe I'd grown used to being invisible, living off the grid so long, but each time I turned down an aisle I felt eyes boring holes into me. Like a celebrity sighting. But not the good kind. More like if you spotted Charles Manson rooting through the cooler for the best deal on booze.

Back at my place, I sat in my junker pickup and cracked open my first beer since yesterday, copy of the *Ashton Herald* splayed on the dash, ready to scour the Help Ads for some entry-level, minimum-wage bullshit. The cab was warm, and I needed a cold one. Being back here was tougher than I thought, too many memories, too many ghosts.

I set the beer on the console and fanned the newsprint, unsure if people advertised jobs in physical papers anymore or if everything was online. I didn't have a lot of time to wonder. The headlights fanned up the lot, stopping behind me. I couldn't tell the make or model of the black SUV, the glare from bright snows blinding. No one knew I was living here . . . Except Turley, who'd directed me here. I braced for the swarm of federal agents with their warrants and affidavits, sunglasses, M-16s aimed at my head, the beginning of the end for Jay Porter.

The door slammed and footsteps approached, crunching snow. When the face appeared in the side-view mirror, I didn't move.

I sat there gawking, which might've been why she felt the need to introduce herself.

"It's me, Jay. Alison? Alison Rodgers?"

Like I could forget Alison Rodgers. I met her a few years back. A boy went missing from a prominent family, hiding out at a rehab she and her husband, Richard, ran. I'd never love another woman like I loved my ex-wife, Jenny. But that didn't mean I didn't try. Alison Rodgers was out of my league, too perfect to touch, which made me want her all the more.

"I recognize you," I said, lighting a cigarette, playing it cool.

"Mind if we talk inside?" She nodded up at my apartment, shivering in her fur-lined ski parka.

"Of course." I hopped down, my nuts retreating into my lower intestinal tract. Having spent the past few months south in Massachusetts, I'd forgotten how goddamn cold this mountain got.

She followed me up the decrepit stairwell, lit by a single dangling bulb, and inside to my dismal little bachelor pad.

"Your sheriff friend, Turley, called me." She shook her hair free from her furred collar, blonde tresses that made my bitter old heart yearn. "I stopped by about a month ago. You were gone." Alison caught my eye. "I had no idea you were in trouble. I don't know what to say."

"Nothing to say. They caught the guys who did it. Big misunderstanding. You want some coffee?" I remembered how much those AAers loved their coffee.

"That would be great. Thank you."

I was glad I'd gone shopping so I could do something with my hands. "Are you warm enough?" I cranked the thermometer back up before she had a chance to answer. I hated getting warm on Hank Miller's dime, but I couldn't let my guest go cold.

I was happy to see her. I didn't say that aloud. All my nervous twitching must've betrayed it, though. She tilted her head, a knowing tell.

"What?" I said.

"I don't remember you smiling. You look good, Jay."

"I'm glad that's what you see." Either she'd make a helluva poker player or my perception of reality was way off. I looked like shit.

Alison helped herself to a seat, and I apologized for not having offered her one, and she said it was okay, and I apologized again but this time with an excuse, mumbling about social graces and time spent alone, her face pinching up, then I found my beer. For a second, I considered abandoning the drink—Alison was in recovery—but I was also sick of running from who I was. I brought her coffee over.

"You lost weight," she said.

"Funny. A friend of mine just said I looked like Fat Elvis."

"Yeah, I can see a little of the King. It's the snarl."

"He meant—never mind. Did you say you talked to Turley?"

"When I saw you weren't living here, I remembered you were friends with the sheriff. Small town, I figured he might know where I could find you."

"Nice to see you missed me so much."

I could've sworn she blushed.

Alison and I *did* have a connection. There'd been something between us before, and there was something happening now, playfulness, banter, flirting. The vibe in the room said it wasn't all one sided, either. Couldn't act on it, of course. She was married. A few years ago, right after Jenny left me for another man, I might not have had a problem sleeping with another man's wife. I'd have a big problem with it now.

"Wait," I said. "Why did you stop by in the first place?"

"I wanted to hire you for a job."

"What job?"

"Doesn't matter now. I already figured out what I needed to know."

"Which was what?"

"Nothing."

"Come on. I'm a big boy." I grabbed a seat at the table, spinning the chair around, straddling backwards. "Humor me." I waved over my apartment. "I've been gone so long. Cable's not hooked up. No Internet. Missing the drama."

"When Turley called this morning," she said, changing the subject, "he told me the man who'd been killed—what was his name? Owen? He said you two worked together."

"Not exactly. The same line of work. Antiques. Estate clearing."

"But he called it something else. Not estate clearing. Ragged something."

"Rag and bone man."

"That's it. Never heard that term before."

"That's because no one under the age of a hundred and twelve uses it."

Alison laughed. She had a great laugh, like her whole body was in on the joke, head to toe. If I didn't know better, I'd say she actually liked me. I tried not to let that lack of judgment make me think less of her.

"So this job?" I said. "I assume it was for money?" I waved an arm over my depressing, musty apartment. "Because if you're hiring, I have to say, you're catching me at the right time. I need to pay this lawyer . . ." I saw her face twist and I backtracked, holding up a hand. "I'm kidding. I don't need money that bad." Nothing terrifies the rich more than thinking someone is after their gold.

"A few months ago," she said, "there was some vandalism. Remember the farms?"

"Sure."

The rehab Alison and her husband ran worked with neighboring farms. The partnerships kept recovering addicts busy, and the farms, mostly sugarbushes, got someone to tap trees for free. Win-win.

"You want me to find out who was responsible for the vandalism?"

"Moot point. I sold Rewrite Interventions."

"Let me guess the buyer. The Coos County Center." Adam and Michael Lombardi. Of course.

"Sale was finalized a couple months ago. The CCC already dissolved the partnerships Rewrite had with the farms, rehousing patients into their facilities." There was that smile again. "I don't think they wanted the competition."

"No surprise." I'd deduced as much. Vandalism, strong-arming. This was the Lombardi MO. "Sorry to hear you lost the business, but I can't say I was a big fan of what you and Richard did."

I liked Alison. A lot. But during that job a couple years back, I learned Rewrite Interventions was involved in some questionable practices, including kidnapping teenagers in the dead of night, against their will. Yes, it was their parents' idea, and was done with explicit permission and blessing. These were troubled kids abusing drugs and alcohol. I appreciated it wasn't black and white. But it wasn't all that gray either.

"I know you were critical of Rewrite's practices," she said. "But our whole business model changed after Richard and I divorced."

Divorced? I hopped up, hurrying to rearrange groceries, hoping I wasn't smiling too wide. Forget personal interests, she'd always been too good for that jerk.

"You know," she said. "Maybe I do have a little work for you to do. Not as glamorous as investigating break-ins, but my house could use a few small repairs."

"I don't need your charity."

"It's not charity. Since Richard left, the house has been falling apart, and I don't have the time. Or temperament. Please. Until you find something more permanent. I assume you're good with your hands?" Was she blushing? Or just heating up from the cold? "I need a fence on the side yard put in. I know it's a bad time of year, the ground so frozen, but a town plow clipped it, and I need it back up. I miss my privacy."

"You could call anyone to do that."

"I could. But if I'm going to pay *some*one, why shouldn't I pay
you?" She smiled, looking beautiful as always; and in that moment
I knew doing busy work for Alison Rodgers was the last indignity I
could suffer.

"I appreciate the offer. It was great seeing you again, Alison."

I'd left town last November a business owner, fifty grand worth
of antiques in a warehouse now confiscated by a shiftless landlord
because I'd broken my lease. I was prepared to start from square
one, ready to re-climb the ladder. But that didn't mean the bottom
rung as a handyman.

CHAPTER FOUR

RESTOCKING MY PANTRY with food, getting plugged back in, landline, TV, Internet, the process of reentering the civilized world, I felt like a newly paroled ex-con. No, I hadn't done hard time, never been convicted of a crime. But I'd watched my share of "man out of prison" movies. And reputation proceeds. Anytime I left the house, visiting the Price Chopper in town or Hank Miller's convenience mart downstairs, I'd overhear the whispers. "Is that Jay Porter?" "I heard he killed a man?" I pretended not to hear. Like I pretended not to care.

I was a broken man putting his life back together, restructuring every detail, however mundane, and paying a pretty penny for the right. Since so many of my utilities had been shut off due to delinquent payment, I not only had to repay what I owed—which was considerable—I also had to double down on deposits, my credit ground into dirt. Meager savings depleted, I had no relatives to turn to for financial help. I had an aunt and uncle I hadn't spoken to in ages. Couldn't imagine they were too happy with me. Plus, I had my pride. I wasn't begging. Working day labor as a bearded bum on the run was one thing; I wasn't taking handouts in my hometown. I used to be somebody.

For the first couple days, I walled myself in, waiting for Mickey Asal to call or the Feds to show up. I wondered how long till Jenny learned I was back. She had a newborn at home. She also had my son, whom I hadn't seen in close to a year. If you don't have kids, you can't imagine what that's like, being denied access to your flesh-and-blood. For a father it was like losing a limb or an organ, and not an appendix or spleen either, but one of the indispensable, important ones. Aiden was living proof I was capable of good. I resisted the urge to drive by his school, glimpse him with my own eyes, catch his laugh on the wind. But Mickey had said sit tight. You listen to your lawyer. I didn't know how much trouble I was in. I didn't need to muddy already murky waters. Family services? Supervised visits? No, that wasn't happening. Not on my watch.

No work. No human interaction. Way too much time trapped inside my head. I was alone.

Besides me, three others had been there at the start. My brother, Chris, who was dead. My best friend, Charlie, who drank himself to an early grave. That left this little tech nerd, Fisher, whom I'd never liked. When I figured out Lombardi knew that ground was poisoned, I'd gone to Fisher. And he ratted me out to the cops, helping land my ass in the state loony bin for three days. Danger-to-myself bullshit.

The snows came. Instead of one big storm, which hits hard and fast and lets you recover, these early blizzards were a slow, steady onslaught. Despite my best efforts to push these theories and conspiracies from my mind, I could not.

While on the run, I stayed in the loop by making a friend in a chatroom. When I first started scouring websites, I was paranoid about a trap, a sting operation, authorities masquerading as allies. At any moment I thought *To Catch a Predator* might kick down my door with a pitcher of sweet tea. Eventually, I decided I had to trust someone; I wouldn't last long on my own. I was in an unfamiliar state, scrounging for day labor, ducking the police. So, like an overweight fifty-year-old working in a comic book store, I made my first virtual friend.

I found Wounded_King1180 one night while in an Internet café in Waltham. I wanted to be around—but not in—Boston because I needed to talk to Bowman. In those early days especially, the more visible I let myself be, the more danger I was in.

I wormed my way around the cyber underground, starting with environmental whistle-blowers, which led me to climate change deniers and all that horseshit, the lefty apologists and right-wing whackos, until I stumbled on a thread about corporate greed and contaminants poisoning the earth. I didn't come right out with what I knew about Lombardi and the Coos County Center.

Took a while but the Wounded_King1180, whatever his real name was, picked up on the clues, directing me to a private server. Turned out he—or she—also operated out of New England but, citing safety, wouldn't divulge which state. Anyone you meet on a conspiracy website is going to be, by definition, paranoid. But the connection proved invaluable. I learned Bowman was dead from the Wounded King, and he or she helped guide me home, breaking the news Andre and Dmitry Volkov's bodies had been recovered, Owen Eaton's murder rightfully pinned on them.

But there was still the greater pursuit.

With the Internet back on, I brought up the private server address I'd been given and left a message for Wounded_King1180. This was our arrangement: drop a note in the rabbit hole, as the King called it, and wait.

I killed time getting my living space back in working order. Snows continued their onslaught, slathering trees, autos, and poles, and I wondered if the power lines would hold.

Half an hour later, a message pinged back.

wounded_king1180: hows it feel to be home?

I grabbed another beer, a seasonal Sam Adams winter ale worth every penny of the extra four bucks I didn't have, and sat down at my computer, lighting a cigarette.

jay_the_junkman: weird. everyone looks at me like a criminal

wounded_king1180: thats what happens when u r accused of murder

jay_the_junkman: i dont think i can let it go, the lombardis, their father, the contaminated job site. i cant unlearn what i already know

wounded_king1180: like i ever believed u would?

jay_the_junkman: you do me a favor? find out what you can about the rewrite interventions sale. theyre a rehab up here that worked with local farms getting ex addicts jobs. i saw the woman who used to own it. she told me someone had been terrorizing the farm owners, hoping to scare them off from working with her clients. i think lombardi wanted her out. it worked. she sold

wounded_king1180: yeah i can do that. u doing like we talked about right? talk to me and only me. dont be sniffing around the lombardi bros, u r lucky u found me. keep everything on the dl until u have concrete physical evidence

jay_the_junkman: everyone thinks im nuts

wounded_king1180: if they didnt u would be dead by now

My signing off coincided with the pounding on the door. And that's what it was—pounding, not knocking, the angry, pissed-off calling card of the authorities. I popped up, peering over my computer, out to my porch and the fields of white. What was I going to do? Jump two stories, hope I didn't break an ankle, and make a run for it? The nerve damage in my left leg made me move about as fast as Big Papi. I was tired of running. That's why I'd come home. I was going to have to answer this call sooner or later.

I pulled open the door, hands high where they could be seen.

"Daddy! Daddy!" Aiden threw his arms around my waist and hung on so tight I thought I'd cry. "I've missed you *so* much, Daddy. Where'd you go? Why didn't you tell me you were back?"

I met my ex-wife's icy glare. If Aiden wasn't there, I was pretty sure she would've slugged me. And she'd have had every right.

Crouching down to eye level, I took my son's hands. "I'm so sorry, little man. I had to go away for work, and I just got back and because I was gone so long—" I glanced up at Jenny, whose anger wasn't abating— "I had to talk to your mom first, but I didn't have any way to get ahold of her." I shrugged, affecting a frown. "I lost my phone."

My son, now almost eight years old, let me know I couldn't get away with those little white lies anymore.

"You know where we live," Aiden said, eyes full of hurt.

"Honey," Jenny said, showing mercy. "Daddy wanted to surprise you!" My ex's eyes conveyed warmth and forgiveness for our son's sake, but I knew what really brewed behind those narrowed browns. "Why don't you tell Daddy all about school?"

Aiden led me by the hand into the living room. I peered over my shoulder at my wife, who went to my fridge and grabbed a beer without asking. Jenny rarely drank, and she'd just had a baby, which meant she was nursing. Two and two added up to one thing: she was furious and needed help calming down.

Fine by me. All I wanted was to spend time with my boy. We started making a fort out of the couch cushions, crawling inside to pretend. He snuggled right up to me, and the touch of his skin made me whole again, as if I just might pull through this.

An hour passed, my ex staying in the kitchen, giving us time alone; and for that I never loved her more. Regardless of my transgressions, Jenny never kept my son from me. She'd driven in the snow and cold, a couple months after giving birth, because I'd been too much of a coward. I wished I could blame my legal counsel who cautioned against making contact. But that directive only made my decision easier. No matter what lies I told myself, I knew the truth: I was ashamed.

Soon Aiden's eyes fell heavy, and my boy lay asleep in my lap. I carried him to my bed and covered him with a blanket. Then I slunk to the battlefield, prepared to face the firing line. Jenny had yet to finish a single beer but she appeared calmer, if only by degrees.

"Thank you," I said, joining her at the table.

"Fuck you, Jay."

"Jesus, Jenny. I wanted to call or send a message, but I mean, fuck, they thought I killed Owen Eaton. I didn't know what they told you."

"You think *for one second* I thought you were guilty?"

"I don't know. The last time I saw you was at a competency hearing, after I'd been locked up in a psyche ward. Which, I mean, let's face it, you had a hand in. You and your husband backed Fisher's play. You all ganged up on me."

"Because you were *acting crazy.*"

"I'm not disagreeing with any of that." I held up my hands, the universal sign that I didn't want any trouble; let bygones be gone. "I'm sorry. Soon as I knew I was in the clear, I came back."

"And are you? In the clear?"

"They know I didn't kill Owen, if that's what you mean."

"You were wanted for murder and fled the state."

"I was wanted for *questioning*. Big difference."

"Are you telling me nothing is going to happen to you?" Her eyes betrayed genuine concern.

"I don't know yet. I got a lawyer. We're working on it."

"How can you afford a lawyer? How did you stay alive for ten months? Couldn't have been working. A social security number would've gotten you flagged in a second. All of New England was looking for you. Unless you were working under the table? I can't imagine you'd be able to save money that way. Not that you've ever been able to do that." Jenny stopped. "Sorry. That was a shit thing to say. I was worried, okay? Every day I waited for the phone to ring or for some state trooper to pull up the driveway to tell me Aiden's father had been shot dead in some hotheaded standoff." Jenny pulled her purse. "You need money." She started counting twenties.

I tucked her hand back. "I'm not taking your money. I *owe* you money. I'll get you the child support."

"I don't need it. Stephen makes more than enough money."

"Do you have any idea how emasculating that is? I know you mean well and are trying to help, but I'm paying for my son. I got caught up in something."

"Oh, I'm well aware. Adam and Michael Lombardi. The same obsession that ruined our marriage, the same obsession you're letting ruin your life. When are you going to stop, Jay? *Are* you going to stop? Or do you have to die like your brother to prove a point? I'm sorry to say it like that but I'm not sorry I said it. Ever since Chris died, you've been a mess." She looked at my bedroom, where our little boy slept. "You missed a year of his life."

I hopped up, trying to keep my voice low so as not to wake him. "What the hell did you want me to do, huh? If I don't run, I am in prison right now. No one was buying my story. Two men dragged me up to the blinds in Gillette Gorge? Tried to frame me for murder? That Lombardi hired them? The police would've looked at me as crazy as you are right now. I can see you don't believe me. And you know me better than anyone on the planet." I closed my eyes and clenched my fists, fighting to keep my cool, unable to keep my legs from shaking. "I have no one. No one. Do you understand that? You have Stephen, your fancy house, your money." I opened my eyes, spreading an arm over my sparse quarters. "This. This is what I have."

"And whose fault is that?"

This was getting us nowhere. I grabbed another beer and saw it was my last. I'd made myself a promise. Six-pack a night. I'd had two beers, which meant Jenny wasn't finishing her first. She was on her third, and for someone so small, who doesn't drink, my ex had to be drunk. Part of me was impressed she held her alcohol so well. The other part wanted to point out she'd fucked up my rations by drinking half my supply.

"I'm going to make it up to you," I said.

My ex didn't answer.

"I owe you a congratulations," I said, trying to make peace. "A baby girl? What's her name?"

"Sophia."

"Pretty name. And where is Miss Sophia tonight?"

"With my mother, at the house." Jenny was back to seething.

"And how is my ex-mother-in-law? Still hate me?"

Jenny didn't answer that either, standing up, silent, stepping closer. Now I smelled the bitter taste of hops on her breath, which brought me back to those banks of Silver Lake when we'd steal away after summer parties to be alone and drink each other in. We could never drink fast enough.

"Listen," I said clasping my hands. "I know you have to get back, but I'm not sure you should drive—"

My ex-wife's kiss caught me by surprise. Not for long. I kissed her back, long and hard. Maybe it was the alcohol, which Jenny wasn't used to. Maybe it was relief I hadn't died. I didn't know. Didn't care. Next thing I knew we were in the living room, on the couch. My wife tugged down her jeans and panties, right there, our son asleep in the next room. She unbuckled my pants and climbed on top, pinning me down, guiding me inside her. It all happened so fast, a whirlwind. Felt like we were done in seconds, collapsing in heaps.

We woke like that a couple hours later, naked from the waist down, Jenny on top, keeping me safe and warm like a cozy afghan.

My ex-wife's eyes caught mine, switching from blissful confusion to wide-eyed horror. She jumped up, as if only now aware that our son could've walked in on us any second, or maybe she remembered she was married with a new baby at home. Whatever the impetus, she buttoned up, bolting into my bedroom, rousing our son awake.

Then I was saying goodbye to my boy as Jenny whisked them out the door, my head spinning. Jenny muttered to call when I got a new number, my sleepy-headed son turning over his shoulder with one last, "I love you, Daddy."

Then both were gone, out of my life again, back into the cold, dark night.

I watched her taillights disappear.

If her scent wasn't on me, I might've thought the whole thing a dream.

CHAPTER FIVE

I'D ALWAYS HEARD how tough it was for ex-cons to get hired. Before I walked that mile, I chalked it up to a lingering Hollywood stereotype. Folks get second chances. Doesn't everyone love a good story of fall and redemption? That would be a big, fat no. Because no one wanted to hire a man falsely accused of murder either. Like news of my pardon hadn't reached the mainland, soldiers unaware the war was over, still carrying on the prejudicial fight.

Trying to find work, I spent the next day pounding pavement, or crunching snow as it were, applying for any and every job. I started out with pride, sights set high. By the end, I was groveling for the night shift at the Gas 'n' Go. People who didn't know me acted disappointed in me, and those I did know treated me like a stranger. Either way, I wasn't finding a whole lot of employment opportunities.

What happened with Jenny last night? Had she left Stephen? Doubtful. Why, after everything, would she want to have sex with me? I couldn't imagine. I was hopeful, despite how much drama it added to an already dramatic situation.

Walking in and out of businesses with a snowman's tan, glassy-eyed thinking about my ex—how much I loved her, how much I'd lost, still high off the sex but carrying the desperation of a man out of money and options—I wasn't endearing myself to employers. I must've looked stoned. Most said they weren't hiring. The rest didn't bother stifling yawns. One threw out the application before I left the store.

Heading back through town, I swung down the Chamberlin Highway to my old shop, Everything Under the Sun. I'd been so optimistic when I opened my own business. Sure, it was small. But it was mine. I was the master of my fate. I'd always been a hard worker. This was my shot. When my old boss, Tom Gable, split for Florida, the move provided a kick in the pants. And I was up for the challenge. I'd been in the process of acquiring merchandise for the Grand Opening when I bumped into Andre and Dmitry Volkov.

The windows were boarded. A "For Lease" sign hung on the padlocked doors. Through dirty windows, I spied the empty floors. No surprise. The guy who owned the building, Daniel Hanratty, wasn't known for doing favors. He controlled most of the warehouse district, concerned with nothing but bottom-line and profit. I owed close to a year's rent. Once I defaulted, all that merch was Hanratty's, and he would've wasted no time selling it to the highest bidder to recoup losses. There was forty, fifty thousand dollars' worth in that warehouse, way more than I owed. But Hanratty wasn't the type to issue refunds.

All the work I'd put in, bidding and buying, going to flea markets and swap shops, clearance sales all over this godforsaken mountain, gone, lining another man's pocket. Story of my life. I wasn't feeling sorry for myself. This *was* life. Born with nothing, there's no point trying to come up. Soon as you get a little something for yourself, they'll be coming for it. If I had my old truck, I'd fire up Springsteen for some empathy, but my new junker pickup only came with radio. The oldies station was the only station that came in. If I never heard the fucking Eagles again, it would be too soon.

I decided to call Hanratty anyway. I had to at least try. If it was just me, I would've let it go, but I needed money for Jenny. I owed back child support, and that wasn't a debt I could forgive. I didn't want the aggravation, but since when did aggravation walk away from me?

"You owe for back rent," Daniel Hanratty said, the response I'd expected.

"Then subtract it from whatever you got selling my shit."

"There's nothing left over. I didn't get enough to cover what you owed."

"Oh, screw that, Hanratty. There was fifty grand worth of antiques in there."

"Says you."

"Says my inventory list. And I kept immaculate records." My "records" were scrap paper and whatever I managed to hunt and peck into a computer that wasn't inside anymore, also confiscated. Hanratty didn't know that. "You can expect to hear from my lawyer."

"Lawyer?"

"Robert Asal, attorney at law. One of the biggest in the goddamn state."

Patting down my coat, I found my Marlboros. I gazed over the horizon of this smoke-choked town, looming mountaintops spearing the northern skies, smothered in cloud, rendering me more insignificant than I already felt.

"You have your lawyer call me," Daniel Hanratty said, calling my bluff.

"I will. And if I don't get a check within the week, I'll have him countersue you for another hundred grand for pain and suffering."

Daniel Hanratty bellowed. "Ha! I think you brought that on yourself."

"I've been cleared of all charges—charges I was unaware of until I returned to town." I waited. "And good luck proving otherwise."

He hung up without a goodbye. Prick.

One option remained, the lone job offer on the table, a pity assignment from Alison Rodgers to do yard work. I'd never have a woman like Alison Rodgers, I knew that, but until now I'd been able to stand tall in her presence, hold my own, cast off witty one-liners, kid myself otherwise. This was me on my knees, hat in hand, the power dynamic shifted and dropped on its ear. But it was either handyman for Alison, or I had to take up Jenny on a loan. I decided to go with the devil I didn't know.

With the last of my cash, I grabbed a pay-by-the-month cell. I made two calls: Mickey Asal and Jenny. Both times I got voice mail. I would've liked to talk to Mickey. I needed his help getting my money from that tight-ass Hanratty. A long shot, no doubt. But without a lawyer, I had no shot. I was glad Jenny didn't pick up. Not that I didn't want to talk to her. I would've loved to get a read on what happened last night. But if she picked up the phone, I knew I'd stumble and say the wrong thing, because I always stumbled and said the wrong thing where women were concerned. There's a definite protocol with that stuff, an order the man has to follow, which questions to ask, knowing when to take charge and when to shut up and listen. This situation required finesse and romantic acumen, tact, none of which I possessed. And I feared confirming the truth: that her drunken come-on and our intoxicating sex was the by-product of alcohol and not something she'd want to face in the sobering daylight.

Alison Rodgers' number didn't make the cut during my myriad phone exchanges—I could barely remember where she lived, this saltbox in the sticks of Middlesex, a snow globe encased by evergreens and granite.

She wasn't lying about the house needing work. The eastern retaining wall twisted in a spiral from where the plow had clipped it, a row of apprehensive wooden slats frozen mid-topple like dominos. The driveway hadn't been properly shoveled, with just enough room to back in and out, leaving the rest of the snow to freeze and affix to the asphalt. Once the heavier storms of December began piling, she'd have a layer of permafrost that wouldn't thaw till spring. Walking up, I saw the railing to her steps had settled and needed to be reset. The porch light was burnt out, and the molding to the door cracked. Nothing imperative. But honest work that would keep me busy.

Alison opened the door with a warm smile. She asked if I wanted some coffee or tea, and I said sure, and when she asked which one I couldn't bring myself to say tea so I said coffee. My nerves were fried. Teetering on edge, humiliated that I needed this job, I wondered if Jenny was thinking about me. Not that coffee made my anxiety worse. I felt so displaced. My discomfort stemmed from more than Alison or Jenny or my being back in Ashton with so little left. I lacked purpose. Being on the run was harrowing but thrilling; in an odd way it offered identity. Now I was just a dude with a hammer looking for work, cobbling together enough spare change to eat, drink, and not be scared.

"I'm glad you took me up on my offer," Alison said.

I pointed toward the damaged retaining wall. "The town did that? I hope they sent you a fat check to pay for the new fence?"

"The first few feet of any property belongs to the town, so technically the part the plow struck belongs to them."

"That's bullshit."

"It is. But it's not worth the hassle for a few hundred bucks."

I nodded like I understood. And I did. For someone like Alison. I'd crawled through rivers of shit for less than a few hundred bucks.

"What do you need to get started?" she asked, checking the time.

For some reason, I'd fantasized about Alison standing at the window with her hot tea, watching me work up a good sweat, cue porn soundtrack. As she put in earrings, the final touch to an impeccable ensemble, sleek slacks, professional blue blazer, I accepted Alison Rodgers wasn't sitting around her house on a weekday. Helming Rewrite Interventions or not, Alison Rodgers had places to go.

"I guess money," I said.

"Right, we should talk about wages."

"No, I mean for supplies. Normally I'd do the work and settle up later, but you're catching me at a bad time." I gestured out the window. "I need lumber, fasteners, a heating system to thaw the ground."

"The hardware store in the center of town—you know the main road?" There was just the one. "I have an account with them. They have a small lumberyard out back. Give them my name. Do you have my phone number?"

I shook my head.

Alison plucked a small square sheet from a Post-It magnet on the refrigerator and scribbled digits. She counted out five twenties, fanning them like a full house. "That okay for now?"

I nodded and scooped up the bills.

"Okay," she said. "Wish me luck."

"What am I wishing you luck for?"

"Getting through a day of headaches?" Alison tried to smile. "Selling Rewrite comes with a lot of loose ends."

"How loose?"

"There was a fire at one of the farms. Part of what made me decide to ultimately sell. Turned into a PR nightmare. Now I have to deal with the insurance end of things, bureaucracy, lawyers and affidavits, liability waivers. Today? Deposition. Oh joy." Alison collected her keys from the counter, slipping one free. She pointed toward the gleaming steel fridge. "Help yourself."

I held up the key. "You always this trusting with strangers?"

"Strangers?" She laughed. I waited for her to add something else, but she just shook her head and walked outside.

I drove down to the hardware store, picking up the slats I needed to repair the fence. I'd already scoped out what Alison had in her garage, which wasn't much. I purchased an insulation blanket and some metal tubing, heat-resistant tape, a three-sided shovel. The storeowner was very helpful once I mentioned Alison's name. No wonder. This town didn't teem with pretty, single women. He let me borrow a ground heater, free of charge.

Back at the homestead, I slipped on the canvas gloves and my knit cap—I was unprepared for how cold it would be, spoiled by the warmer fall of the greater Boston area. I lay down the blanket, cutting a hole for the tubing, fired up the ground heater, and got to work. Three of the supporting posts had suffered irreparable damage. I knew I'd be there most of the day, the earth impenetrable bedrock.

Evening fell fast. Alison hadn't returned. The winds picked up, swirling snow, spitting ice, stinging exposed flesh, temps nose-diving below freezing. Being so close to finishing—and being such a hard-headed sonofabitch—I wanted to wrap up the project, cross it off my to-do list. I headed for the garage. Earlier, when I'd been scoping out supplies, I recalled seeing a battery-powered floodlight. Now that it was dark, I couldn't see as well. Another joy of pushing forty: my eyesight was turning to shit. I was feeling for the lights on the wall when I caught movement out the window, a shadow slinking along the back edge of the property.

My first thought: an animal, fox or coyote. I wasn't sure how high up the mountain coyotes ventured, but Alison's place in Middlesex

was still the flats as far as Lamentation was concerned. February saw
the bulk of coyote sightings. During mating season, it wasn't un-
common to spot one walking down Main Street. They never bothered anyone, clocking from afar, worried more about you than you are
them. It was possible one could be scavenging in these lean months.

But it wasn't a coyote. The figure moved like a man. My fears
flashed on those Feds Turley warned me about, a task force sent
two by two, securing the perimeter with night-vision goggles,
waiting for the cue to raid the garage and apprehend the fugitive.
But there was only one man, far as I could tell. Besides, if they
wanted me that bad, I'd been sitting, alone, in my one-bedroom
apartment above a gas station, for the better part of a week, doing
fuckall. Why a lone gunman in the dark? In the event of legal
fallout, I doubted a message would arrive via carrier pigeon. Maybe
the shadow man was a neighbor on a mission to borrow butter or
sugar, even though the closest house in either direction was at least
three quarters of a mile and slinking around the woods out here
was a good way to get yourself shot, Middlesex the preferred residence of 2nd Amendment crackpots.

The man crept closer to the back door. My junker pickup sat in
the driveway. The kitchen light was on. He was right above me,
shadow splitting the mudroom pane, distorted shape, ragged and
formidable.

A handle jiggled. Followed by a loud crack and crash. Shattered
glass, broken by an elbow or something harder. Robber? Out here in
Middlesex? This town wasn't like Ashton, where you got junkies
and lowlifes slithering in from the Desmond Turnpike, aiming to
swipe an iPhone for a quick fix. No bus lines ran through Middlesex.

I felt in the dark for a wrench or shovel, a weapon, prepared to
push open the door and confront this guy, whoever he was. Personal
welfare be damned. I might get my ass kicked but I'd at least be a

man about it. But I couldn't find a weapon, or the verve to make my move empty-handed. Instead I sat there, cowering in the dark. Maybe self-loathing would've eventually forced me into action, but I never got the chance. After the glass broke, nothing happened. No one entered the house. I peered through the window, and the man was running off, ducking into the woods.

What kind of a break-in was that?

I picked up the biggest shards of glass, sweeping the rest in a dustpan. Like an idiot, I ran a finger along the floor to make sure I'd gotten it all. I hadn't, and I pricked my thumb, dribbling blood all the way to the sink. One tiny pane. Of course, I'd slice my thumb. I paper-toweled a Band-Aid around the cut and went to fix the window. Too late to go to the hardware store now, I'd have to make do with what I had. Nursing my throbbing thumb, I dug out an old, oil-stained cardboard box from the garage, measured a square, cut it out, taped it up. The Mickey Mouse job resembled a low rider with its back window blown out, but it would hold for the night.

After I mopped the blood, I sat in the kitchen to wait for Alison, drinking mineral water out of fancy blue-tinted glass bottles, one eye on the knife block, the other watching the window for any unwanted visitors. A couple hours passed, and no one returned.

When Alison finally got back, she seemed surprised to find me sitting at her kitchen table so late. I guessed from her point of view, my being there could be construed as presumptuous.

"You're here, Jay?" She said it like a question.

I pointed at the broken back window. "Somebody tried to break in."

Alison stared at me, doubtful.

She wasn't looking where I was pointing, so I stood up, walked to the cardboard-replaced window, speaking more clearly. "Somebody. A man. Broke this window."

Alison went over to the back door, touched the cardboard. "Are you sure?"

"Well, I didn't do it myself."

She sighed with parental exasperation. "I didn't say you did. I meant—"

"What? The wind? A stray buck sewing wild oats?"

"Don't be ridiculous. Maybe, I don't know, you opened it for a cigarette and slammed it too hard?"

"I already told you. I didn't do it." I led her to the mudroom, pointing into the adjacent garage. "Was in there, trying to find a lamp to finish the fence tonight—"

"There's no timetable, Jay. I don't want you freezing. This is—"

"A handout. I get it."

"I didn't say that."

"These 'loose ends' with Rewrite?" I said. "Is there more to the story?"

"There is no 'story.'"

"When you left earlier, you seemed stressed out." I moved closer to take her hand, reassure her, comfort. "I'm here for you. You can talk to me."

"Talk to . . . you?" She laughed, pulling away. "Who are you, Jay Porter? I don't remember you being so . . ."

"Concerned?"

"Touchy feely."

"I'm trying to help. Someone was trying to get in here. Maybe he heard me in the garage and I scared them off." Which was a lie since I hadn't moved a muscle. "The bigger question is why he was breaking in to your house in the first place. I don't think this was a random robbery."

"It could've been." The expression on her face told me she didn't believe that either.

"Tell me about the vandalism at the farms."

"Before I sold Rewrite? Maybe vandalism's too harsh a term. More like harassment, nuisances." She took my hand, squeezing like a mother placating a little boy. "I doubt that has to do with this."

"If you tell me more about 'that,' maybe I can figure out 'this.'"

She wrinkled her nose, in that adorable way of hers that I'd managed to forget. "There is nothing that requires you to dust off those old investigator boots of yours."

"Those boots don't fit anymore, trust me. But I don't feel great leaving you out here all alone."

"Would you feel better if I told you I keep a gun in my bedside table?"

"I'd feel better if you told me more about this fire you're dealing with."

She grabbed a stool at the counter, patting the seat next to her.

"You remember the farms Rewrite partnered with?" Alison said.

"Of course. The sugarbushes." Sugarbushes were maple syrup processing plants, and a huge part of New Hampshire's and Vermont's economy.

"Besides sugarbushes, we also worked with other types of farms, cow, dairy. The fire was at a dairy farm, and because there was fertilizer there, it turned into a hazmat situation. Which changes the insurance, which is still tied to Rewrite. Or I should say tied to *me*. Since Richard left me high and dry. Because the authorities determined it was arson . . ."

"Arson?"

"I know what you're thinking. And, no, this is unrelated to Adam and Michael or any harassment to get me to sell."

"How can you say that? They are trying to force you out. This fire is what made you decide to cut bait." Two and two, Occam's razor, whatever you want to call it, answer plain as day and noses on faces.

"They already caught who started the fire. The owner of the farm owed a lot in back taxes. He torched the place to collect the insurance money, a straight-up cash grab."

"Then why are you involved at all?"

"One of our clients was there when the fire started. A sixteen-year-old boy."

"What's the boy say?"

"Nothing," Alison said. "He's dead."

CHAPTER SIX

No matter how many times I told Alison I felt uncomfortable leaving her alone, she didn't invite me to spend the night on the couch. And you can only push so hard without looking like a creep. People always assume the worst intentions. She didn't seem worried, so why was I? She'd hired me to fix up the house, grunt labor. Why was I itching to make more work for myself? I flashbacked to something Jenny said a long time ago, when she'd shown up on another cold winter's night to find me in the middle of another clusterfuck.

"I swear you seek out trouble," my ex said. "You want this. You yearn for drama, pain, tragedy."

Maybe Jenny was right. Maybe I did feast on problems. Made sense. Trouble gives you purpose. Trouble gives you direction. You either run toward it, or you're running from it, but at least you're not standing still with your dick in your hand, wondering what you're doing with your life.

A small avalanche diverted mountain roads. I got back at midnight. Soon as I stepped inside, the scent of my ex-wife hit me hard. Wasn't any particular hair product, lotion, or laundry detergent; her taste lingered beyond lavender oils and notes of warm vanilla sugar. Her presence was defined by the empty space left behind. She'd been here last night, her smell stamped, reminding me how much of my life was defined by absence, these people and things that once were everything to me, evidence of their removal painful, permanent, like the way you tongue the hole in your gums after a tooth is ripped out.

Pouring a cup of coffee, I checked my burner phone for messages. Nothing. Not sure what I was hoping for but I still managed to be disappointed. I didn't want to talk to anyone, didn't expect any fanfare over my return; I wasn't demanding a pie baked or parade thrown in my honor. Yet my feelings were hurt no one welcomed me home. If I hadn't been wanted for murder, would anyone have noticed I was gone?

My burner rang, and I took the call before registering the number. Hoping for Alison Rodgers, I instead got Mickey Asal, my lawyer on retainer for less than a Subway foot-long. Because, you know, tax.

"Apologies for calling so late," he said. "I didn't get your message. Different line. I have a few." He didn't need to explain why he'd need more than one telephone. "Anyway, you're good to go."

"Go where?"

"Anywhere you want," he said. "You're in the clear, Porter. Of course, the boys in Concord are pissed—I wouldn't get caught speeding there anytime soon. But their hands are tied. Like I thought. Any action runs the risk of a lawsuit. No one wants to take that chance."

Was Michael Lombardi afraid to poke the bear? Or did he have something worse in mind? Let me keep running in circles, drive myself nuts, pop in when I least expected. Or maybe I wasn't worth the aggravation. Not like I had jack on the brothers anyway.

I lit a smoke off the stove. "Could you do me a favor?"

"I think I already did you one."

"I know. And thanks. A lot. Huge weight lifted. This is something else—do you handle other areas of the law besides drunk driving tickets?"

"I handle a lot of different areas of the law."

"How about property law? The owner of the space I was renting sold all my shit while I was gone. We're talking, like, forty thousand dollars' worth of antiques. Even subtracting the year's lease, there has to be a few grand left. Can you make a call, write a letter, threaten legal action? Means more coming from a lawyer." I waited. "Of course, you get your cut. Whatever you think is fair." Half of something's more than half of nothing.

"Who owns the property?"

"Daniel Hanratty."

"That asshole?" Mickey said, chuckling. "Sure, I can do that."

Property law made me think of something else.

"One more thing, Mickey."

"You don't stop, do you?"

"A friend of mine, Alison Rodgers, she owned this rehab. Rewrite Interventions. She sold her interests, and now the rehab is being incorporated into part of the Coos County Center."

"And?"

"There was a fire at the property before the sale. It's complicated because her place, Rewrite, they partnered with farms throughout the state, and—"

"This doesn't sound like something I can help you out with."

Writing a letter for fifty percent of several thousand? That he was up for. There was no money in this, which is why I'd led with the moneyed gig. Lawyers.

"I want to know if my friend could be on the hook?" I said.

"I suggest asking your friend."

"It's a touchy subject. She's divorced. Her husband was a partner in the business. I'm worried about her safety."

I explained the scene tonight, the aborted break-in, how Alison was worked up over dealing with insurance companies, the impression of more than met the eye.

I heard Mickey take a deep inhale, the sucking, agitated breath people take when you ask to borrow large sums of money or want to use their truck to move shit.

"You've seen my law practice. It's budding and booming, brother."

Budding and booming, my ass.

"Sending off a quick letter on embossed legal letterhead? No problem. But I am too inundated to work pro bono."

"What if I hired you? For the little brother of old wrestling buddies discount?" I chuckled, laying on some of the ol' Jay charm.

Apparently, that well had run dry.

"You just said you're broke. Sorry, Porter. But doing favors for the baby brothers of old wrestling teammates doesn't pay the bills."

I thanked him for his time anyway, then cracked a beer from the day's six-pack and headed to my computer, dropping a message for my friend, The Wounded King. Waiting for him to respond, I poked around the web. I felt like one of those sad, pathetic losers who Googles their own name. But it was that kind of sad, lonely night.

Pick up the phone and call her, little brother.

The question was: Which one did I want to talk to?

I gave up thinking about the women driving me crazy, instead surfing the last year of my life, the details of a scandal I'd never escape.

The majority of articles focused on all the ways I'd failed as a man—shit husband, deadbeat father, lousy brother. I wasn't throwing myself a pity party either. The authors of these online pieces didn't pull any punches. Whatever happened to presumed

innocent? Most insulting of all, every one of these reports butch-
ered my occupation. Estate clearing involves skill, an ability to locate hidden gems—you have to make worthwhile what others have
dismissed as worthless. But in the papers, I was a "jack-of-all-trades"
or, my favorite, "Fix-it Felix," which is from this movie I once took
Aiden to see about a misunderstood cartoon character that gets sick
of always being the bad guy and decides to flip the script.

Seeking redemption from the public, I made the mistake of
reading the comment section. The comment section is not something anyone should ever read. Vicious. I could pretend these in-
sults didn't hurt my feelings—no one was around to see me crack
another beer and slam it—but it stung to be pushing forty and
reading the opinions of strangers that I should kill myself. Some
nights you want to pile on the pain. I queued Dylan's *Blood on the
Tracks*. If you want to feel like shit about all the lousy decisions
you've made in your life, you can't beat that particular record for
pure, unadulterated heartbreak.

Out of beer, all the stores closed, I switched over to the real killers,
Andre and Dmitry Volkov. I'd already read up on them from the
road. Not that it did any good. Might as well have never existed. No
origin, no history. Just two dudes from the former Soviet Republic
hunting moose out of season in Bumfuck, New Hampshire. Keyser
Soze had a more credible backstory. No one asked what they were
really doing in our quaint mountain town; no one offered a motive
for murder beyond run-of-the-mill robbery. I had my own theory—
shadowy operatives, enemies with agendas, a mission to bury secrets
in toxic sands. But that's all they were. Theories. Everything about
the past seven years of my life: a theory.

My computer dinged.

wounded_king1180: glad to see u r taking my suggestion to
heart

jay_the_junkman: leaving the past behind is easier said than done

wounded_king1180: as long as u r not talking to strangers on the internet. at least no stranger than me. lol

jay_the_junkman: i told you i wouldnt. any luck?

wounded_king1180: about the rehab? not really. corroborated everything u said. the rodgers woman sold it. guess she got it in the divorce

jay_the_junkman: her husbands a drunk

wounded_king1180: not surprising the coos county center would buy it, theyve been buying up rehabs in the area

jay_the_junkman: anything about a fire? one of the farms associated with rewrite interventions burnt down, i think it mightve sped along the sale

wounded_king1180: and u r wondering if the lombardi bros employed some muscle to commit arson?

jay_the_junkman: wouldnt be the first time they used scare tactics. remember the guy who got stabbed in prison, bowman? he started out doing that stuff for them, clearing riff raff from old truck stop motels when they wanted the real estate. fire is bad press

wounded_king1180: buying up the competition is solid business strategy. whats Alison say?

jay_the_junkman: shes tight lipped. plus its weird with her

wounded_king1180: what isnt weird with women? lol. give me a couple, ill see what i can find out

jay_the_junkman: i know weve never met but i owe you king. you kept me alive out there

wounded_king1180: dont go getting all mushy. ill see what i can do. stay safe porter

What did it say about my life that the best friend I had was on the flip side of a computer monitor, a cypher in the ether?

I pulled my chair next to the window and watched puffy balls float down as I sucked the dregs from the last bottle.

* * *

I woke with the dawn's first light, consumed by a ravenous appetite. I headed for my favorite restaurant. In high school, we practically lived at the Olympic Diner, the twenty-four-hour dinette on the Turnpike. When all this shit with the Lombardis started to go down, Charlie, Fisher, and I reconvened at our old stomping grounds, plotting for the future as we relived glory days. Now? Chris and Charlie were dead, Fisher out of the picture, and I was the last man standing. How long till I, too, was snuffed out? I wasn't being morbid or fatalistic. In my family, anything beyond forty constituted borrowed time.

Everything on the menu sounded delicious. My belly rumbled as I took stock of the last time I'd eaten a real meal. I ordered damn near the entire menu. Pancakes and corn beef, hash browns and mushroom omelets. Sausage links. Bacon. English muffin, bowl of fruit, Danish. You could still eat like a king for ten bucks at the Olympic. I slurped my coffee with renewed vigor, because sometimes just the act of nourishing a body constitutes victory.

I never got a chance to swallow a single bite.

My phone rang before the food arrived.

"Hey, Alison," I said, pouring a thick stream of cream. "I was planning on getting there by nine, if that's okay. Need to stop at the hardware store and—"

"Jay, can you come now?"

The fear in her voice was palpable.

"Did something happen?" I asked.

"Yes."

CHAPTER SEVEN

ALISON GREETED ME in the driveway, rattled and distraught.

"Thanks for coming so fast," she said.

"I'd just stopped off for a little breakfast first."

"Hope you got something in your stomach before I called?"

"Yeah," I lied. I studied her expression, which lingered between motherly concern and shell-shocked, abject horror. "You okay?"

She pulled me along with her head, beckoning me to follow around the side of her house, which splayed out much bigger than advertised. I'd only spied the backyard from inside or at night, and during such times perspective gets skewed.

Downslope, the property extended to the edge of the forest, the middle of the valley hidden, creating an optical illusion; its borders expanded with each step, fresh snow covering up any boot print. The landscape was so expansive, in fact, that the red stain didn't come into view until we were almost on the body.

A coyote. The animal hadn't met its fate naturally losing a show-down with a bobcat; its throat had been cut with a sharp blade, ear-to-ear, left to bleed out, slow, tortured, painful, as if to prove a point. Folks hunt up here. It's what they do. Not sure a bullet from a tree's any more humane. But there is a special place in hell for people who are this cruel to animals. The dead coyote had been dragged onto Alison's property from the forest to send a message. *Why would Lombardi and his boys still be harassing Alison after she'd sold them the business?*

"You get a lot of coyotes out here?" I asked.

Alison gestured to what at first I thought was a tool shed, one of those thousand-dollar extravagances you find at the Home Depot. Upon closer inspection, I saw the structure was an elaborate doghouse.

I glanced from the poor beast to Alison. "You have a dog?"

"Used to. Died last summer. Kept the coyotes away."

She glanced down at the cold, lifeless thing, which seemed to evoke a melancholic remembrance.

"What breed was the dog?"

"Huh? Oh, Shepherd Vizsla mix."

I thought about whether to mention the similarity in appearance between breeds. Could mean something. Or nothing.

"Poor guy had the onset of mange, shed everywhere." Alison was staring at the doghouse, correctly assuming what I was wondering. "I think he liked it better outside," she said. "Richard insulated the doghouse. Swear it retains heat better than my house." Alison glanced up at me. "Of course, we'd bring him in in the cold."

I returned my attention to the slaughtered coyote. A slick sheen of blood from the flayed skin glistened off the gray ice in the dim morning sun. Who would do this?

I thought back to the intruder, how at first, I'd confused him for an animal. I looked back at the doghouse, to the edge of the woods, traced the tree line to where the coyote had been deposited. I'd never heard a dog barking, not any of the times I'd been out to Alison's house. The trail of blood stopped before the forest. Which meant someone had killed the coyote out there, carrying the carcass and depositing the body by the doghouse. A lot of effort. This was personal.

"I have to ask . . . where is Richard?"

"Why?" Alison acted offended. Given my relationship with the guy, how our last interaction ended, the hostility wasn't entirely misplaced. "My ex-husband is living in Oregon. With an old drinking buddy. He calls some nights when he's had one too many, which is any more than zero, crying, blaming, bargaining, swearing he's getting sober. It's pathetic." Alison gazed wistfully into the woods. "I recognize the 541-area code." She stared at me, to the quick. "That's how I know Oregon. This wasn't Richard."

"Okay," I said. "Who was it then?"

Alison shook her head, covering her mouth, not able to look at the dead coyote.

"You sold Rewrite Interventions," I said. "If this is continued harassment—"

"This isn't about the rehab, Jay. Everything isn't about your hatred of Adam and Michael Lombardi. Can you just bury the damn thing? Get rid of it. Seeing it is making me sick."

"Sure, I can do that."

"You're not going to dump the thing in the woods, are you?"

"Of course not." What kind of man did she think I was? A rotting coyote carcass would attract every wild animal on the mountain.

"You'll bury him?" She pointed to the back edge of the property, beyond her markers. "Anywhere over there is fine."

Glad I had all the tools left over from digging posts. This was going to take a while.

* * *

By the time I wrapped up, my hands were blistered and bleeding. No one digs graves in the cold shadows of Lamentation Mountain, heavy-duty canvas gloves notwithstanding.

Alison sat at the kitchen island with her hands cupped around a mug of hot tea, her attention slow to return. Her eyes were bleary and red, as if she'd been crying. I was about to ask if everything was all right, but she cut me off.

"Done?" she said quickly.

"All set."

"Thank you."

"Alison, if this isn't about the vandalism—"

"The vandalism at the farms was months ago. Minor nuisances, meant to aggravate, hasten my decision to sell. This has nothing to do with the Lombardis or Coos County."

"What about Rewrite?"

"You know the work we did there. It was controversial. We boasted a high success rate, but I can't say every case was an unmitigated success."

"Some people walked away less than happy with your services?"

"Of course. It's the nature of addiction. A lot of times we were hired by well-meaning parents, but their kids weren't ready, or able, to get clean. Sometimes the children were stuck in the middle of a divorce or some other drama we didn't know about."

"Like Crowder?" Phillip Crowder was the boy I helped locate a couple years ago, the teenage son of a wealthy family harboring dysfunctional skeletons, albeit better dressed ones.

"Yes, like Crowder."

"Do you have names?"

Alison laughed. "Of addicts who relapsed? Drunks who couldn't keep the plug in the jug? Jay, the nature of the work my ex-husband and I did was defined by failure. About five percent of addicts clean up, five percent of programs work. Doesn't matter what the program is. This is one of the things I learned as I moved Rewrite away from a strictly twelve-step model, trying to

incorporate other disciplines, philosophies, approaches. Change
rankles people."

"A lot of unsatisfied customers, got it. Any standout examples?"

"I want to put this behind me. I don't think I'll ever get that coyote's cut throat out of my head. I hired you to do work around the
house, not investigate, all right? You don't need to 'figure it out.'
Thank you for taking care of . . . that . . . out there. I appreciate it.
I'll have more work for you tomorrow, if you want it. I need to get
this house in shape to sell."

I pulled back. "Sell?"

"Yes. In the spring. To get ready for the move."

"You're moving?" I didn't know why the news should surprise me
so much. Or why it felt like such a kick to the gut.

"I have a sister in Colorado. Going to stay with Annie and her
family for a bit." Alison forced a laugh. "Been a rough couple of
years."

Alison cupped her tea, staring out to the cold, gray day where I'd
buried a slaughtered coyote beyond the doghouse. I waited for more.
But she didn't say anything else, which I took as my cue to leave.

Walking out to my janky pickup, my burner buzzed. My initial
hope it was Jenny abated. Because Jenny calling could only be bad
news. The faint flicker that had buoyed me these past couple days
had been replaced with an inevitable truth: Jenny was married to
another man, with a newborn at home. Whatever the other night
had been about, it wasn't about me. Didn't matter. It was Mickey
Asal again.

"What's up?" I said, taking the call and climbing inside the cold
cab.

"Wanted to tell you I sent a letter to Daniel Hanratty," my lawyer
said. "Not sure what will come of it. But good luck."

I stole one last look back at Alison Rodgers, ensconced inside her warm home. Mickey didn't say goodbye, hanging on the other end.

"Was there something else, Mickey?"

I appreciated the update, but he'd already said he would draft a letter. Calling to tell me he'd done so seemed pointless.

"After we talked the other night, I dragged out the old high school yearbook. Guess I got a little sappy. Man, I miss your brother."

"I miss him, too." As crazy as Chris could drive me—and my idiot brother drove me nuts—not a day went by where I didn't think about him. Chris and I talked more now that he was dead. In death I could tell him all the shit I didn't have the guts to say when he was alive—that I loved him; that, no matter what he'd become, there was a time when he was my hero; that I would give up everything besides my boy to have him back. If you've never lost a sibling, maybe that won't make sense. But losing a brother is like being shorn a limb, and you know that no matter what you do, you will never, ever be whole again.

"I didn't know until the funeral," Mickey said. "How bad his life had gotten. None of us did. After high school Chris disappeared from our lives. Truth is, he'd already begun fading while we were in high school. Our last year wrestling, he'd started messing with drugs, distancing himself from the rest of the team, and, fuck, I wish—"

"There was nothing you could've done." I knew what he was thinking. The two biggest emotions experienced when someone dies: guilt and regret. For years I'd been choking on both.

"Anyway, this fire you wanted me to look into. The woman. Alison Rodgers." The call started to break apart, the mountain disrupting cellular signals. "Arson for sure. The Davidson County Fire Department's treating it that way."

"Who started the fire?" I'd heard the theory from Alison. I wanted corroboration.

"Billy Joel?" Mickey laughed. "Sorry. Shouldn't make a joke. People died. Besides, Billy Joel sucks. Whittaker Pruitt. Insurance grab. The farm had been underwater. Pruitt died in the fire, so he's not talking."

A raw howl ripped through the ravine. I tried to steady my hands to light a cigarette, the heat in the cab slow to warm.

"Got anything on this Whittaker Pruitt?"

"Fifty-nine years old," Mickey said. "Third-generation dairy farmer. Not married. No kids. But," Mickey added, "he had help setting the blaze."

"What makes you so sure?"

"Davidson County said Whittaker was halfway across town when the fire started. Seven witnesses place him at the Chili's in Littleton when he got the call."

"How'd he die then?"

"An explosion. An accelerant was used. Davidson County thinks he went in to retrieve something from the inferno. Evidence probably, cans of whatever that accelerant was. Blew up in his face. From what I hear, Whittaker Pruitt was a mean SOB. Never wanted to be partnering with a bunch of drug addicts. He'd been trying to dissolve the deal. That had been his father, Jewett's, arrangement."

"How did his father die?"

I couldn't hear Mickey's response, the connection interrupted; I waited for the transmission signal to reestablish.

"Mickey?"

"Pneumonia. Couple winters back. Whittaker had been trying to repair the damage. Jewett left them in debt up to their eyeballs. Checked the Davidson County tax records. That farm was being foreclosed on any day."

"Start a fire, get the insurance money." Like Alison said.

"Looks that way."

"Okay. Thanks, Mickey. I owe you lunch and a beer."

"I might take you up on that, Jay. Stay out of trouble."

I told him I would. But I knew I was right back in the mess.

CHAPTER EIGHT

MORNING WAS MET by an overnight sloppy storm, the wet goopy kind where the weather gets stuck in that in-between state, too warm for snow, too cold for rain. What you get instead is slush weighing down branches and antennas, sleet slicking street, saddling worlds. Nightmare for drivers, travel on the mountain a pain in the ass, detours in and out of valleys, two-lane backed up for miles.

Making my coffee, preparing to head to work, I got a call from Alison. She wasn't feeling well and said to take the day off; she needed a break. I started to say I'd be working outside and would leave her alone, when I realized that maybe the break she needed was from me. I'd pressed her hard about the fire yesterday, which, in hindsight, might've been the wrong move. I was trying to help but I'd grown lousy at picking up on social cues. I was trying my best to be more amenable, more likeable, but a year in isolation, washing up in gas station bathrooms, hardly improves interpersonal skills.

Hanging up, I was startled by the heavy fist on the door. I didn't need the calling card to identify Sheriff Rob Turley. I could hear him huffing. A big man, Turley didn't have an easy time climbing the two floors to my apartment.

I swung the door wide. Turley remained hunched over.

"I was making some coffee. Want a cup?"

"No. Thank you."

I resumed pouring a mug full, my back to him. "What can I do for you, Turley?"

"Car crash on Dead Man's Curve, up in the foothills." He stepped inside, trying to talk while still catching his breath. "Two dead. Including the drunk driver."

I took my coffee to the table. "Anyone I know?"

"Doubt it. One of the vics was a mother. Leaves behind a little girl. Eight years old."

"That's terrible."

"Mom was coming back from the mall in Meriden. Guy had no business being behind the wheel. Some sleazeball lawyer got him off."

I knew there was a reason he was telling me this, and no way the news wasn't biting me in the ass.

"Your pal, Mickey Asal," he said.

Since coming back, I'd resolved to be nicer to people, especially Turley. Most of the problems I'd had with the guy stemmed from him doing his job. I could be impetuous, impulsive. I ran hot, a real red-ass. Returning with my tail between my legs made it hard to hold my head up high. Which helped with the humility. It's a fine line, though, balancing the requisite amount of responsibility, being deferential while not letting people walk all over you.

Shit like this only made it harder.

"Why are you here?" I said. That the child was the same age as my son struck close to the bone. Turley knew it would. That's why he said it.

"Mickey Asal is a real piece of shit. You know that, right? You know how many DUIs he's gotten thrown out on BS technicalities?"

"How would I know that?"

"I know you went to see him," Turley said, oozing authoritative preachiness that pissed me off. "Care to tell me why you were talking to him?"

I ground my teeth and swallowed my grit.

Stay calm, little brother.

"Jay?"

"Because he's a fucking lawyer and *you*—you, Turley—told me to talk to a fucking lawyer last time I saw you at the precinct—"

"I didn't mean a low-rent dirtbag like Mickey Asal—"

"Don't like my choice in legal counsel? Sue me."

"I find it very coincidental that you didn't return to Ashton until *after* we nabbed the Volkovs." Not a question.

"This is what's got your panties in a bunch?" I got it now. Must've stuck in his craw that I escaped on his watch. And this was not an insult he planned to suffer lightly. "Because you didn't get the chance to jam me up for a crime I didn't commit?" I pushed up from the table. "I have to get to work."

"Got a job already, eh?"

"Yeah, I got a job. Or is that against your laws, too? Want me to sit around my apartment waiting to die?"

"Where you working? Stocking shelves at the Best Buy in Pittsfield?"

"Why do you give a shit?"

"Or is it out at Alison Rodgers' place?"

"None of your business. What are you doing? Keeping tabs on me?"

"Where Jay Porter is concerned, I'm making it my business."

"Where 'Jay Porter' is concerned? I'm standing right fucking here. Why are you talking about me in the third person?"

"Answer my question."

"Yes, Alison Rodgers. Who lives in Middlesex, which, last I checked, isn't in your jurisdiction." I snared my winter coat off the back of the chair, dumping the coffee in the sink. Out of commission so long, the coffeemaker wasn't producing its finest work. "I need to go."

"Please tell me you're not playing private investigator again."

"I don't have to tell you anything. But, no, I'm fixing up her house."

"Anytime I hear the word 'rehab' where you're concerned—"

"For one, Alison sold Rewrite Interventions."

"And I know who she sold it to, too. The Coos County Center. And we *both* know who runs that."

"Adam and Michael Lombardi. So? They run half the goddamned state. Listen, man, I'm trying to get back on my feet. And I need money to do that, okay? So if you don't mind, I have a job to get to."

"I have a job to do, too. And that's keeping this town safe. For the year you were gone, know how many people died in Ashton?"

"Zero?"

"Zero," Turley repeated with profound satisfaction. Then, just to bug me, he okayed his sausage fingers into an "o." *Then* repeated "zero" again, this time mouthing the word, silent. "I don't need you causing trouble."

"Causing trouble? Right. I'm a real bad-ass dropping fence posts."

Turley shook his head, fishing expedition low on line. "I don't know your game, Porter . . ."

I waited for him to fork his fingers, motioning between his eyes and mine, pantomiming he'd be watching. Instead, he swatted his sheriff's hat, tugging it back on his fat head, tipping the wide brim, exiting without another word.

I slammed the door shut after him. Asshole. I checked my phone, although I wasn't sure why. Alison didn't want to see me. Nobody wanted to talk to me. Why was I here? I felt like Phil Collins making a new record, the comeback nobody asked for. I dropped a note in the rabbit hole. Waiting for a reply, I scoured news about the fire in

Davidson County. Good thing it happened while I was away, or I would've gotten blamed for that, too.

I didn't need Mickey Asal's help. The bulk of the story was right there, if I wasn't so fucking lazy.

My mental state had improved a lot since last year. I no longer needed anti-anxiety meds, lingering panic attacks easily managed by sticking to my "six-pack-a-night" diet. I wasn't going anywhere today. I got a head start on the beer, reading up on details of the fire. The accelerant used was a compound of various heating oils, including kerosene. Which was also the problem, since among accelerants kerosene is the most likely to explode. Two dead: Whittaker Pruitt and a sixteen-year-old boy whose name was being withheld because he was a minor. Plus, he'd been sobering up at the farm and rehabs are confidential, even in death.

I needed food, stomach roiling. I braved the snow and slush and hit the grocery store for easy-to-heat meals. While I was there, I bought a case of Michelob, because that made more financial sense than purchasing a six-pack at a time. I'd have to be more disciplined. I opened one in the parking lot, fighting off the creeping sensations that threatened profound moments of lucidity—and after a few beers, I was feeling pretty fucking lucid. Paranoia. But unlike my previous battles, the paranoia didn't attack from the peripheral; it hit head-on, all at once, descending through windshield and roof, a slow-rolling wave rising up beneath the thin metal of this piece-of-shit truck, through the soles of my big, brown boots, travelling along my nerve-damaged leg. Like the limp left in its wake, the injury had become such a part of me I sometimes forgot it was there.

Mothers loaded stuffed sacks into their cars, wholesome shit like vegetables and milk, fresh meats, staring at me, scowling, and I couldn't tell if their stink eye was because I'd become notorious in this small mountain town, another no-good Porter brother accused of murder, or because I was dressed like a bum, in a rust-bucket truck, drinking beer in the parking lot at nine a.m. during a snowstorm.

When I thought I saw the ghost of Erik Bowman, with his shaved head and neck tattoos, standing by the Price Chopper automatic doors, I accepted my tolerance wasn't what it once was and slammed the truck in drive, heading home.

Back at my place, I made for the computer and found a message waiting in my in-box. My invisible friend, the Wounded King. I filled him in on the latest, the visit from the dipshit town sheriff, Mickey Asal's client's car accident, the accelerant used in the fire. I had a good buzz on so I rambled longer than I'd intended. But the Wounded King was good company. How fortuitous, I wrote, using my favorite ten-cent word, that I'd found him lurking on conspiratorial websites—one targeting corrupt politicians like the Lombardis. Thirty-seven years old (can you imagine?) and my only friend could be a twelve-year-old boy or a seventy-six-year-old woman, who's to say? For all I knew, the King could be part of a sting designed to take me down . . .

Wounded King1180: u okay jay?

I pinched the bridge of my nose, willing myself back to sobriety.

jay_the_junkman: sorry. lot of shit going on bro. no one in this town understands what were up against

wounded_king1180: lombardi

jay_the_junkman: who else? ive been doing this dance for almost a decade man. close to 1/4th of my life. i know they are guilty but i cant prove it. maybe its time i bypass the law, take matters into my own hand. did you ever see the dead zone?

wounded_king1180: stephen king?

jay_the_junkman: he wrote it, yeah. but im talking about the movie with christopher walken. johnny smith, christopher walken in the movie, he sees something no one else can, an undeniable evil, and knows that no one will believe him. he talks to his psychiatrist who basically gives him permission to assassinate the guy

wounded_king1180: what guy?

jay_the_junkman: the guy in the movie! martin sheen, the one whos going to start a nuclear war! whats his name, greg stillson. walken knows because he touches his hand and sees the future

wounded_king1180: sorry, not following

jay_the_junkman: maybe i need to do what walken does

wounded_king1180: what did walken do?

jay_the_junkman: shot the mutherfucker

wounded_king1180: i think its time we meet face to face

CHAPTER NINE

SINCE THE OLYMPIC Diner served breakfast all day, I ordered the same meal I did the other morning, the one I never got to eat, plus an extra pancake. I needed the afternoon grease and carbs to sop up the too many beers I drank killing time before the meet and greet.

When I got to the Olympic, I'd been riding a good beer buzz. Meeting the Wounded King face-to-face, I'd soon have an ally. The Wounded King had been fighting the good fight from afar, committed to stomping out the same injustices I was, working to see the same criminals held responsible. Now he was stepping out of the shadows, into the light, making our mission real, satisfaction within reach, possible. Thank God New England was so small. The King said he could be there within three hours. I'd been lying to myself that I could forget what the Lombardis had done. I would never be able to rest until I saw them pay. This realization, coupled with the evaporating alcohol sucking me dry, brought me crashing back to Earth.

Sobering up with a bottomless cup of coffee, I wasn't surprised to see Fisher standing beside my table. I wasn't angry with him like I'd been last year, when he'd ratted me out to the cops. I just didn't want him to run into the Wounded King because then I'd have to explain who he was and what we were doing there, introductions and that whole headache, which would've only added to the one I already had, the hangover that comes from draining piss water and the faint aroma of diesel fumes wafting in from a busy thorough-fare. Fisher didn't wait for a hello or an invitation; the little runt plopped right down, flagging the waitress for a coffee.

He'd ditched the glasses he didn't need, but the ponytail was longer. Sideways move. Just seeing his ugly mug again gave me angina. I waited till the waitress left.

"Hey, man," I said. "I don't have time to talk." He didn't budge. The nerve of the guy. What was he waiting for? Absolution? Fine. If it would make him leave. "Listen, we're good, okay? Last year? Ratting me out to the cops? Water under the bridge." I glanced at the front door, waiting for the bell to ding. "If you want to talk, call me later. But you need to leave now because I'm meeting someone."

"I know, Porter."

When revelations hit, they don't always come all at once. Several smaller reveals can filter in slow and steady, incrementally, mingled with the mundane, dripping like a leaky faucet. For instance, have these walls always been blue? How old is that waitress? Why did my ex-wife jump my bones the other night? How would Fisher know anything?

How had I not made the connection before?

"You've got to be shitting me," I said under my breath.

The waitress came back with his coffee and a menu.

He wasn't going anywhere.

"You're lucky I don't kick your ass right now."

"For what?"

"Lying to me, for one."

"I kept you alive. Jesus, man, I found you on a website, bitching about the Lombardis—you were going by the handle 'Jay the

Junkman.' You were wanted *for murder*. How long till the Feds found you? Do you know they have entire divisions, agents whose sole job it is to infiltrate chatrooms? I did you a favor."

I knew Fisher was right: without the Wounded King, I wouldn't have lasted long, wandering New England, clueless and inept, calling attention to myself. Maybe I should've shown appreciation, acknowledged these harsher truths. But having such insight is tougher when you're sitting there, slack-jawed, holding a bag of magic beans with a giant L stamped on your forehead. I felt like such a chump. And Fisher, the smug little shit, didn't make it easier.

"And don't blame me, man," he said. "You were on *my* website. How's it my fault you didn't catch on?"

"How was I supposed to know that?"

"How many times had you been at Charlie's when I was working on my e-zine, *Occam's Razor*?"

"I didn't keep a log."

"That's probably how you knew to go to that web address in the first place."

"I was looking for a community of like-minded people—"

"Like me."

"Yeah. Like you. But not you."

Fisher wrinkled his nose, leaning over the table, sniffing. "Are you drunk? It's barely noon, man. You want to end up like Charlie?"

"Fuck you."

The waitress stopped by with my food, which I no longer wanted. Recognizing the tense situation she stepped into, she set down the food, backing away, without bothering to get Fisher's order.

When I didn't touch my meal, Fisher asked if I minded.

"Go ahead," I said. "I've lost my appetite. But you're paying the bill."

Fisher started shoveling grub into his pie hole, without an ounce of remorse. I didn't think I could feel worse about myself. Broke, divorced, chasing rainbows, and now catfished.

"You lied to me." That was the best I had.

"Shit, Porter. Wounded King 1180?"

"What about it?"

"Do you, like, even *know* the story of the Fisher King?"

"Why would I?"

"Read history sometime."

"I'm not interested in solving riddles."

"Hey, man, if you'll recall, back when the Wounded King started helping you, no one knew you were innocent."

"But you did?"

"I never thought you killed Owen Eaton, no. I thought you were cracked out, drinking again. Which you are."

"Go to hell, Fisher."

"I thought you needed a friend and could use someone looking out for you. Charlie would've wanted that." Fisher speared a hunk of hash. "And you're damned lucky I found you before the cops did. You can thank me now, if you'd like."

"Gee, thanks." I wished they still let you smoke indoors. "Why now?"

"Why now what?"

"Why did you want to meet face-to-face? To rub my nose in what a moron I am?"

"Nobody thinks you're a moron, Porter. But to answer your question, numbnuts—because you just told a stranger, on the Internet, that you intend to shoot—" he leaned in and lowered his voice— "Adam and Michael Lombardi, the latter of whom by the way is a goddamn state senator."

"I did fucking not."

"Yeah. You fucking did. And if I hadn't directed you to my own private server, someone else would have that admission in a chatroom, preserved on *your* hard drive, and you *would* be in custody." He waited. "Do you have access to a gun?"

I thought about Alison's gun in her bedside table. "No," I lied.

"I'm trying to help you."

"I don't have a gun. Never wanted to be that jackass who forgets to lock his box or leaves the safety off. I have a son."

"That's good," Fisher said, softly. "That's good."

"I don't need your approval. And I don't want *your* help."

"I don't like Adam and Michael any more than you do, but for fuck's sake, when are you going to let this go? Don't you ever get sick of having those two define your entire existence? Remember when Chris was alive?"

"No, I've forgotten my brother."

"You used to say Chris was obsessed with that family and that his infatuation ruined any chance he had at happiness."

"Man, when did you and I talk?" I seldom spoke with Fisher.

"You'd tell Charlie. Charlie would tell me."

I arched over the table, stabbing a finger in his face. "Chris *was* obsessed with that family. But that began in high school, when my brother got left off the all-star team. A little boy snubbed. What I'm dealing with isn't some bullshit teenage drama. This is grown-up shit. Abuse. Murder." I began ticking items off my fingers, one by one. "Pedophilia. Kids for cash. Toxins in the soil. Someone's got to do something. That family has to pay."

"At what cost, Jay? I'm not denying the Lombardis are greedy, capitalist pricks. But we never had proof that their dad, Gerry, was molesting kids—"

"We had pictures from a hard drive."

"Those were inconclusive. And where is this hard drive? Your buddy Bowman was shanked in the prison showers. Info *I* found out for you. Another thank-you I'm not getting. And the rest of this shit you are fixated on, their rehab, the Coos County Center, all the shady, underhanded crap the brothers pulled to get that mill running? Nothing illegal about it. The price of doing business in this fucked-up system we have."

"Killing men isn't illegal? Bribing judges to incarcerate kids isn't illegal?"

"It's not about what you know, Porter. It's about what you can prove."

"Why did you come down here? You could've told me this online."

"I'm trying to talk sense into you before you make a mistake you can't come back from. This story doesn't end with two graves; it ends with three. I think you want that. I think you want to go out in some grand, dramatic fashion. A martyr. Which you think will make you a hero. It won't. It will cost your son a father, and no one will herald you as anything but a lunatic with a gun."

I pulled on my coat to leave.

"Hold on." Fisher fumbled for his jacket, patting pockets. "Do you have a new number?"

"Yeah. I do."

I walked out the door.

In the parking lot, I lit a cigarette and drove straight to the bar.

CHAPTER TEN

WHEN MY BEST friend, Charlie, was alive, he used to be a permanent fixture at the Dubliner, the miscast Irish-themed bar in the middle of the northern New Hampshire wilds. I'd hang out with him, winter through the summer, fall and spring, smoking cigarettes on the bamboo Tiki porch, surrounded by kitschy license plates from all over America, all the roads and routes I'd never travel on, all the places I'd never see. I wasn't leaving Lamentation. I'd die on this mountain. I knew that now.

In the two years since I'd last been to the Dubliner, the bar had undergone a radical makeover. The former Irish pub had been rechristened Scarlett O'Hara's, although I failed to see how a character from a Civil War novel set in the South made any more sense. They'd ditched the shamrocks and shillelaghs, gone, too, the Tiki smoking porch, in their place a bunch of brightly colored, mismatched crap that made the place look like an Applebee's on steroids. Random red typewriter glued to the wall. Oversized fork and spoon. An old macaroni and cheese advertisement. A duck. How did any of this represent the Grand Ol' South? And who gave a shit about the ol' South in the frigid Northeast? They had decent beer on tap for reasonable prices.

I asked the bartender, a mustached '70s porn star look-alike, if Liam or Rita, the former owners, were there, but he said they moved away after selling the place. By my second shot and pint, I learned that Scarlett O'Hara's was part of a small chain throughout New England. I didn't know why the thought depressed me so much. But it did. Just like the new décor and layout and clientele. My despondency transcended my best friend drinking himself to death, went further than the years and miles on this ravaged, broken body. Change should invite hope. This new bar affirmed what I already knew: that everything dies, that's a fact. And we were a long way from Atlantic City. Slap a button on the servers, stick a toothpick in the sandwiches, we were done.

With the last of Alison's money, I started drinking in earnest, beginning with shots of Jameson to prime the pump, and then a steady stream of pitchers until I was good and ripped. As the alcohol took hold, I surrendered any search for closure, let go of my brother, Charlie, the Lombardis, Fisher, the past, fuck 'em. Instead, I watched wheels out the window, minivans and 4x4s spitting snowy muddy sludge along the dirty boulevard, hunchbacks in parkas, the sun having long ago abandoned the fight, surrendering to night.

The night got confusing, my timeline fucked up. I was in and out from the smoking area, now a tiny roped-off section by the garbage cans, freezing my ass off for a hit of nicotine. Eventually, like a fighter with a busted hand, I grew numb to the pain. I knew hours passed, but when I reassembled the parts in my brain, the span felt more like seconds, snippets of conversation, trips to take a piss, conflated memories, Jenny, my boy, Chris as a kid. Then I'd be lucid again. It wasn't a blackout because I remembered stuff, was aware of what was happening, just not *how* it was happening, or in what order.

When my friend Charlie was alive, we used to discuss the poetry of the movie *Rocky*, in awe of how a single film could distill the American aesthetic so poignantly. At one point, being as wasted as I was, I felt extra chatty, like Colin Hay with a good cup of coffee. I made friends, college kids from White Mountain Community Tech. Lots of pretty girls. Some had their douchebag boyfriends in tow, but I didn't pay them any mind. I was at least fifteen years older than these kids, but bars are the great equalizer, and I was in fine form. Talk about *Rocky* and Stallone's Cinderella story— "Did you know that, flat-broke, living in a shitbag apartment, after, like, having to sell his *dog* and shit, man, *his dog*, dude turned down, like, three-hundred thousand because those studio fuckers wanted Ryan O'Neill to play Rocky? Sly was, all, Fuck. That. Either I play the part, or no deal. You know the balls that takes? The integrity when you don't have a pot to piss in? Turning down that kind of cash? *Those* are mutherfucking ideals. People used to have ideals. People used to believe in shit before all this, like, bullshit"—turned to my year on the run. My wife. Alison Rodgers. Getting weepy about my boy. Mickey Asal and drunks slipping off the icy road. Fisher making a fool of me. The Lombardis. Adam, Michael. And this time they'd killed a kid—a kid! I didn't have any proof but hell yea I was certain they'd put Whittaker Jewett up to torching that farm. The ploy *so* obvious. To me. I was trying to help these people. Couldn't they see that? I was the good guy, looking out for the downtrodden and trampled upon. The persecuted! A mutherfucking hero. Ideals! I need a beer. Who do I have to talk to around here to get a beer? Where's the fucking beer, John? Ha ha fucking ha.

And, yeah, I was hammered, blotto, good and gone, slipping in and out. But I wasn't unconscious. I registered the change in people's reactions. I'd gone from mildly entertaining old guy to that crazy drunk uncle everyone avoids at Thanksgiving.

But laughing and getting loaded makes for a good time. For the few who remained, who could handle when shit got real. People howling and whooping and pounding shots and getting flirty, because people were drinking, and when people are drinking, people are loving life, man, having fun. We were young. I was ... young-ish. But as I cracked jokes, I accepted, on some level, I was masking the pain. I floated high outside my body, seeing this sad wreck of a man, this pathetic asshole who'd been fighting the same losing battle, and who was not going to stop until he killed himself. No money. No friends. No future. No problem. I knew my fixation on the Lombardis and the past was counterproductive. But I wasn't going to stop. Fisher was right. This story ends with me dead.

Sometime around midnight, I got friendly with a new group of coeds, which included a girl named Marie. Or maybe it was Maria. If pressed, I might've been able to give a physical description, except the girl I was making out with had four eyes and two noses, double vision augmented by bar light. Closing time, we were in the corner, and she was all over me. Fucking Charlie, man. He was as much a brother as Chris ever was. Why did everyone I love leave? How the hell was I getting home? I couldn't see straight. What was this girl's name? Was she even the same one? I was beyond blitzed.

The hand on my shoulder told me I had the wrong girl.

Then we were outside, on the sidewalk, around the bar, in the parking lot. Me and two other guys. A crowd had gathered to watch the fight. The two guys were a lot younger than I was, and both their legs worked. Fucking showoffs. There was a time when I would've held my own. That time was a long time ago.

After a lot of yelling for everyone to go fuck themselves, someone threw the first punch. Could've been me. I'd like to say I got in a few good shots. I threw some real haymakers. Not sure I landed any.

Next thing I knew I was slumped in the corner by the big blue dumpster, on my stool. "Cut me, Mick."

"Huh?"

"What the fuck the old dude talking about?"

"Cut me, Mick."

"Dude is whacked, yo."

"I think you gave him a concussion."

"I didn't give him a concussion."

"You cracked his head off the edge of the dumpster."

Blood dripped in my eyes. Shadows danced through the bright lights. I staggered to my feet. I wasn't quitting. I didn't have to win, only had to survive till the final bell, go the distance . . .

Fists flew. The sound of bone on bone. I heard cries in the night. The voice doing the crying wasn't mine.

* * *

I woke in my own apartment, head throbbing with the pain that comes from dehydration and repeated punches to the face. I touched the swollen parts—ballooned lips, eyes slit like ripe plums. But I also felt some pride. There had been two of them, and one of me. I must've held my own. Better than that if I got out of there.

Feeling hope that I might have some fight left in me yet, I pushed myself up, favoring my ribs, which didn't feel much better than my skull. I wasn't wearing a shirt. I must've used it to mop up the blood. I saw the wadded ball of red-soaked fabric in the garbage bin.

I flicked on the bathroom light and checked my face in the mirror. After thirty rounds with Apollo, Rocky hadn't endured this bad a beating. I flinched with the stitch in my side, recognizing the sting. I'd cracked ribs in a snowmobile accident once. Other side. Maybe this latest thrashing would even me out. Opening the medicine cabinet, I hoped Hank hadn't tossed the ibuprofen. Not only had he left the Motrin, there was also a prescription bottle with a couple old anti-anxiety meds and, blessed be Heaven, a pair of painkillers from ages ago when I'd fallen through the ice. I tossed it all back, headed to the fridge, grabbed a beer, cutting into tomorrow's allotted supply, slamming it down with one long swallow. Something felt off. My ass was uneven.

Where was my wallet? A Costanza-sized monstrosity jammed full of crap—scraps of paper, tabs ripped from coffee shop walls, advertisements for random jobs—the wallet had left a permanent indentation in my ass cheek. I patted myself down. Wasn't there. I started to panic. Had those little shits at the bar rolled me? Like a bum tossed at a bus stop?

I flicked on all the apartment lights, searching high and low, couch and closet—I didn't remember driving home, let alone climbing the stairs—my memory of last night ending with my late-round resurgence. No wallet.

I caught the clock above the stove. Almost seven a.m. I would've guessed two or three in the morning, middle of the night, skies burbling black with storm clouds. I found my cleanest dirty shirt, one of the three I'd brought back to town for my inglorious return. Bundled up, I stepped on my stoop. There was my truck, parked perfect in the filling station below. I didn't park that well sober. I ached all over—bruises, gashes, punctures. I remembered the hydrogen peroxide in the cabinet. Stepping into the tub, I uncapped the bottle and started splashing my wounds, picking dumpster dirt from the assorted abrasions and cuts.

A hard knock sounded on the door. "Hey, Jay, open up." Turley.

I winced, sliding the shirt back down. I stepped out of the tub and opened the front door.

"Jesus, Jay, what happened to your face?"

"Nothing. No big deal. Got in a fistfight at the Dubliner."

"Aren't you a little old to be getting in fistfights?"

"What do you want, Turley?"

"You said to come back in the morning."

"When?"

"Last night. When you and your buddy were up here, rocking out."

"I wasn't here last night. I told you. I was at the Dubliner."

"There is no Dubliner. Closed down. Did you get a concussion? Maybe I ought to give you a ride to the hospital, get that checked out?"

"Gee, lost my insurance card." I'd made so many trips to the ER over the years, never paying any of their astronomical fees; the hospital gave up siccing their collection agency on me. "They changed the name—bar's still there, though."

"You don't look so good."

"What buddy?" I asked, catching up to the conversation.

"Huh?"

"You said when me and my buddy were up here. What buddy?"

"How am I supposed to know?"

"Till twenty minutes ago, I was knocked out."

"What you want me to say? I came by, about two o'clock, saw you two climbing the steps to your place. Swaying and hooting. You had the music blaring and shouted through the door to come back later."

"No, I didn't."

"Okay. I'm lying. Maybe it was your buddy."

"Stop saying buddy. I don't have any 'buddies.'"

"You was walking up the stairs with someone."

Did one of those little assholes from the bar feel bad about knocking me around and drive me home? Could've gotten my address from my driver's license. *Before stealing your wallet?*

"How old was my . . . buddy?"

"I don't know. It was dark. Just the light from the well. You were leaning on him pretty hard." Turley glanced down with better judgment at my breakfast beer. "Figured you'd tied one on."

"Young or old?"

"Huh?"

"The guy, my buddy. Was he older or younger than me?"

"Older. I think. Had a bunch of tattoos, shaved head. Pretty jacked."

"Tatted and jacked?" Like Bowman. *Bowman is dead.* "Wait," I said. "You saw some tatted, jacked-up stranger carrying me to my apartment, and you didn't do anything?"

"I knocked."

"You have to be the worst cop in the history of cops, Turley."

"Who knows why you do what you do? I've stopped asking."

"Why did you stop by at two in the morning in the first place?"

"I had a question."

I cracked another beer, not feeling so bad anymore. Last night was today, meaning I wasn't cutting into tomorrow's stash. "What?"

"Mickey Asal."

"Jesus, not this again. What about him?"

"Did you know his law license was suspended until last summer?"

"How would I have known that?"

"Mickey likes his drink, too. Got a couple DUIs himself. Some other shady shit. Might've perjured himself in a case. Twelve-month injunction from practicing law." Turley seemed so proud of himself. "Told you he was a sleazeball."

"Who gives a shit?"

"Just sayin'. You might want to do a better job vetting your next legal counsel."

"Thanks for the unsolicited advice." I walked to the door, paving the way to get lost.

Turley slapped on his hat, nodding at the hamburger that used to be my face. "Might want to splash some peroxide on that. Looks infected."

CHAPTER ELEVEN

"WHAT A STORM yesterday, eh?" Alison stood inside her cozy, warm doorway as I bulled up the sidewalk. The gusting winds spat ice and rime in my face, the never-ending insult. All traces of hostility wiped clean, she was back to perky All-American cheerleader, right as rain. "I hope you didn't try and drive in that—oh my God, Jay. What happened to your face?"

I could lie and say I walked into a shelving unit. But I was too tired to lie. "Said the wrong thing to the wrong guys." I needed to head back to Scarlett O'Hara's once they opened. I was hoping my wallet got knocked out in the fight and some Good Samaritan had returned it. *While you, somehow, drove home without killing anyone?* I knew that was wishful thinking. Whoever my "buddy" was, he must've needed it to see where I lived. *So he jots down your address, drives you back to your place, tucks you in, and then steals your wallet?* That made less sense. You don't do nice things for people and then steal their wallet. What kind of friend does that?

"Where?"

"What?"

"Where did you say the wrong thing to the wrong guys?"

Or was Fisher mistaken? Could Bowman be alive? Tatted and jacked, shaved head, sure sounded like Bowman. Bowman knew where I lived. If he hadn't been shanked in the shower, I still had a chance.

"Jay?"

"Don't worry about it, Alison. What's on the docket today?"

By the way her face twisted up, I could see the nurturing, recovering addict take over, the pressing need to save the sick and suffering because no one gets their ass kicked like I had in the produce section of the supermarket. My face—and I'd taken a good, hard look in the harsh morning light, and it was worse than I imagined—carried all the hallmarks of a drunken bar fight.

Maybe she was too tired to waste the effort. She dropped her haunches, resigned, leading me inside. She listed items—cleaning the lint from the dryer vent; new door hung to replace the old one in the guest bedroom; extra paint cans to dispose of, busywork.

I grabbed what I needed from my truck, screwdrivers and steel duck clamps, two-hole galvanized strap, heading to the basement to start on the vents first. When I got there, I found Alison sitting on the bottom stair, chewing the cuticles of her thumb. I sidestepped her and started dismantling the vent to see how much lint had accumulated before I hit the hardware store to get the vacuum and hose I'd need.

"Good thing I'm doing this," I said. "Got about three inches, caked. At best, you blow a fuse. Worst case, you have a fire on your hands."

Alison sat there, staring straight ahead, expression troubled. I wondered if she was working through the ways to save my soul, a conversation I was not having sober.

"Alison?"

She stopped daydreaming, or whatever she was doing in her head, and glanced over.

"Tell me about unsatisfied customers."

"Huh?"

"I'm thinking you might be right," I said, unscrewing a brace. "Someone is seeking revenge on Rewrite."

"Let it go, Jay."

"But I am worried. I might be able to write off a break-in as a random robbery." I didn't believe that for one second. "But killing a coyote and leaving the carcass beside the doghouse is personal. If you don't want to go to the cops—"

"You know Rewrite's reputation with the local police. I can't." She walked over as I struggled with a striped head. "It's not your problem."

"I'm making it my problem."

"I just need some work done around the house," she said, dispassionate to the point of disdain.

"I won't let it affect my daily chores."

She didn't laugh at my lame attempt at a joke.

"Don't worry about money," I said. If she were worried about incurring the cost of a lengthy investigation, I wanted to set her mind at ease. When I *was* dabbling in amateur investigating, I'd never gotten a handle on what to charge, selling my services short, fees seldom commensurate with the effort and time I put in. I'd always been lousy at managing money. "I'm doing this because we're friends."

"Is that what we are?"

I squinted up from my knees, unable to see much through my swollen eyes, swallowing back a gob of snot and blood clot that slipped down my throat, a slimy ball of mucus and cranial fluid tainted by metallic tang. I wasn't at my sexy best, and taking handouts from a rich, beautiful woman had me feeling extra insecure. Alison Rodgers had been out of my league three years ago, when I had nothing, and back then I had a helluva lot more than I did now. But, damned, if I didn't catch her playing with her hair, biting her lip. You'd have thought I was quarterbacking the goddamn team. I didn't know much about women, but there're a few signs even a blind man can pick up on. I read *Cosmo* at the dentist.

With brain function so compromised, I chalked it up to selective memory.

"There's three or four people over the years," Alison said, getting back to my original question.

"Folks you pissed off more than most?" I extracted the screw.

"Who were more upset with Rewrite's practices, yes. Parents, not patients. Even the most rebellious kids had a way of coming around in the end."

"You remember who?"

"I can't exactly give you names, can I? There's such a thing as professional ethics."

"This again?" When I was looking for the missing Crowder boy a few years back, Alison cost us precious time by clinging to the sacred tenets of doctor-patient confidentiality. "You dissolved Rewrite Interventions."

"The company. Not my integrity." She caught my eye. "Sorry. I want to be done with this."

"I'm sure you do. But someone else doesn't. You're right. You can't call the cops." I put down my tools, wiping dirty hands on dirtier jeans. "I'm not restricted in the same way. Give me the names. Let me take a look. On my dime. It'll give me something to do, keep me out of trouble." I smiled. Or best I could with my mangled mug.

Alison spun on her heels and headed upstairs. I figured I must've overstepped my bounds again not to get a goodbye. I caught my reflection in the cellar window. The halo of the basement light shone a perfect circle around the beleaguered head of a beat-down man. I didn't want to alarm Alison any more than necessary but I couldn't shake what Mickey Asal told me, how Davidson County suspected two men started that fire on the farm. Someone assisted Whittaker Pruitt, who witnesses placed too far away at the time. Whoever that second person was, they were still out there. A pissed-off parent working in collusion made sense. Unless I was overlooking the obvious and it was just one of Lombardi's thugs. Then again, who's to say those two couldn't be the same thing?

I'd have to pay a visit to Davidson County. That side of the state was far enough away that maybe my tarnished reputation wouldn't precede me.

The basement door opened, and Alison descended the stairs, handing me my daily cash. When she passed the bills along, her hand lingered, and I felt the electric charge. She swept hair out of her eyes, which fixed on mine. The moment didn't last long. But it *was* a moment. I didn't make a move. The thought of pressing my lips against anything right then hurt, my mouth so swollen.

I could've sworn she looked disappointed.

"Do you need more money?" she asked, backing up, turning from me, letting me know I'd blown whatever chance I had.

Did I have a chance? No way. Must've misread the situation. *A blind man, little brother, a blind man.* What was I supposed to do? Make a pass at her, with a face like roadkill? I shook off feelings of uncertainty as easily as I did confidence. First Jenny— now Alison?

"Jay?"

"Sorry. Forty bucks is fine."

"That's it?"

"We can settle up at the end." I pained a smile through the scabs. "I'll charge any tools to your account at the hardware store." I tucked the two twenties in my pocket, patting it. "Incidentals," I said.

We both knew the incidentals I needed. Beer and cigarettes, food a distant third. I wished I could've taken the high road. But after last night, I didn't have two dimes to rub together.

* * *

The winter night fell silent, unforgiving. Alison had headed out after our moment, if that's what it was, and I spent the rest of the morning completing the oh-so-romantic task of vacuuming dryer lint. After I was done with that, I slogged back to the hardware store, spinning mud and spitting sludge, to hang a door.

Alison didn't return. When I accepted that she wouldn't until I was gone, I set to lock up. I had a few screws in my pocket and opened a couple drawers in her kitchen, looking for the junk drawer. Of course, this was Alison Rodgers, a woman too well maintained to have anything as pedestrian as a "junk drawer." But I kept opening drawers anyway. I wasn't exactly snooping, just curious, the behavior addictive, like mandatory checks of the medicine cabinet when you are taking a piss at a party. I made it to her office. Checked a couple drawers there, too. If anything was that important, surely doors would be locked. I opened the top drawer, and there was a scrap of paper with three names and addresses, beneath a scribbled heading, my name, and underlined: *Disgruntled Customers* with a question mark. It looked like it had been recently written, and I reasoned, obviously, this was something Alison wanted me to have—my name was on the goddamn thing—these had to be the former clients unsatisfied with Rewrite's services. I flashed back on our earlier conversation where I was asking for a list, her response about doctor-patient confidentiality and sacred oath business. She must've written these names down when she left the basement. Technically she didn't *give* me anything, so she was in the clear, in terms of conscience and the law. More importantly, now I could investigate.

Leaving Alison's with the list of possible conspirators in my jeans pocket, I broke the stalemate and called Jenny. After she left my place the other night, I felt hope, like this nightmare might end. When you have the history Jenny and I did, there's no such thing as "just sex." Being together again wasn't like hooking up with college girls at the bar. She and I belonged. Jenny was my home.

I'd been expecting the call to go to voice mail. By calling first, I was capitulating, waving the white flag. Picking up would be gloating. But she answered. Which threw me off, and when she didn't say anything after "hello," I was left stuttering and stammering, like asking Gennifer Colaresi to Homecoming Dance all over again.

"Jenny? It's me." I didn't know what else to say to the dead air reception.

"I know, Jay. What's up? I'm in the middle of cooking dinner. Stephen's going to be home any minute."

"Um . . . how are you?"

"Fine. Rushing to get this in the oven. My mother's dropping Aiden off in a few, and like I said Stephen should be pulling up any second." She waited for me to respond. When I didn't, she added, almost whispering, "It's not a great time to talk."

"You just said no one's home?"

"No one is home," my ex-wife responded in that pedantic, didactic, infuriating tone of hers. "But they will be. Soon." She exhaled her exasperation. "Did you need something?"

How the hell was I supposed to answer that? Did I need something? Like the other night never happened.

"Yeah," I said, "I'm wondering why you haven't called."

"Was I supposed to? If you're ready to talk about resuming your visitation schedule, we can do that. But let's table that discussion for another day, okay?"

"Did we have sex the other night?"

"Excuse me?"

"We had sex, right?"

I could hear the phone being covered and her voice lowered. "Stephen just pulled in. We are not doing this right now."

A baby cried in the background.

"Great," Jenny said, "you woke her up."

I had forgotten about the baby. I couldn't remember her name at the moment.

"It's just," I started.

"It's just what?" Her hand cupped the receiver. "In here," she called out. Then something else I couldn't hear, but she was obviously talking to the jerkoff, adding, "It's Janice. From school." Then back to me. "I need to go."

"I want to talk about the other night," I said.

"The other night was . . . a mistake."

Then my wife, my ex-wife, my whatever the hell she was, hung up on me.

What the hell? I knew I hadn't been the greatest husband in the world, but I also didn't cheat, didn't gamble away our savings. I wasn't a thieving, lying piece of shit. Her new husband, Stephen—the father of her new baby—was no better than the Lombardis or the rest of the vultures. Before I split last year, when I was investigating those workers who got sick, I found a paper trail linking Stephen to the payouts. Or rather the company he worked for.

Alliance Life handled the annuities. Maybe he didn't know the ground was poisoned, maybe he didn't personally know workers were dying, but he was part of the same machination, the same system of oppression.

I needed a drink.

CHAPTER TWELVE

I COULD'VE CALLED Scarlett O'Hara's and asked if they had my wallet, but I didn't feel like shouting my humiliating defeat over raucous background chatter. I could use a beer anyway.

A few older-model cars cluttered the lot. Light snow started to fall. I was bundled in my coat, jingling the change in my pocket. Knowing I shouldn't splurge on a draught beer depressed the shit out of me.

"Yo, Adrian!" the bartender called out in his best Sly Stallone when I walked through the door. "What can I get you?"

I ordered a pint.

He slid the beer in front of me.

"You saw the fight the other night?"

He nodded at my face. "If you want to call it that."

"I got in my shots, too."

"Maybe we were watching different fights." He laughed. "Sorry, man, but those two boys handed your ass to you. If your brother didn't show up when he did, I'm not sure they were showing mercy." He leaned over. "That girl you were fingering in the corner, bro? His wife." He pulled back with a wince, reaching under the counter.

"My brother?"

He returned with my wallet, flipping it on the counter. "I assume that's what you're looking for?"

I slipped the wallet back where it belonged, filling in the indentation of my left ass cheek. I shouldn't have been surprised someone would turn it in. No cash. Didn't have any credit cards, just a bunch of coupons I'd never use, loyalty cards I'd never fill, forever three sandwiches short of a grinder.

The barkeep thumbed over his shoulder, through the repainted walls. "Someone found it under the trash bin." He nodded at my face. "You get that checked out? Looks infected, bro."

"Appreciate the concern. Why did you say 'thank my brother'?"

"Because he saved your ass? Those two guys weren't taking it easy on you, and when you got up off the ground—don't ask me how—they went at you twice as hard."

"You watched the whole thing?"

"Only a couple of us left in the bar."

I raised my beer. "Thanks for the help."

"Hey, you had the mouth. You said, and I quote, 'You stop this fight, I'll kill ya.'" I mean, you'd think, even by mistake, you'd have landed a punch."

"I get it. I lost. Tell me about . . . my brother."

"You want me to tell you about . . . your brother?"

"I had one brother. His name was Chris. He died seven years ago. Whoever that was, he wasn't my brother."

"That's what he said. 'Don't worry. This's my brother. I'll get him home safe.' Goddamn lucky he did. He whooped their asses, too, before scraping you off the pavement."

"What he look like?"

"Brick shithouse, lots of tattoos. Bad mutherfucker. He fought those two guys off in a tank top." He shook his head. "Minus twelve degrees and he's wearing a wifebeater. Didn't break a sweat."

"Did he have the Star of David tattooed on his neck by any chance?" Bowman wore that indistinguishable marker. "Shaved head?"

"Yeah, his head was shaved." The bartender laughed. "I didn't get close enough to make out any neck tattoo. Possibly. He was covered in the things."

I drained the dregs and nodded thanks. I would've left a tip. But I was running low on cash. And my restored wallet didn't magically come with more.

Some stranger who resembles a dead man—the same dead man, Bowman, who I once believed could help lock away my enemies forever—plucks me from a bar fight, says he's my brother, and brings me home. Then splits before I can ask any questions. Never mind the mind fuck with Jenny, the mixed signals from Alison—forget my financial woes, my drinking problem, the son I felt slipping away—if this *were* Bowman, I was still in the fight; I had a chance.

I wouldn't have minded calling it a day, packing it in, except I had this list of names I needed to check out. Alison wasn't paying me for the overtime. But I still had a job to do. We are our work.

Behind the wheel, I inhaled the clean, crisp scent of evergreens and snow leaking through the vents as I waited for better days to kick in. Alison Rodgers. What happened in that basement? Was my take on reality so skewed that I was fantasying rich, beautiful women throwing themselves at me? Me, Jay Porter, handyman at large. Have hammer, will travel. The only thing that separated me from full-blown vagrant status: a one-bedroom apartment above a gas station, which would soon require rent. Forty fucking dollars a day wasn't cutting it.

The first of the three names, Dave Fontaine, lived south of Pittsfield, in the bucolic suburbs of Marymount. To get there, I had to pass the exit to my ex-wife's palatial spread. Far from the beaten path, high in their ivory tower, she and her new husband nestled warm indoors with my son.

I jerked the wheel, skidding into the right lane, causing a tractor-trailer to swerve and blast its horn. Fuck 'em.

I found a small grocery store and picked up a six-pack, cracking a cold one in the parking lot. I also grabbed a tin of breath mints.

The Fontaine homestead was only eight miles southwest, but I needed thirty-five minutes to get there. The routes wound around boulder and stump, depositing me in the clouds along the outer rim of the range.

The last thing I felt like doing was traversing no-man's land, but telephone calls were a dead end. Too many telemarketers, too much reliance on Caller ID these days for folks to take a chance on a number they didn't recognize. What would I say over the line anyway? "Do you remember paying someone to abduct your junkie kid? Yeah? Great! Doing a follow-up Q&A. Mind taking a survey?" True, I didn't have a better approach in person, but one thing I'd picked up during my short stint as an insurance investigator: people are quicker to slam a receiver than they are to shut a door.

Lucky for me, the two beers I guzzled injected some much-needed confidence. Unfortunately, the buzz obscured all self-awareness of just how bad I looked.

"Jesus, kid," the man who answered the door said. "You get the license plate of the truck that ran over your face?"

"Traffic accident," I said. "Are you Dave Fontaine?"

"I am."

A thick, heavyset man, Dave was at least sixty. He spoke with a slow drawl as if he were chewing rebar taffy.

"Mind if I ask you a couple questions regarding your experience with Rewrite Interventions?"

If I'd been anticipating hostility, I'd come to the wrong place.

"Our son, Jacob, went there," Dave Fontaine said before dropping his head, mournful and lachrymose. "Didn't work out."

"How so?"

"My boy died."

I fumbled for the right words—of which there were none.

"Jacob was troubled from a young age," Dave Fontaine said. "A good boy. But different. Had a harder go of things, y'know? Just livin' seemed to wear on him. I saw the signs, stealing beers, money, pinching his ma's pills. By the time me and the wife decided to try Rewrite, it was too late."

"I heard you were unsatisfied with Rewrite's practices?" How do you couch that better? I waited for him to demand my name or scream to get the hell off his porch. But either Dave Fontaine wasn't the skeptical sort or he wasn't in the mood to argue. Maybe he just needed a friendly face to talk to. In lieu of that, I'd have to do.

"At the time, I wasn't nice to that couple who ran the place, Richard and . . ."

"Alison."

"Right, Alison. I liked her. He was a bit of a jerk. But Jacob's problem existed long before they got their hands on him. They did the best they could." Dave broke into a pained grin. "He made it almost a year. Those nine months were as happy as this family had been in a long time. He was making coffee at the meetings, helping cut the birthday cakes. We were so proud of him."

He didn't need to add the rest. I'd read this story before. Gonna stop off for one drink on the way home, only get high on the weekend; and you pick up right where you left off.

"How long ago was Jacob there? At Rewrite, I mean."

"Would've been . . ." He did the math in his head, subtracting sobriety date from death. "Four summers ago."

"He was assigned to a farm?"

"Sugarbush, just over the border."

"Not a dairy farm?"

"Nope. A maple syrup farm. First time he got a pass to come home, he brought them sugar candies. Fourth of July. My wife liked them candies."

I didn't ask Dave where his wife was. I knew she, too, was gone, a pall of guilt and regret cast over the entire home.

"Did you hear of any other parents, clients who were unhappy? Maybe when you were researching where to send your son?"

"There were a handful of bad reviews for Rewrite Interventions online, if that's what you mean. You can always find someone grumbling on that Internet. But overall people seemed satisfied, which is why we tried them. In the end, Jacob wasn't able to stay sober. And that wasn't nobody's fault but his."

CHAPTER THIRTEEN

THE NEXT MORNING, I skipped the face-to-face, calling the two remaining names on my list. Time heals all wounds, and like Dave Fontaine these other parents had also gained perspective, eliminating the need for scapegoats. Both families I spoke with that morning took all the heat, accepting the blame for the shortcomings of their addicted children. I started wondering if Alison really left those names for me to find. There was nothing here. No scorn, no outrage fueling a need for vengeance. But for me, the fire remained.

Why was I obsessing over a job I hadn't been hired to do? I needed something permanent to sustain me. I *might* be able to get Alison to keep me on for the winter; I wasn't bilking her—there were plenty of legitimate repairs to get the house in working order to sell. The deeper I probed, the more I risked pissing her off; and then I could kiss my steady payday goodbye. But when you open certain boxes, a peek isn't going to satiate; you need to throw back the top, open her up, let the light flood. Never be satisfied any other way.

Walking around my meat-locker apartment, bundled in my winter coat and long johns, I didn't know how I was going to settle

up with Hank Miller or pay back Jenny for child support—I sure as
hell couldn't afford extravagant luxuries such as heat.

Internet, however, was essential.

I headed to my computer. I'd exhausted every avenue available to
me via search engines, and I'd milked all the free legal advice I was
getting. I was pissed at the subterfuge—but the guy *had* helped me
for the better part of ten months. Hitting up random websites,
asking questions about the Lombardis, using Jay the Junkman as a
moniker? Should've landed my ass in jail. Fisher was right: I'd been
lucky. I didn't feel so lucky anymore.

> **jay_the_junkman:** you there?

Now we wait . . . I don't have anywhere else to turn. *I know that.
No worries, little brother.* Nobody seems to care. Not about Rewrite.
Not about the fire. *Why do* you *care so much? Your girlfriend sold the
business.* One, she's not my girlfriend. And, two, right is right. *And
wrong is wrong. Sure thing, little brother.* Someone tried to break
into her house. And then they killed that coyote, left the dead thing
right by the doghouse. *I'll give you the coyote, but, dude, you were
crouched in the dark, it was storming, a piece of hail could've smashed
that window.* Right. *I think you're pushing so hard for another reason.*
Goddamn right I am. Because we both know Adam and Michael
were behind terrorizing Alison. They're trying to corner the entire
market. *But why do* you *care?* Because they killed my brother!

My computer dinged.

> **Wounded_King1180:** u couldve picked up the phone.

> **jay_the_junkman:** couldnt. i traded in phones and dont
> know your number

> **wounded_king1180:** would it help if i gave it to u?

jay_the_junkman: i prefer this. i feel like less of a chump

wounded_king1180: i never thought of u as a chump. i was glad i got to u first and we kept u alive long enough to clear ur name

jay_the_junkman: you really believed i was innocent?

wounded_king1180: always. u r alot of thing porter but u r not a killer

jay_the_junkman: are you sure bowman is dead?

wounded_king1180: um yeah

jay_the_junkman: how?

wounded_king1180: hes listed as deceased by the state for one. why?

jay_the_junkman: nevermind. i need to know about a fire, arson

wounded_king1180: the pruitt dairy farm, over in davidson county

jay_the_junkman: you know about that?

wounded_king1180: i read up on it the other nite, when u asked me to look into the partnerships rewrite had with the farms

jay_the_junkman: alison said the authorities pegged whittaker pruitt as the arsonist. we sure hes good for the crime?

I imagined the clacking of keys on the other end, picturing Fisher with six monitors, eating Chinese food out of a take-out container as screens rained Matrix codes. I waited for him to say, "I'm in," like every hacker in every cheesy cyber-fueled flick. Instead he came back with the *Ashton Herald*, online edition.

wounded_king1180: yup, insurance scam, says he was in deep with the bank, 2nd mortgage, losing money, had a large policy. makes sense

jay_the_junkman: whatever happened to the most logical solution usually being the correct one?

wounded_king1180: u got something more logical than greed?

jay_the_junkman: the authorities think pruitt had an accomplice because he was far away when the fire started

wounded_king1180: thats what i read too

jay_the_junkman: what if pruitt was far away because he had nothing to do with the fire?

wounded_king1180: so someone else started the fire. any other suspects in mind? let me guess. couple brothers maybe? let me ask u something

jay_the_junkman: shoot

wounded_king1180: if what u have been saying about adam and michael lombardi is true, all of it, the last seven years, from ur brother, to the dead workers, to this fire

jay_the_junkman: it is true

wounded_king1180: okay, fine. but u have been on their asses a long time

jay_the_junkman: ive lacked that one piece of ironclad
evidence to put them away

wounded_king1180: right. but if that evidence exists, and if
u r the one person out there trying to find it, why havent
adam and michael killed u already and been done with it?

* * *

Despite the dismal forecast, I couldn't skip out on another day of
work for Alison. What would I do with a day off anyway? I'd poke
around the fire, kick up dirt on the sale, chase smoke, all for free.
Right now, I needed cash more than satisfaction.

I had to call Jenny and work out when I could next see my boy. I
was still Aiden's father. But I didn't have the stomach for another
knockdown, drag-out fight with my ex. I was livid she'd hung up on
me, treating our night together like an unfortunate anecdote she'd
laugh about with friends over brunch at the Avon Old Farms Inn.
The thought of having my son for a weekend felt so far away.
Accusations stick. Presumed innocent my ass. Didn't matter if I'd
been cleared, perception is nine-tenths of the law. I'd been branded
a killer in the court of public opinion, which in a small town like
Ashton is the only court that matters.

I tried not to think about that, or Fisher's question. But pink elephants are tough to ignore. Several examples existed of when Adam
and Michael tried to kill me. Phony detectives. Dirty cops. Russian
hunters. I'd slipped out of some sticky situations. But I also operated a long way from ninja stealth. I was just a shit-kicking country
boy who spent a lot of time doing what I was doing now: sitting
alone in my apartment, drinking beer, hiding in plain sight. Either
I'd been very lucky, or I was very . . . wrong.

I went to the window to scope surroundings, trying to shake off that creeping sensation of being clocked. Hank Miller waved up from the filling station lot. I waved back, letting the blinds fall, ducking into darkness. Maybe right now my place wasn't the safest place to be.

On my way to Alison's, I stopped by the hardware store, adding an extra padlock and dead bolt to the day's purchases. I wasn't sure how much that would stop ghosts or doppelgängers from breaking into my apartment. But in lieu of a gun, extra locks were the best I could hope for.

I didn't like someone knowing where I lived. I hadn't driven myself home from the bar the other night. Then again, if Lombardi was sending someone to take me out for good, I failed to see how tucking me into bed served as an intimidating message.

CHAPTER FOURTEEN

AFTER CUTTING OUT of work early, I refortified my front door. Changed lock, added dead bolt. I also brought a hefty wrench with me from my truck, keeping it within reach, a cowboy and his six-shooter, like that would matter if someone got inside with a real gun.

Fisher's question burned front and center: Why was I still here? If I were any threat to Adam and Michael, I'd be gone by now. The brothers *were* murderers. I could tick off five, six, seven people I knew, certain as I was still living and breathing, the Lombardis had killed. Or at least they had played some role in their deaths. Everyone who crossed them ended up six feet under. All but one: me. Why had I been spared?

Bounding down the rickety old steps, out to my junker pickup, I set off for the Davidson County offices. I wanted to see just how far underwater the Pruitt Farm had been. Braving rush-hour traffic, I arrived with five minutes to spare, my skin-of-the-teeth timing pissing off the clerk, an old lady with a dowager's hump and lung-butter hack.

I extracted every public record I could access on the Pruitt Dairy Farm. Lots of numbers and zoning ordinances, shit I didn't understand. What was crystal clear: the reports were true. Bank was about to foreclose any day. Whittaker owed close to sixty grand. Powerful incentive to make a man torch his own place.

"Where's the Pruitt Dairy Farm?" I asked the old lady.

"You got questions," she said, "ask during working hours. The county doesn't pay for overtime. Why you so interested in the Pruitt Farm anyway?" Either she'd had a tracheotomy or gargled nightly with glass shards. Tom Waits would've been envious of that rasp.

"A friend of mine worked over there," I said. Not that it was this woman's business. But sometimes the quickest way to get what you want is to play along, give them what they're asking for, let folks feel important. How much did this woman's life have to suck? Shuffling papers for minimum wage at eighty. "Can you tell me how to get to the farm?"

"Why? There's nothing left of it. Whole thing up in ashes."

"Like I said, helping out a friend. Maybe I poke around, I find something the fire department missed."

"What makes you so special?"

I attempted a smile, the effort cracking the scabs around my mouth.

The old lady grumbled under her breath and snatched some scrap paper to scribble directions. She took forever writing them though. She kept getting distracted by something in the back room, shuffling back and forth, leaving me to wait. What choice did I have? GPS wasn't working out here.

When she finally passed along directions to the Pruitt place, she nodded at my face. "You outta put some antibiotic on that. Looks infected."

*   *   *

A slim wedge of white moon peeked around a wall of encroaching storm clouds, charcoaling skies promising another long, serious night. Too many routes, roads, missed connections. Three point five miles turning into twelve, take a left at the collapsed barn, don't run over the three-legged dog bullshit. Abandoned harvesters rusted in fruitless fields, rock face lacking distinction. I fiddled with the radio, stuck on a dark, deserted highway. I switched it off before the warm smell of colitas. Fucking Eagles. How many times does someone need to hear "Hotel California" in a lifetime?

Took a while but I found what I was looking for. Despite the fire being months old, the smolder lingered; the charred remains seeped into the battlefield, blood and death and mulch.

Though located in the southwestern flats, Davidson County saw more snow cover than Ashton, the region catching the brunt of the jet stream. Snows fell harder in the colder months, the landscape defined by white-on-white contrast. You'd think cows would freeze to death in this weather, but I wasn't a farmer. All the cows were gone now anyway.

Kicking against the prickers, I wasn't sure what to expect, how badly operations had been affected—by all accounts the fire had been devastating—but when I got on actual Pruitt property, I saw it was worse than that; the farm had been decimated, leveled, lost. A larger farm might've been able to absorb the blow, but this operation was too small to take the hit and continue on.

I took in the vast terrain, the collapsed barn smack dab in the middle, ground zero, fire-scorched stumps and felled trees detonated in expanding waves, the aftermath of a bomb. That's what the papers compared the explosion to, a mortar shell dropped, the kerosene accelerant acting like a blasting cap, pines and shale projectiled. The explosion, not the flames, was what killed that boy. I knew Lombardi was behind this. But that didn't mean Whittaker wasn't complicit. With this much money at stake, I couldn't rule out anything. A crazy thought popped in my whirling mind: What if this kid was the one who helped start the fire? Other than money, I didn't have a motive, but if kerosene was that unstable, maybe their plan backfired?

I slapped the head of my flashlight till the beam started working properly and panned the scarred remains. Fractured posts. Splintered studs. A pivot hinge was out of its hole, gate waving in the mountain gale. I had the source of the smell wrong. I didn't smell ash. The lingering stench owed to the singed remnants of fertilizer, shit now trapped in the frozen ground. I spread my flashlight down dale, up surrounding rocks, toward the sky. The moon had disappeared, lacquering the country night black. Above the ridge, I caught a flicker of light. Then it was gone as quick, leaving me to wonder how a shooting star could penetrate a sky so dense.

Nothing to find here among the wreckage. No one was leaving a typed confession, which would've been burnt to a crisp anyway.

Turning to go, I heard a pop, the far-off bubble of trapped gases. My brain didn't register rifle till the first bullet ripped past my ear, tearing out a chunk of tree stump.

Instinct kicked in and I dropped my flashlight, ducking for cover, slithering on my belly as another errant shot zipped past, this one closer to the mark, pinging off my rusted ride. I scrambled behind the engine, before realizing I'd left the flashlight blazing bright, giving the shooter an easy target. I scuttled, a demented crab, reaching, one eye on the dark hill, the other coveting the cover of my truck, neither on the actual flashlight. Finally, I got hold of the damn thing, chucking it far in the woods.

The shots stopped. Feeling around the back of my truck, I wrapped my fist around the first piece of heavy metal I found, my oversized crescent wrench.

Over snowy hills, through the bramble of decaying, felled forest, wrench in hand, no light, I stalked sightless, mentally calibrating the source of the gunfire. Not the smartest move, running toward the shooter. I should've been more concerned with getting away, but I didn't have the option of calling the police. I itched to get my hands on the SOB taking shots at me, beat some answers out of him if need be. Was this the same man from the bar? The one pretending to be my brother? Had he been involved in the fire? How did those two things tie together? Why save me from an ass whooping, carry me home, only to take low-percentage shots in the dark?

Without gloves, my hands were ragged and raw—I was dressed for winter but not prowling in the wilderness. Coming over the crest, I made out a vague shape. A small house. Ranch-style, one floor, with vines up the sides and across the roof. More shack than house, helpers' quarters.

Closer now, I heard a generator thrumming. Ear to the door, I heard the sound of a television playing inside. Soft murmur, canned laughter. I two-fisted my weapon as though it were a gun.

I squared myself in front of the door, praying the shooter was distracted by that TV and not eyeing me through a peephole. There was no one to mouth a countdown to. Lifting my good leg, I cocked it high for extra torque and kicked the door in. If the door had been well made, I would've been screwed. But this was old wood, freeze dried, brittle. It gave, splintering in twelve different directions.

The room stank like dirty motor oil. A shapeless man stood in the dark corner, big beard covering most of his face, wool cap pulled low to protect his face from the wintry elements. His eyes registered shock. He hadn't anticipated me running toward the ring of fire. The only light came from the portable TV, the kind you don't find anymore, aluminum foil rabbit ears, dials the size of egg timers.

Average height and weight, indiscriminate, the man cowered. Although I couldn't see much of his face, I knew I didn't know him.

The shack was dark as hell; I was lucky to see my hand in front of my face, but you sense familiarity. This man was a stranger. A slice of moonlight shone in and I caught the glint of a rifle propped against the wall. He darted for it. I did, too. When his hand fell on the stock, I brought down the crescent wrench with mighty fury, rapping his knuckles good, like a parochial school nun beating out impure thoughts.

"Ow!" he squealed, jumping back.

I snatched the rifle, sticking it out of reach.

"I think you broked my hand," he blubbered.

"That's what you get for taking pot shots at me."

"Can I get some ice?" He nodded sheepish at a cooler, which like the rest of the small house was bathed in the blue-gray cadaver light of late-night television. "Please? It really hurts."

"We can swing by the ER on our way to the police."

"The p-police?"

"You tried to shoot me. I'm guessing because of the fire you helped start. I think the cops would like to talk to you."

"I didn't start no fire! And I wasn't trying to kill no one! I'm caretaker of this property. I saw someone trespassing. Wanted to scare you off, is all."

My eyes adjusting to the light, I saw the man couldn't have been much older than me, but he looked a lot older. The way he carried himself, irresolute as a shamed priest, doughy, a sad sack of a man. There weren't many places that made me feel better about my life.

"What do you know about the fire?" I said.

"What everyone knows. Whittaker started it. He's a mean man, a bad man."

"Then why you working for him?"

"I didn't work for Whittaker. I worked for his deddy, Jewett. Jewett was a good man. An honest man. A righteous man."

"What's your name?" I said.

He didn't answer. I panned the room, spying a wallet on an up-ended cardboard box that was being used as a coffee table, and snatched it up.

"Hey!"

"Shut up." I flipped open the wallet and out slipped a card. Small, square, simple design around the edges. At first, I thought it was a coffee card but looking closer I saw I was holding an NEUCA card. The New England Utility Contractor's Association. A union membership card. Clearing estates, I'd dealt with plenty of union guys over the years.

"Give me that!"

I held up a hand and fanned through the wallet till I found a driver's license, face distorted beneath the scratched plastic covering. I tilted the license till I caught enough light to read the name. "Peter Pugh." I panned over. "That's a rough one."

"Please, mister, my hand really hurts."

I tossed him back his wallet. "Stay there." I didn't know if he kept an extra gun in the icebox. Crescent wrench trained on him like a pistol, I back-stepped to the cooler, peeled the lid, grabbed a handful of ice cubes floating between the cheap six-pack of beer. "You got a dishrag in this dump?" I said. "Washcloth?"

Nursing his smarting hand, which flopped limp as a dead fish, he nodded at the ground. I plucked a swath of dirty rag. Twisting the ice into a ball, I dipped the makeshift icepack in the cooler to get it wet, tossing along the wad.

"Put that on it," I said. "Keep the swelling down."

"My hand feels broked." Peter started sniffling. "Can I sit down?"

Only place to sit was a filthy, fire-scorched La-Z-Boy bursting stuffing.

"How do I know you don't have a gun stashed in the cushions?"

He nodded sideways at the chair. "You can look and see for your-self but please, mister, let me sit. My hand is throbbin' and the blood rushing to my head is making me feel dizzy. I'mma pass out. Plus I got the arthritis. Makes standin' on my bones hard—"

"Fine. Just shut up."

"You want to check—"

"Sit down, Peter." I had a good enough handle on which people were dangerous. And Peter Pugh, with his old arthritic bones, wasn't getting the jump on me.

He sat, creaking with gratitude, thanking me, profusely.

"Yeah, yeah. Now you want to tell me why you were shooting at me?"

"I already told you. I'm caretaker for Pruitt Farms."

"There's no farm, not that I can see."

"Property still theirs. Gotta job to do. Gotta protect it."

"Protect it? From what? Wild turkeys?" The television light flick-ered and dimmed, swallowing the man in its shadows. "And for who?" I said. "From what I've read, Whittaker didn't have any family to leave it to."

"Why you reading about the Pruitt Farm?"

"None of your business, Pugh."

I had a hard time buying his story, but I didn't have another one to swap in its place. I sure wasn't going to spend all night in that shack.

Reaching back, I retrieved the rifle, making for the door.

"Where you going with my gun?"

"I'll leave it at the bottom of the ravine. You can walk down and get it after I'm gone."

"I think my hand is broked," Peter Pugh whined again.

"Maybe next time don't be so trigger-happy."

Using the rifle as a walking stick, I descended the ice-slicked ter-rain, one eye peeled on the road and my truck, the other casting back to make sure Peter Pugh wasn't getting a second wind with a concealed firearm.

At the bottom of the hill, I popped the shells and set the rifle on a burnt tree stump. Then I stashed the crescent wrench in my back pocket, before climbing in my cab and heading home, feeling oddly comforted by the progress I'd made.

When people start taking shots at you, you know you're getting closer to the truth.

CHAPTER FIFTEEN

I LEFT FOR work at sunrise, hoping to catch Alison before she bolted. But I got tied up having to change a flat on the side of the snowy Desmond Turnpike. The tire popped when I hit the on-ramp, leaving me to wonder if it had been slashed or tampered with in some way. Then again, I had been driving fast, primed by too much coffee, up half the night, scouring the Internet. How could I sleep? I was amped, on edge. Which is what happens when some-one points a gun at you. And that was another thing that bugged me: letting Peter Pugh walk. I should've turned his ass over to the cops. Except I'd been the one trespassing and didn't have a good reason for being there.

By the time I put on the spare, turned around to get a proper tire from Hank's, and made it to Middlesex, I was pulling in as Alison was pulling out. I held up a finger, slammed it in park, and jogged over.

Alison rolled down the window. "Can we talk later?" She was all done up. Hair, makeup, professional pantsuit, a grown-up. What did she do with her days? How many depositions can one woman give? I smelled the dishonesty on her. Not like she owed me the truth. But something was up. She went for her purse. "Right. What do I owe you?" The rich always think money is the answer to every problem.

"Like I said, we can settle up when I'm done."

She pulled the forty bucks, passing it along. "For today's incidentals."

I didn't appreciate the condescension. But integrity wasn't putting fuel in my tank or food in my belly. I stashed the bills in my shirt.

"I wanted to talk more about the fire."

"This again?"

"How well did you know the owner of the farm, Whittaker Pruitt?"

"We did business together. I wouldn't say I knew him well."

Alison waited for more. I couldn't think how to word what I wanted to ask her. I hadn't gotten a malicious vibe off Peter Pugh but I couldn't shake this nagging malaise gnawing at me since I left the farm. When I got home last night, I'd dropped a note for the Wounded King, supplying the name I'd read on the driver's license. As of this morning, Fisher had yet to respond to my request.

"I visited the Pruitt Farm last night."

Alison set down her chamomile tea in the traveling mug. "All the way out in Davidson County? Why were you there?" Snow gusted in through the open window. Alison glanced at the dashboard clock, a not-too-subtle cue to hurry the fuck up.

"I met the caretaker."

Alison's face screwed up. Then she nodded through the wind-shield. "I hate to ask. But can you double-check that grave? Make sure that it's not too shallow? There've been bear sightings in the area, and I don't want to walk out and find a dead coyote carcass dragged on my lawn again."

"He took a shot at me."

"Who?"

"The caretaker. At the farm. He shot at me. Twice."

"Did you report the incident to the police?"

"I was on private property. Besides, my relationship with cops isn't any better than yours."

"I don't know what to tell you," she said, losing patience with the little boy who keeps asking why the sky is blue or fish can't talk. "The Pruitt Farm was one of many Rewrite partnered with. I dealt more with the business end of things. Contracts." Meaning her ex-husband, Richard, handled the face-to-face and day-to-day. And even if he wasn't out West, Richard wasn't talking to me.

Alison touched my arm, cool and removed. "I appreciate your taking your own time to look into this. But it's unnecessary. Whoever was out here the other day isn't coming back."

She rolled up her window and drove off.

* * *

I rechecked the grave. Nothing had disturbed it. Bears did venture down here, from time to time. By Thanksgiving, they should be hibernating. Poking around the edge of the forest with a stick, I found an empty bottle of Southern Comfort. On top of the ice, the bottle hadn't been there long, almost certainly dropped by whoever had tried to break in. Which didn't tell me much—I wasn't lifting prints with superglue and bringing them to Turley to run through the police database—except that whoever had been out here was trying to keep warm and had shitty taste in alcohol.

When I was done checking the grave, I spent the rest of the day painting chairs in the basement. As usual, Alison remained out, like she had a regular nine-to-five somewhere in the city. Outside of those fleeting exceptions where she seemed into me, she treated me very much like an employee.

I went upstairs to use her bigger bathroom, surrounded by fluffy towels and creamy white soaps. There, I convinced myself of something that, later on, I would realize was wish fulfillment. But in the moment, I started asking myself: Why is Alison leaving me alone every day? Giving me the run of the house. Unsupervised. All day long. Me, a guy just off the hook for murder, a man who, in her book, was in active addiction. Even if that was bullshit recovery code and a couple beers a night didn't mean jack, I knew *in her mind* she considered beer an addiction. So why the extra rope? Then it hit me. *She knows you, little brother. She knows damn well you don't let anything go. That is why she hired you in the first place, to get to the bottom of the break-ins, punish the people pushing her around, the assholes that forced her to sell her company, the same pricks who ruined our lives.* She didn't need me to mend fences. Or if she did, there was no urgency to start in the dead of winter, hammering hard earth, wrenching lumbar and straining shoulders, slicing my hands, not when she wasn't planning on selling it till the spring. She *had* left those names for me to find. Like she was giving me access to her records now. She couldn't come out and ask because an investigation would require her to break confidentiality oaths. So it was a wink and a nod, a secret handshake.

There wasn't anything in her office, but I found a filing cabinet in her bedroom. Standard, small, black. The kind you find in any superstore for thirty bucks and change. I tried the handle. Locked. No surprise. I encountered them often at estate sales, keys seldom included.

Tilting the cabinet, I searched under the lip for the hole. With my pinky finger, I pressed the bar, and was in.

A lot of paperwork. Requisite licensing and insurance information. Taxes filed, 509 application—the nonprofit status hysterical, given how the Rodgers lived. Alison was nothing if not meticulous. Starting with year of inception, she'd paired each client with a farm, everything slotted in its proper place. I only had to locate the year

Rewrite began working with Pruitt, and I'd have everything I needed. Of course, it would've helped if I knew how Lombardi connected to all of this.

Headlights fanned up the drive. I fumbled to shove everything back, panic gripping, heart jammed in throat. I hurried from the room, trying to come up with excuses about why I needed to be in Alison's bedroom that didn't involve pervy shit and her underwear drawer.

When I got to the kitchen, I peeped through the drapes. The headlights were still on but no one was getting out. I saw right away it wasn't Alison's SUV.

"Fisher? What the hell are you doing here?" I bounded down the steps, out into the cold, wearing only a tee, the rest of my layers peeled off in the toasty house.

Fisher emerged through the settling gloam, bundled in a pea coat, a tiny sailor of shore leave.

"I've been trying to reach you all day," he said. "You haven't been online."

"No," I answered, blowing on my hands, trying to calm down, having almost been busted. "I've been here. How did you know where to find me?"

"I'm the one who told you where Alison Rodgers lived in the first place, remember? When you were looking for the Crowder boy." He pulled back, taking in the damage from the bar fight the other night. "You okay, man? Looks like you've taken too many punches to the head."

"I got in my shots, too."

"I bet."

"I'd rather not explain to Alison who you are."

"Why? Isn't this all for her benefit?"

The question was fair, and on the surface, he may've been correct. Except I didn't know what Alison wanted, my actions based on conjecture, and if I were being honest with myself, which I could be, depending on the time of day, this was for one person's benefit and one person alone, driven by the singular desire to thrust a knife into the heart of my enemies.

I jammed hands in pockets. "What do you want?"

"That guy you met at the farm."

"Peter Pugh. What about him?"

I waited to hear all the ways he was connected to Whittaker Pruitt. Maybe they'd spent time together in the Army, blood debts. Or better yet, a direct line to the Lombardis. A former employee with a criminal record would be nice. I was buying the loyal servant routine less and less.

"Where did you meet him again?" Fisher asked.

"I told you. A shack about a quarter mile up the hill, maybe less. Why?"

"And how old was he?"

"How the fuck should I know? My age?"

"You saw his license?"

"I was lucky I could read the name, so dark in there. I didn't catch a date of birth. What's with all the questions?"

"Because Peter Pugh wasn't the caretaker."

I wasn't following.

"Peter Pugh is the name of the sixteen-year-old boy who died in the fire."

CHAPTER SIXTEEN

AFTER I WHISKED Fisher out of Alison's driveway, I scampered back upstairs, returning to the filing cabinet to finish what I started. If the man at the caretaker quarters wasn't Peter Pugh . . . who the hell was he? I felt a sucker for buying his aw-shucks, humble routine. He got me. I could drive back and ask what was going on, but we both knew he wouldn't be there.

I got home late, tired, feeling the cumulative effects of several beers and a ravaging week that had taken its toll. Seeing Hank Miller's light on reminded me I needed to figure out how to pay him his rent. As I took the stairs, thinking about the cold, empty apartment waiting for me, I ached to reset the clock. Let me start over, chart a new path. I wanted my brother back. I wanted my wife back. I wanted my newborn son back. Another chance. Let me go back seven years to when this all started and take a different road, make better choices, give me something worthwhile to hold onto.

Flicking on the light, I saw him sitting in my kitchen chair, smoking. I was pretty sure those were my cigarettes.

Prison-chiseled body, tattoos up and down beefy arms, curly-cue script scrawled across his thick neck. So much like Bowman. Except he wasn't Bowman.

"You're the guy who brought me home the other night." I asked the question but I didn't need the answer. "From the bar."

All this time, trying to shove the paranoia out of my mind—I'd been right; I was being watched.

I studied him through my still-puffy eyes, trying to shake the déjà vu. "Do I know you?" I watched him, unsure whether I'd need to fight or bolt. I didn't see any scenario where I came out on top. He looked in peak physical shape. I felt like I had six body parts still functioning adequately.

"Nah, bro, you don't know me. But I know you." He leaned over for a respectful handshake. "Travis," he said. He didn't look like a Travis. Travises lived in trailer parks down South and listened to country music, ate crawdads, ran a trawler. This man was correctionally raised. Sometimes a name doesn't fit a face.

"You've been following me?"

"Nah, bro. Not following. But you may have seen me around Ashton. I had to find you. Didn't have much to go on. Just a name and town." He lowered his stare, fixing his eyes on mine, and my skin chilled from the inside. "I have a message for you."

I glanced around my apartment, wondering if this was it. Had Adam and Michael finally sent someone to shut me up once and for all? I gauged the distance to my cutting block. Not that it would do much good. The blade on my one steak knife couldn't pierce tomato skin with a running start.

"Relax," he said, picking up on my unease. "Why don't you have a seat?"

I pulled out the chair and reached for the cigarettes. Travis passed along my own pack, which was big of him.

I thought back to the fight. "What happened at the bar that night?"

"You were getting cozy with the wrong girl. Her man got pissed. You did all right inside the bar. But then him and his buddy handed you your ass in the parking lot."

Inside the bar? How long had the dude been watching me? "There was two of them and one of me."

"I'm not sure you would've been able to lick a chair, drunk as you were. Don't worry. I took care of those punks." He nodded through the front door. "I drove you back in your truck, carried you up the stairs."

"Why did you leave if you wanted to talk so bad?"

"I was planning on sticking around till the morning, when you were in better shape, but then that fat cop come by. Figured you two was friends the way he acted. I turned up the radio, told him to come back in the morning." Travis shook his head. "I can't be talking to no cops."

When I thought back to the fight, I remembered hearing screams. They weren't my screams I heard. I wasn't the one landing the punches, either. I stared at Travis' scarred, calloused knuckles, fists that carried the remorseless weight of many split skulls.

Travis nodded at a mug of cold, black coffee, left over from this morning. "Drink up. We need to talk."

Tasted like shit then. Tasted worse now. I choked down the swill until my head cleared. Then I asked the question I should've asked fifteen minutes ago when I'd walked in on a strange, yoked convict kicking it in my apartment.

"Who the hell are you and what are you doing in my kitchen?"

"Let's say we have a mutual friend. Or did anyway." Travis struck up another cigarette, waving out the burning sulfur head, using an empty beer can as an ashtray. I tried to pay attention to which one so I wouldn't take a wake-up swig and get a mouthful of ash. "I was Erik's celly."

"Erik Fingaard? Bowman." My heart sped up, the fleeting hope that comes with promises before they are broken.

"He told me you called him that."

"You guys talked about me."

"Erik was a good dude. I owe him a lot."

"He's dead?"

Travis nodded the solemn confirmation.

"Who killed him?"

"Some other prisoners. Jumped in the showers. Stuck him fifty-nine times, bled out. It happens."

"Who were they?"

"Some guys."

"I mean, were they, like, carrying out orders? Was there a hit or something?"

"People get killed in prison for all sorts of shit. Nobody calls it 'a hit' except in the movies. But did someone want him dead? Maybe. Probably. Yeah, sure, why not. Like I said. Happens all the time. He knew it was coming. But before they got him, Erik made me promise to do him a solid. He knew you were looking for him."

"I needed something I thought he might have."

"A hard drive," Travis said. "Contains evidence about a family you both hated."

"The Lombardis."

"Yeah, that's them." His face coiled rattlesnake mean. "Erik told me about the old man. Pedophile fuck."

"You don't have this hard drive, do you?"

Travis' stone-cold face betrayed the stone-cold truth, one I'd known all along.

"Gone, man. Destroyed long ago. That's what Erik wanted me to tell you. Get on with your life, bro. I've spent most of my life behind bars, locked in cages, seething to get even with everyone that done me wrong." Travis panned around my sad, dismal apartment, under-furnished, musty from the sealed-up year, my own prison.

"You came all the way from Massachusetts to tell me this?"

"I didn't know where you lived. Like I said, I had the town. Erik did me right. He asked me to do this for him. I am repaying a debt."

Ass-kicked by a couple college kids. My man behind the scenes, the Wounded King, one of my least favorite people on Earth. My wife, who'd had sex with me a few nights ago, couldn't be bothered to return a call. Alison Rodgers, good to go one minute, condescending and distant the next. No money. No job. No future. All I had was revenge. And now they'd taken that away from me, too.

Travis got to his feet, clasped a hand on my shoulder. "I got a sister in Fall River. I'm not supposed to be crossing state lines. Conditions of parole. I need to get back. Can I give you some advice?"

"You don't owe me anything."

"No," Travis said, matter of fact, "I don't. But I owe Erik and he liked you. Let it go. Give up. Or get right with the Lord. Fast. I've met too many men like you, full of anger and self-righteousness, feeling wronged, hell-bent on payback. Like drinking poison and expecting the other person to die."

I nodded thanks for stopping by but didn't do a good job of hiding the fury brewing in my gut.

"All right, brother," he said. "Have it your way. You know what they say about revenge, right? Good luck digging an extra grave on this ice block."

CHAPTER SEVENTEEN

PURSUIT IS PURPOSE. The chase. That's most of this life, chasing after the shit you want and will never get. Sucks. But if you're not doing that, you're standing still, in a holding pattern, and that sucks worse. It's like that Dr. Seuss bedtime story I used to read to Aiden, *Oh the Places You'll Go*: The Waiting Place. For people just waiting. Waiting for someone else to determine their future and fate. A phone call. A favor from God. Lotto. I'd rather be the one doing the chasing, the one in control. Win, lose, draw, it all comes down to me. But to chase, you need a goal, an objective, an end-game; otherwise you're spinning your wheels and chasing your own tail like a dipshit. This is the reason we lie to ourselves. To have an excuse to get up and keep moving. Better job, more money, unrealistic lifestyle upgrades, vacations, whatever, as long as there's a reason to gaze upon the horizon hopeful, regardless how soon the sun will set. While I appreciated Travis risking the conditions of his parole to tell me my dream was dead, I couldn't get too excited about his parting advice. I believed in God, or my version of it, but waiting to collect my winnings until after I died felt like the ultimate sucker's bet.

Gathering the pages of notes I copied from Alison's cabinet—patient names, more parent addresses, farm alliances, insurance information, details that just yesterday I thought might be important or lead somewhere, I walked to the trash and threw it all away. There was nothing to investigate. This was a dead end.

I pulled open the fridge door. Today's beer gone, I tapped into the next.

A knock on my door was followed by Fisher bellowing to let him in. I'd had no choice but to call Fisher after Travis left and fill him in on the visit. I couldn't sit alone with this.

"Your place stinks, Porter. You should open some windows."

"It's twelve degrees outside."

"Sorry, man," he said removing his miniature pea coat. "I know how much finding that hard drive meant."

"If a dream don't come true, it's a lie, right?"

"Isn't that a song?"

"Used to be."

Fisher came over to where I sat, letting his gaze linger on the coffee maker.

"Have a seat," I said. "I'll brew a fresh pot. Warning you though. Tastes like ass."

"I take it black. Always tastes like ass."

Mr. Coffee sucked up water, spat out steam, coughing, chugging back to life on the assembly line.

"What are you going to do now?" he said.

"Sleep a couple hours. Get up, go to work at Alison's, I guess."

"Yeah, about that . . ." Fisher thumbed his eye, stalling.

"What?"

"Alison Rodgers' ex-husband. Richard? You sure he split town?"

"That's why I'm working for her. Fence is falling down, steps loose, dryer clogged. Left Alison holding the bill to move out to Oregon and get soused."

"Not according to his latest arrest report." Fisher reached inside his coat pocket and pulled out a copy of the *Sugar Hill Gazette*, slapping the paper down, page open to the local police log. "Drunk and disorderly. Three nights ago."

I read the name. Age was right. "Maybe this is another Richard Rodgers?"

"Could be. Common enough name. Except the paper lists his last known address as Middlesex. Pretty small town to have two Richard Rodgers."

What the fuck?

"Sugar Hill," I read. "What county is that?"

"Davidson."

"Of course. Same county as the Pruitt Dairy Farm." I fetched Fisher's coffee for him.

"You sure that wasn't Richard Rodgers up in those caretaker quarters?"

"It was dark, hard to see, but no, it wasn't him." I didn't know Richard that well, our limited interactions coming a few years ago, but no one is that good an actor. "Richard's smaller but stood taller than this guy, if that makes any sense."

"Not really."

"The man in the caretaker quarters was like a kicked dog. Hunched over, beaten down." I snagged a beer from the fridge. "But he was stouter than Richard. Plus, he had a big ol' beard, and Richard Rodgers couldn't sprout facial hair if you smeared his face in chia pet and left him on the sun. I'm not standing in the same room with the man, having a conversation, and not recognizing the guy."

"This insurance grab," Fisher said. "Why Whittaker Pruitt started the fire."

"What about it?"

"He left no beneficiaries."

"So?"

"So why would he run into a burning building?"

"Authorities think he forgot incriminating evidence."

"What could be so damning he'd risk his life? He had no kids, no wife. He dies it's over. Davidson County owns the farm now anyway. All for nothing. Some coward torches his own place to get out from under the bank's thumb? Then he rushes across town, headfirst into the flames, for a couple gas cans?" Fisher shook his head.

"What are you saying?"

"There was another reason he ran into that burning barn."

"Like what?"

"Fuck if I know." Fisher waited. "Maybe Whittaker Pruitt didn't have anything to do with the fire."

He waited for a reaction. I didn't have one.

After a moment, Fisher hoisted the mug. "You weren't kidding. Tastes like sewer backflow." He got up and dumped the swill down the sink.

Fisher grabbed his coat off the back of the chair and slid it on. "I've been staying at my mom's up here. But I should hit the highway and get back home. And you look like you should get some sleep." He got that overly concerned look in his eyes, the one I hated. "You going to be all right?"

"I'll be fine. I appreciate you driving over."

"Maybe we can grab breakfast at the Olympic next time I'm in town."

"Sure, man."

"Take care of yourself, Porter. You know where to find me." He double-knocked the table, his signature move.

After Fisher left, I was struck by the stark realization that I might never see him again.

More surprising was how much that thought bothered me.

* * *

When morning rolled around, I helped Hank Miller shovel his lot. We didn't talk. We rarely did. I smiled, like everything was wonderful in my life and I'd have his money any moment. All I needed was a miracle. Too bad Christmas had cornered that market. It wasn't even Thanksgiving yet; I wasn't sure I'd last that long.

Upstairs I packed a butter and jam sandwich for lunch and made ready to ship off to work. I reminded myself to stay cool but knew I wouldn't be able to pretend. No way Alison didn't know her ex-husband was still in town, which meant she'd lied to me. How long had Richard been back? Had he ever left? Why not tell me? Unless she was covering for him. For the break-in, the coyote . . . for the fire.

I had to go to her house because I needed to get paid. Knowing my temper, my short fuse, how I wouldn't be able to bite my tongue, the impending conflict burbled in my belly like gas station sushi. I'd been running around trying to find who'd been harassing her, putting myself in harm's way, looking like an idiot trying to solve the mystery, when she'd known all along it had been her shitbird ex-husband in the kitchen with the candlestick, the lamest game of Clue ever.

That fire has nothing to do with you, little brother. Let go, Let God. Haha. I wish you'd paid attention to your bumper sticker faith when you were alive. *It works if you work it, so work it, you're worth it, wait for the miracle to happen. Haha.*

Halfway to Middlesex, my phone buzzed. I didn't recognize the number.

"Porter here." I slid out a smoke.

"I'll give you your money," Daniel Hanratty, ex-landlord from my old storage space, said. "Tell your lawyer to stop with the goddamn letters." He muttered something I couldn't make out, then said, "Seven. High as I go. Take it or leave it. Out of the goodness of my heart."

I dropped the smoke between my legs. "Sonofabitch!" I plucked the burning cigarette, swatting ash.

"Fine," Hanratty said. "You win. Eight. That's it, though. Otherwise I take my chances in court."

"Eight works." I gave Hanratty my address, before he hung up, cursing.

I'd probably have to wait a few weeks, but the promise of eight hundred bucks? For someone in my spot? Like manna from the heavens to a starving man.

*   *   *

Alison greeted me at the door, same as usual. Seemed like she was always fitting an earring or buttoning her blouse, in a perpetual state of mid-dress, racing to be somewhere else. Today I hadn't shown up till almost eleven. Yet, there she was, waiting by the door to leave. I swore she timed her exit to correspond with my arrival.

I waited till she gave me my forty bucks.

"Why didn't you tell me your ex-husband was in town?" I said, pocketing the cash.

"Excuse me?"

"Richard. Your ex-husband. He's in town. Or the general vicinity."

She didn't bother denying it.

"He was arrested in Davidson County the other night."

"Why are you checking up on Richard?"

"I'm looking out for you. That's what you're paying me to do."

"No, Jay, that is not what I am paying you to do. I am paying you to get this house in order so I can get out of here. And as for *why* I didn't tell you Richard was in New Hampshire, I didn't want you getting in some pissing contest with my ex."

"Or figure out who tried to break in to your house? Who killed that coyote?"

"You don't know that. And I'm not sure someone *did* try to break in."

"And I'm thinking he's good for the fire as well." I didn't have any proof of that last one, a shot in the dark, but I wanted to see her reaction, if she'd give something away. She didn't.

"Why would Richard want to set that farm on fire?" she said.

"He must've got paid from the sale. Seems pretty obvious to me."

"Two people died, Jay. I know you don't like my ex-husband, but he's not a murderer."

"He pulled a gun on me once."

"That wasn't loaded. And you were trespassing—"

"He's a drunk."

Alison stared, pot-calling-the-kettle deadpan.

"Don't compare me to him."

Alison nodded at the wad in my jeans. "And where's that forty dollars going? I can smell the beer on your breath every day."

"Nothing illegal about a man having a couple beers."

"Couple," she repeated. Like I'd told her I'd seen a yeti skiing in her attic.

"I'm not the one getting arrested for public disturbances, spending the night in the drunk tank."

"No, Jay," Alison said, pedantic bordering on boredom, "they didn't catch you, did they?"

"When was the last time you saw him?"

"Are you asking me the last time I saw my husband?"

"I thought he was your ex-husband?"

"What's yours called again? Jenny?"

Alison stepped to me, and I couldn't figure her angle. She was close enough to kiss with a face looking like she wanted to drill a hole in my heart.

"Why don't you get to work?"

"You fucking rich people are all the same."

Alison stepped back. "On second thought, I think we're done. I'm not sure I feel comfortable having you here, walking around my house, going through my things." She extracted her checkbook. "What do I owe you?"

"Nothing. Forty dollars a day, we're square."

"Don't be a martyr, Jay. You need the money."

"Not that bad, Alison."

I turned and walked out without looking back.

Yeah, I'd screwed myself out of a few hundred bucks that I could use and Alison Rodgers didn't need. But it was worth every cent to buy my dignity back.

CHAPTER EIGHTEEN

I STOPPED AT the Price Chopper to pick up a sandwich and a six-pack. At least I'd answered a few questions. I knew who'd been watching me—Travis—and who was breaking windows, smashing doors, slashing tires, and slitting animal necks—Richard Rodgers. I didn't think that would be the last I saw of Richard Rodgers. I'd gotten in the middle of a rich couple's nasty divorce. I wasn't sure how I'd let that happen other than I had feelings for his wife and needed work, so shame on me. Richard Rodgers may well come up behind me one of these nights, jump me from the shadows, and then we'd see who was tougher. I'd put my money on me. If I had any to spare.

Outside my dashboard window, snow tumbled through the tall supermarket lamps as bundled moms trundled babes. I unwrapped my sandwich and set my tall boy in the console.

Investigation is its own high. It's why people read mystery novels, watch whodunit films—uncracking the unknown provides a kick. When I broke into Alison Rodgers' filing cabinet, I didn't know she'd been lying to me, that her husband, ex-husband, was very much still in the area. If I were being honest, which wasn't high on my priority list at the moment, I knew Richard Rodgers had to have seen me at the house. Maybe that was why Alison hired me in the first place, trying to make him jealous. Who knew what she was thinking? My motives weren't altogether altruistic.

After learning the man in the dark caretaker quarters was not Peter Pugh—that Peter Pugh was, in fact, the boy who'd died in the fire—I wanted to talk to his parents. I *thought* that's what Alison had wanted, too. Now I had no idea what Alison did or didn't want. I wasn't working for her anymore. I was on my own time. Why did I care who started that fire? Because solving mysteries was what I did; it's who I was, what I'd become. Pursuit is purpose. Like a shark, I had to keep moving or I'd die.

I was about to put the truck in gear, when knuckles rapped on my glass. I panned over to find Sheriff Rob Turley in his furry town browns, coat and hat, shivering through a burr. I rolled my eyes before unrolling the window.

"Hey'ya, Jay," Turley said, teeth chattering, waiting for an invite inside the cab. Which he wasn't getting. This wasn't going to be a long conversation.

"I just stopped for lunch," I said. "Have to get back to work. Good seeing you." I made to punch it in drive.

Turley reached his hand—inside my window—stopping me from shifting.

"What the—?"

"I need to talk to you about something."

"You mean you didn't randomly bump into me at the town grocery store? First my apartment. Now the Price Chopper. If I didn't know better, I'd say you liked me. If you need to talk, call next time."

"I don't have your new number."

"No, you don't." I wasn't giving him my cell. When he realized that, he got to the point.

"Adam Lombardi and his family are in town for the holidays."

"Wonderful. Thought the whole brood was down in the big city?"

"Everyone's living in Concord, yes, but they still have their property on Elton Drive. Same house they grew up in. Guess they wanted to celebrate Thanksgiving this year in their childhood home."

"They?"

"Michael is here, too." Turley took a deep breath. "Now, Jay, I don't have to tell you—"

I held up a hand, stopping him there. "No trouble."

Turley whittled his brow, scowling, trying to deduce how full of shit I was. Which might've been a lot. I'd figure that part out later. Right now, I had somewhere I needed to be. I waved goodbye, waiting for him to take the hint. Turley glanced at the beer in my console.

"You sure you're okay to drive?"

I picked up the beer, which I hadn't opened, thank God, or I probably would've been written up for that, too.

"Put the beer back in the bag," he said. "It's illegal to drive with an open container."

I saluted thanks, before rolling up the window, blasting the heat, and inching forward over packed snow.

The world shrouded in white, I left Turley in the dust, heading home to dig through my trash and fish out the paperwork I'd stolen from Alison Rodgers. I was back on the hunt.

* * *

Peter Pugh's mother, Mary, lived in Crimson Peak, an affluent section of the Mountain. Dad, Larry, wasn't as well off, with residences listed as a string of single-room occupancy motels on the Desmond Turnpike. Last known whereabouts: unknown. Chances were he was still down there, somewhere; those SRO hotels are the last stop before the soup kitchen line. I wasn't up for checking each out, one by one, bribing residents with schwag beer and fast-food combos.

Which was why I decided to see Mary first. I'd been up to Crimson Peak a few times in my life, most recently a few years ago on the Crowder case. More often though, anytime I had occasion to venture up here, I was clearing out some dead rich person's mansion, a sewer rat hoping someone dropped a French fry.

Crimson Peak, like its name implied, sat high on the hill, and was where the richest of the rich on Lamentation Mountain lived. Alison Rodgers had money. But not Crimson Peak money. This was old money. This was heirs' money, trust fund money, my-grandfather-invented-some-chemical-company money. Up here was a different breed. Residents used summer as a verb and knew which fork was intended for which variety of lettuce, shit I'd never have to worry about.

Set back from the street, Mary's house gleamed a sparkling cube, all glass and metal, the shiny, unspoiled parts of a museum, sharp angles violating harmony as they cracked the sky, entitled.

Several new cars hogged the drive, including an Infiniti Genesis G80 and a just-out-of-the-box Humvee. I was interrupting some sort of party. Drunken highball laughter broke through the box and wafted down the drive, rising up to meet me, the shrill of joy knifing a hole in my belly a mile wide and an anchor deep.

Took five minutes of relentless ringing to get anyone to come to the door, and another six trying to explain to the lithe man with the coifed hairdo and alabaster complexion why I was there.

Morrissey said to leave my boots by the door. Everyone else had on their shoes, but I couldn't blame him; mine looked like they were covered in frozen cow shit.

He led me through the floor of partygoers, about a dozen total, all gesticulating, conversing wildly with animated zest about something hilarious that I knew wouldn't be funny, and into the kitchen, where sat a woman who could've been Alison Rodgers in another life, had Alison not been grounded by the humility and losses of alcoholism. Another tiny man handed off a tray of hors d'oeuvres, miniature mushrooms stuffed with pimentos, and Morrissey scampered away to be with others of his ilk. Judging by the way she perched high in her throne, I knew this had to be the queen.

She didn't confirm that right away, leaving me standing around, calculating the value of wainscoting and things forged of precious metal.

"Terry tells me you're here about my son?" Mary Pugh said, condescending to speak.

I had to assume Morrissey was Terry, who now had the name to match the face. I'd given him a quick overview of why I was there, stoking interest and piquing enough curiosity that Mary would agree to see me.

"I'm looking into the fire at the Pruitt Farm."

At her long, polished kitchen table, Mary Pugh crossed and uncrossed her long legs, then gestured for me to take a seat. I took off my stained hobo cap, bunching it between my hands, kneading the ball to remember everyone grieves in different ways, each method with its own merit. Peter hadn't been dead long. There was no law against a woman, a mother, moving on with her life, but I couldn't imagine losing my boy and hosting a party. Maybe my projection wasn't fair. I was guilty of being a class warrior, and that envy wasn't limited to politics or position; I didn't like people with this much money.

Mary reached her slender arm into a cluster of wine bottles and high-end liqueurs, a perfect circle in the center of mahogany, plucking a particular red, presenting the bottle, but the Olde English name meant nothing. I'd never been much of a wine guy. I

couldn't afford the good stuff, and the cheap varieties gave me a
headache. I had no doubt Mary Pugh's parties featured high-end
and top-notch. The effort would be wasted on me; all wine tasted
like spoilt grape juice to my unsophisticated palette.

Pouring a steady, measured glass, Mary projected an air that said
I wasn't to talk until she'd sampled the goods. I waited. I had nowhere else I needed to be.

She swirled the wine in a whirlpool. Then, like a bird testing the
waters of a new birdbath, she took a teeny, tiny sip. Before tilting the
whole thing back, healthy swig bordering on lusty glug. She set
down the glass with a return to delicacy.

"What did you say your name was?"

"Jay Porter." One of these days, I'd learn to use an alias.

"Who did you say you work for?"

"I didn't."

Mary Pugh had to be at least fifty, but she carried those years
well, wrinkles Botox-smoothed to minuscule spider threads, shoulders yoga-honed. But the obvious plastic surgery on her face tugged
pencil-thin eyebrows toward the bridge of her nose, creating the
sense she was forever displeased, as if she had just encountered an
unexpected, foul aroma. Either way, she didn't come easily undone.

"What would you like to know, Mr. Porter?"

"I don't want to bring up painful memories—"

"Then why are you?"

I got the feeling that if I hadn't stumbled in during the middle of
a party, those words would've been followed by a histrionic "Can't
you see I'm a grieving mother?" But any sorrow was drowned out by
the high-society soiree in the next room.

"I apologize, Mr. Porter. I don't mean to be rude." Mrs. Pugh let
her eyes linger on the glass of wine. "You must think I'm terrible,
hosting a party so soon after my Peter was taken from me."

"I don't think anything, Mrs. Pugh."

"Please," she said, brushing my arm. "Mary."

Another man, as delicate as Terry, peeped his head into the kitchen. "Is everything all right?"

Mrs. Mary Pugh presented the back of her hand, and the man skittered away.

"Can you tell me why you sent Peter to rehab?" I asked. "Rewrite Interventions is a last resort, no?"

Mrs. Pugh finished her wine and refilled her glass. "Peter had too much of his father in him."

"You two are divorced?"

"Twelve years now. Twelve of the happiest years of my life." And then catching herself, adding, "Until recently, of course."

"What did you mean about Peter being too much like his father?"

"Have you spoken with my ex-husband?"

"No, not yet. I was hoping you might know where I could find him?"

Mrs. Pugh peered past my shoulder, flicking a loveless finger. "Down there in the flats, on the Turnpike. He switches up motels, trying to avoid paying his child support. He never moves far. Has to stay near his coke dealers who sell him broken promises. Last I heard, he was at one called the Sunset Motor Inn. Claimed he had a job for some heating company or some nonsense. My ex-husband is a liar."

Inside her well-lit, opulent home, Mrs. Pugh didn't hide her disdain for Larry's lower class. I wondered how the two ever met in the first place and how she expected to get blood from stones, but the interworking of their brief marriage and subsequent divorce settlement wasn't any of my business.

Then as if she knew what I was thinking, Mrs. Pugh said, "Terms of our separation were agreed to a long time ago, when I wasn't doing . . . as well financially. Doesn't matter though, does it? Have you ever known drug users, Mr. Porter?" She sipped her wine down to a manageable single serving size.

"A couple."

"They are incorrigible, incurable," Mrs. Pugh continued, schooling me on the subject before she swallowed another mouthful. "No, I don't *need* Larry's money. But I'm doing him a favor. If he wasn't paying for the care of his biological child, the man would give every penny from his sporadic employment to his drug dealers." Mary poured another glass. "Doesn't matter how much drugs cost, Mr. Porter. They could cost a penny. Just means addicts would have bigger habits."

"Did Peter get along with his father?"

"Does any troubled boy get along with his father?" Mary closed her eyes, lids fluttering. "They got on all right, I suppose. Peter had begun smoking, sneaking pills from the medicine cabinet. We were stopping *that* behavior. Now." The punctuated fury ended with Mrs. Mary Pugh staring past my shoulder. I couldn't tell if she was sedated on pharmaceuticals, alcohol, or checking out for another reason. But I'd lost her. I watched her eyes glass over, like a patient when their doctor tells them they need to quit smoking.

Terry and his friend stomped into the kitchen, glowering as if I were a monster.

"I think you should leave," Terry said, as the second man lifted Mary to her feet.

"I need some sleep," Mary Pugh said.

The second man guided her to another room at the end of a long hall, before closing the door.

* * *

Driving home, I thought about Mrs. Mary Pugh and her poor bastard husband on the Turnpike. I didn't know these people, had no skin in the game; how Mary and Larry met or dealt with their lives had nothing to do with me. But I had a tough time dismissing parallels as I took the stairs and picked up today's mail, one handwritten envelope that didn't register right away. Since being back, I'd yet to run to the post office, waving my arms to bring on the bill collectors. Was I any better than Larry Pugh? I owed Jenny back child support. Mary and Jenny shared the same returns of better fortune. Larry and me? Both men of lesser means. But I was going to pay back Jenny what I owed, just needed to get a leg up, a few bucks, a lucky break.

There was no return address on the envelope, only my name, no stamp or postmark, meaning someone had personally delivered it. Holding the letter up to the light, I saw the check inside. Mickey Asal must've put the fear of God into Daniel Hanratty to get him to hand-deliver payment so quick. At the moment, eight hundred dollars was going to change my life. Except it wasn't eight hundred dollars; the check was for eight thousand.

I'd had nothing but rotten luck for so long. Even if I had five times that amount in inventory when I split last year, I owed a year's lease, and I expected pinching and skimming, grifting and theft. Eight grand was fair. You don't get a whole lot of fair in this life. For me, fair was a lucky break.

CHAPTER NINETEEN

"Now's NOT A good time," my ex-wife said.

"I have the money I owe you."

"Use it to get back on your feet."

"I'm using it to pay for my son."

"I don't need your money."

"You know how that sounds? Like my contribution to our son's well-being doesn't matter. It's emasculating."

"I don't have time to deal with your insecurities right now, Jay."

"Oh, such a sweet thing to say!"

"Fine. You want to pay what you owe? Write a check, stick it in the mail." Muted conversation escalating on the other end of the line.

Then she hung up. Without a goodbye.

Mother of my kid. Last week we'd had sex. I wasn't cursing her name or speaking ill of her. But that was some cold shit. She knew I didn't have a checking account.

Not that I was letting that stop me. I raced over to the grocery store, fuming, prepared to get a money order for what I owed, plus next month, slap on a stamp and mail my child support, on the spot.

But by the time I got there, I changed my mind. I wasn't using the US Postal Service out of spite.

No, I was going to deliver the money in person.

I grabbed more beer and headed for the Desmond Turnpike, steering south toward Pittsfield, seething over the mistreatment at the hands of my ex, the way she'd dismissed me so cavalierly.

Up and down the boulevard, cars and buses, trucks and people with purpose, men on their way to jobs, making money. I used to be one of them. I understood the other side, too, the men not going anywhere. The motels along this strip never changed: run-down, dilapidated, soul-crushing. Despite the holiday season, there was no mirth or joy, no gratitude in the air. The bums sat outside these motels in lawn chairs, trucker caps pulled low, used up, broken-down men, trapped. Winter winds whipped. Withered bodies, empty vessels, slipped in and out of rooms, stays lasting five or six minutes. You didn't need a flashing neon sign to advertise what was being sold here. The easy answer, the one most glommed onto—drugs, sex, bad people doing bad things—only told half the story. Yes, these were bad people doing bad things, but not because they were *bad* people; they were bad at living, bad at making decisions, bad at being human.

I'd done almost a year at AA. After a few months, I got more involved, volunteering for tasks like arranging cookies and making coffee. I began opening up, sharing, testifying. The overarching sentiment in the rooms: life is better on the other side. And maybe that was true. For most of the people. Most of the time. But how many of these people were getting to that "other side"? And when they did—*if* they did—there was no guarantee of anything better waiting for them.

Whenever a celebrity, a rock star, actor, Nobel Prize winner dies, the world at large mourns. There's this tremendous outpouring of collective grief and lament, people talking about how much David Bowie meant to them. I liked Bowie; I was a fan of the Spiders from Mars *and* Tin Machine. But the people I cared most about, the ones

I'd lost—Chris, Charlie, my girlfriend Amy—no one was eulogizing them. There'd be no movie or book about them. If I were to describe their lives, these people who meant something to me, the story would be received with polite attention, maybe a "that's a shame" or "he was *so* young." Then everyone goes on with their fucking lives; they won't give them a second thought. These losses defined me. I wasn't putting their memory behind me. I was never moving on. These forgettable existences were not something I'd ever forget.

As I passed the Sunset Motor Inn, last known residence of Larry Pugh, I jerked the wheel, skidding into the snow-covered lot, slamming my truck in park.

On the snow-packed walkway, three men sat in folding chairs, in front of rooms four through six. Without factoring in wind chill, I'd put temps at ten degrees tops, the afternoon gray, gusty, miserable. Big rigs blew past. Twenty-two-inch rims spat castoff, oil, mud, sludge mixed and redeposited in a fine carcinogenic mist. The men didn't move, except to trade swigs from a colorful bottle of Cisco, another day at the bum beach. Each man had the gaunt, sallow complexion of the recently deceased, embalmed, waxen skin aggravated by finer bones.

"I'm looking for Larry Pugh." I could've been talking to all, one, or none.

The man in the middle nodded. But not in a happy way.

"Don't know no Larry," he said.

One of the men held up the bottle. I shook him off. I appreciated the gesture, even if that meant they had me confused with one of their own.

I started for the office, despite the headache that would invite. These were the places people went to disappear. Good luck getting a desk jockey to talk.

A door under the walkway opened up.

"What you want?"

The man standing in front of Room Number 7 shielded his eyes from a sun that didn't exist, the skin on his face opaque, as if he'd just shaven off a decades-old beard and this was the first time his skin had glimpsed the daytime in ages. Aside from the ghostly complexion, I couldn't see much, the natural gray throwing shadows, me backlit, him submerged in dim quarters. I couldn't tell how old he was, but his presence projected a shell, an echo, a sad facsimile. This was me in a couple years unless something drastic changed, a cautionary tale of what becomes of broken men.

"You know Larry Pugh?" I asked.

"I'm tired, man. I've worked thirteen days straight. Gotta another shift in a couple hours. Why you out here hollering. What you want with Larry?"

He wore gray coveralls, pulled up to the waist, unbuttoned at the belt, top flopping down. I smelled fossil fuel and industrial oil, trapper doors slathered in grease, a man who worked in the infernal tar pits and vats of noxious solvents.

"He don't live at the motel no more," the man said.

"When did he move out?"

"I don't know. Maybe a month ago?"

"You know him?"

"You could say that." He squinched an eye. "Use to work together."

"You work together?"

"Used to." The man's shoulders slagged once he accepted I wasn't going away. "Got fired. Too many jobs, too many hours. Man worked his fingers to the bone. Got a second shift position at an appliance store. Plasterville or some shit. Poor bastard. Child support bleeding him dry." He rubbed a stained, inky finger in his eye. "Who are you? What do you want with Larry?"

"I'm not here to cause him any trouble," I said. "I need to talk to him. You have the name of the appliance store?"

The man hesitated, poking his head out, panning up and down the walkway, before waving me in, extending a hand. "Bill," he said. "I don't want to talk in front of those assholes." Bill nodded through the wall at the men in the lawn chairs. "I'm pretty much Larry's best friend. Anything you need to know, you can ask me. But, no, I don't got the name of the store. I can find out, though."

He didn't turn on any lights, the inside of his motel room as dark as the caretaker shack. In fact, a strange similarity hung over both places. More than the lack of light or the fact that I couldn't see any better in the day than I could in the night, the eyes of each man possessed that same haunted, vacated gaze. Thin strips of day blazed around the curtain. Trash piled at my feet, soiled laundry spread out in small clumps. The room stank like a rest stop on the Turnpike. There was nowhere to sit, the lone chair doubling as junk drawer with socks and underwear, other stained fabrics I wouldn't poke with a stick.

Bill tried a couple open cans of beer, holding them up to his ear, swishing the dregs back and forth, calculating risk versus reward.

After taking a swig of piss water, he released the empty can to the rest of the garbage on the ground, turning my way, as if just now remembering I was here. "What you want to talk to Larry about?"

I could see he expected bad news. Money owed, deal falling through, maybe someone's sister or girlfriend was pregnant. Whatever the case, the news wasn't anything anyone would want to hear. Good things didn't happen to men like Bill and Larry.

"I don't want to bring up a painful subject—"

"Say whatever you gots to say, man." He turned back to his unmade bed, covers twisted in a ball, the telltale signs of a man besieged by nightmares and night sweats.

"His son. Peter. The fire."

"What about it?"

"I want to know what happened."

"Read the papers. Watch the news. Ask that fucking rehab place." He shook his head, anger escalating. "What the hell would you come around asking a man about his dead son for?"

"I'm an investigator."

"For the insurance company? They gonna pay out?" He sounded hopeful.

"Maybe. I need backstory. Anything you can tell me? The more information I have, the better I'll be able to piece this stuff together."

"Talk to his bitch ex-wife."

"Mary. Yeah, we already spoke."

"Rich bitch," he repeated. He stepped forward and held out a hand. "Hey, man, I get one of your smokes?"

Not sure how he knew I had a pack on me, Marlboros tucked deep inside my winter coat pocket. Maybe I looked like the type of guy who smoked. I passed him the cigarettes. He took one and then, like an innocent oversight, slipped the rest of the pack into his dirty coveralls. I let the theft slide, the price of doing business.

"You went to her house?" he asked. "Nice place, eh? What you think that place is worth on the open market?"

"I don't know."

"Sure you do. Guess. Three-quarters of a mil? More?"

"Sounds about right." Crimson Peak sported houses in that range.

"Bitch has so much fucking money." He seethed. "Cars, vacation spots, that house. Throws fancy parties with her boy toys night after night. How's that make her a fit mother?"

"Not my call."

"All off the books, man," he said, outraged over the injustice committed against his friend. "She bleeds men dry. Larry can't afford a lawyer. Where's that leave him? Child support, brother." He gazed down at the soft paunch poking out his unzipped coveralls. "How's a man like that supposed to afford child support?" He stopped, remembering the real tragedy, a son, a father. "His boy," he said. "His only boy . . ."

The shame of not being able to pay for one's own child. I knew the feeling. "I have a son," I said. "Younger. I'm divorced from his mom, too. If I were to lose him . . ." I didn't have to finish the sentence.

"Eats him alive," Bill said, "what that woman did to him."

"You got something to write on?"

He sifted through the crap on the table, passing along a scrap. I scribbled down my number. "When you talk to Larry, have him call me."

Walking outside to my truck, I should've felt better about my situation. I didn't. I had the money to pay my child support, but I still couldn't see my son.

Back at my place, I saw Hank Miller moving oil barrels and went to give him a hand. When we were done, I pulled my wallet. Hank tried to refuse the money.

"Jay, you're just getting back to town," he said. "Have you found steady work yet? Hold off for now."

"I'm good." I pressed the bills into his liver-spotted hands. "Please." My eyes told him: I needed this. I was done with charity; I had to pay my way.

"Okay, Jay," Hank said, tucking the money in his bib.

Heading upstairs, I was feeling all right again. Weird that settling a tab would bring such satisfaction. Not like this money made my life all rainbows and puppies. My credit was still shit and collectors would get this new number sooner than later and start harassing me. And I still couldn't get money to Jenny. At least on my terms, which were the only terms I was interested in. I should've mailed a money order, but why should I have to do that? I'd known the woman since we were kids, and here she was hanging up on me—after we'd had sex—for him, that jerkoff? Denying me access to my boy. And that's how I rolled, at the mercy of my moods, because thinking about that bullshit got me thinking about how my body was breaking down. Saddling up each day, feeling my bones give a little more, losing the fight against gravity and barometric pressure. Up on the mountain, that pressure was intense. The leg where I'd severed the saphenous didn't work so well anymore. The pain lingered, gnawing on my best days, dragging me down on my worst. Which were any cold ones. In other words, most days and months of the year.

I went to grab a beer, but remembered I was out. So I had to bundle back up—because you can never wrap a light jacket on this frozen hunk of rock; everything is a production, layering long johns and double-capping. I started off for the grocery store but knew I'd just turn around to drink alone in my sad, depressing one-bedroom above a gas station.

For once in my life, I wanted to be around people. I didn't have any friends. The bar was my only option.

CHAPTER TWENTY

AFTER SUBTRACTING WHAT I owed, I had a surprising amount of money left over. I didn't plan to drink away every cent—but I also had nowhere else I needed to be. I didn't want to think about my future. My visit to see Mary Pugh had left me disgusted, and my attempt to talk to her ex, Larry, offered an unflattering glimpse into my future. How soon before I ended up on that Turnpike? What was the difference between a bum and me? A better break? I'd been down to nickels and dimes. Until this unexpected gift from Daniel Hanratty. Luck. *But for the grace of God there go I.* Oh, yeah? Then what about the poor bastard over there? *You worked hard for that money, little brother.* Man, no offense, but I just want to have a drink in silence, if that's okay with you?

"Who are you talking to, Jay?"

I glanced up from my pint. There were a few folks I wouldn't have been entirely surprised to see at Scarlett O'Hara's the Wednesday before Thanksgiving. Turley. Fisher. Alison. Even Jenny.

But not Adam Lombardi.

He took the stool next to me, beckoning for a pair of beers, a couple old pals catching up over the holidays.

I hadn't seen Adam Lombardi since my brother's wake, six, seven years ago. I'd *seen* him around town, but I hadn't spoken with him.

I'd spy him at the Price Chopper or Best Buy in Pittsfield, with his trophy wife and two popped-collar kids, and he'd shoot a smarmy smirk in my general direction, wave hello, and there was nothing I could do, no matter how much I would've liked to strangle him. I'd scowl or squint or ignore him. Then he moved away. Now he was two feet from me.

"What are you doing here, Adam?"

"In town for the holidays. Michael and I. At the old family house. This is our hometown, too."

"No, I mean, why are you *here*. In this bar. Now. Talking to me."

The girl tending brought the beers. Adam handed her a twenty, flashing that winning smile when he told her to keep the change.

He hoisted his glass, waiting for me to return the gesture.

I took a swig of the beer I already had, staring straight ahead into the mirror above the bar, wondering who the dead man was.

Adam carried on with the toast. "To letting bygones be bygones."

He drank his celebration alone.

Some college-aged kids came in, home from the better universities to hang with old buddies stuck in Ashton, the loyalty of friendship tested before the reality of paychecks set in.

"I was talking to Turley," Adam said. "He was telling me about how rough things have been for you of late. I was hoping you'd let me help out?"

"I'm fine." Which most days would've been a lie, but I was almost five grand in the black, as much cash money as I'd ever had. The world was my goddamn oyster. If I hadn't taken Lombardi blood money when I was flat-ass broke, why would I accept it now? I raised my glass for a new beer. No way was I touching the one Adam bought me. I didn't want any part of this conversation sober.

"We have a lot businesses, interests around the state," Adam said, "this town, other parts of New England. I could always find a job for a man of your talents. Maybe you need to branch out. What would you like to do? You're not getting any younger. Opportunities like this won't keep popping up."

Keep talking. In another minute I was cold-cocking this asshole.

"Last year, Jay, those men Turley was telling me about. The ones they say killed your coworker?"

"Owen Eaton wasn't my coworker. We both dealt in antiques."

"Whatever he was, these men—Andre, Dmitry Volkov, the two Russians? The ones you told Turley tried to . . . kill you?" The pause betrayed his disbelief, and hearing these outlandish claims aloud, I started having doubts, too.

"What's your point, Adam?" I drained the pint.

"You think they worked for me and my brother?"

I narrowed my stare, felt my right hand clench into a fist. One more word . . .

"I'm sorry," he said.

That wasn't the word.

Adam spun his stool sideways. There was no confrontation in him. There was nothing but pity, compassion, the way you consider something smaller, weaker than you, a wounded bird, an oil-slicked gull, a helpless kitten abandoned in the rain, incapable of defending itself.

"You have my brother and I employing hit men? Police officers on our payroll ordered to murder and dump your body in the lake? Now you think what? We hired two Russian . . . assassins . . . to frame you for murder? Do you know how crazy that sounds?"

I wished I'd ordered food, just to have something to do with my hands, a place to divert attention.

"Turley said you think this was all part of a cover-up? Because of toxic dirt—for the Coos County rehab, a business venture I am no longer part of? I'll be straight up with you about that last one. Yes, there were contaminants discovered in the soil, but they were discovered too late. And not by Lombardi Construction, because I'd already sold the company to Tomassi, who, to their credit, addressed the situation and, without being ordered to do so by any court, made fair and sufficient restitution to the families. And what I'm telling you now is not any secret, this is all matter of public record, but hearing about what you're doing to yourself is awful. You need to stop. For you. For your son."

I knew lip service, could tell when a man was blowing smoke up my ass. Adam Lombardi believed what he was saying. Such concern colored his face that, for a moment, I wondered if he were right. What if I had been wrong all along? What if I, not Adam or Michael, was the bad guy here?

"My brother and I live an hour and a half away," Adam said. "We still get calls about you and the trouble you are trying to cause. I don't like to hear it. Michael doesn't either. It's making us sick."

My head started to pound, too much warmth and dehydration. "Why don't you get back to your wife and kids? Say hi to your brother."

"I remember you as a boy. You were always hanging around." He laughed. "You looked up to Chris like nothing I've ever seen. Boy, you idolized your big brother. And he was a helluva wrestler. One of Ashton High's best. He should've gone to State, not me. A misunderstanding. One slight. Cost him everything." Adam spun sideways. "I don't want to see this happen to you, contrary to what you think. Forget me and my bother—you think Chris would want to see you like this?"

I staggered to stand, gathered my coat to leave, reaching for my wallet, fighting to stay steady.

Adam held up a finger for the bartender. "On me."

I waved her off. "I got this." Then to Adam, "Keep your fucking money."

* * *

I was lit up when I drove out to Jenny's, along the straight, flat plains of Pittsfield. The snows were swirling. Sucking nicotine, drinking the warm beers I stashed under the floorboard, augmenting, amplifying the effect with a slug of scotch from the half pint I picked up at the liquor store.

The country roads out of town were slick and slow, and the busier Turnpike offered little relief. The rush hour slogged with heavy flow, red rings of breaking lights bleeding through the silver, trucks and big rigs, sedans and utility vehicles, a glut of immobility. I swerved and veered, hand on horn, trying to gain separation, a man on a mission, the questions coming strong, fast, relentless. I couldn't block the inconsistencies puckering holes in my brain. Once I hit Pittsfield proper, I opened up the engine, flooding the two-lane with octane, radio cranked.

He's right. If all these men were hired to kill, why not you? They tried! *Not that hard. These were professional killers. Trained hit men. Paid assassins. Mowing everyone down—Bowman, those construction workers, Owen. Me. And, yet, here you are.* Maybe I'm tougher to get rid of. Maybe I'm not as ineffectual or easy to dismiss, you ever think of that? That maybe I'm too important around here to go belly-up and not have it cause a stink? I matter! *Or maybe you've never been a threat, Jay. Just a grumbling nuisance.*

Stephen's car was in the driveway. My ex-mother-in-law's, too. Through the big bay windows, I could see them all inside, smiling, laughing, silhouettes glowing in the warm, seasonal home. Sounds of joyous evening conversation drifted out to my cold cab, a family gathering at the end of the day to share stories. My wife carried a plate of food to the table. I saw my son race by the window. A pair of pumpkins perched on the porch; horns of plenty hung from the door, decorative gourds.

For a moment, watching them inside, happy, content, better off without me, I reconsidered. Did I really want to do this? Now? The day before Thanksgiving? *This will accomplish nothing.* I put the truck in reverse.

Then I slammed the shaft in park.

I killed my beer, jumped down, flicked my burning smoke into the snow. Gusting winds assaulting me, trying to persuade me to turn back, get in my truck, *not to do this.* If I had anti-anxiety medication, I'd have taken a pill; my pulse spiked, banging on eardrums like floor toms.

I pounded on the front door, and when no one answered in one second, I kicked the base, repeatedly, quaking the frame. Jenny opened, pushing me out onto the porch, slamming the door behind her. I'd taken the liberty of counting out the money I owed her, adding two months in advance. I thrust the cash at her hands.

"What are you doing here, Jay? Are you drunk?"

Shaking my head, too angry to talk, I tried to make her take the cash, form her hands closed around the bills, but she wouldn't take my money.

She pushed me off and started to back up inside, imploring me to stay silent with her eyes, whispering, "Call me later." Such urgency but so, so cold. Where was the passion of the other night?

I pushed past her into the house, Jenny shouting after me. My son jumped up from the dinner table, rushing to my side. "Daddy, Daddy!"

I flung the cash on the table. My ex-mother-in-law, Lynne, sat there, nestled beside Stephen. This had all been Lynne's idea, introducing my former wife to the hotshot banker next door. Jenny and I had been going through a rough patch, and my mother-in-law, who'd always thought her daughter could do better than some manual labor monkey, jumped at the chance. She'd itched for the opportunity to erase me from the picture. And she'd gotten what she wanted. She didn't hide her delight, satisfaction smeared across her cracked old-lady face, oozing out her pores.

"Please?" my son said. "It won't take long, Daddy. It's a really cool game. Please?"

"Listen to Mom," Stephen said.

If he'd said, "Listen to your mother," I'd have let it slide. Maybe. I was pretty ripped. But it was the "Mom," the direct address, the colloquial, familiar term of endearment, a cohesive family unit minus its inconvenient biological father.

I leapt across the kitchen table, grabbing Stephen by his shirt collar, lifting him out of his seat and flipping him over, slamming him down on the tabletop.

The mashed potatoes and pork chops sprung in the air. The crescent rolls tumbled out of the breadbaskets. Milk spilt onto the floor.

Jenny and her mother screamed. I couldn't make out exact words, blood pressure spiking between my ears. I kept lifting Stephen up, slamming him back down. He covered his face, squealing.

"You knew Lombardi was paying those dead workers' families, you sonofabitch!"

"I don't know . . . what you're—"

"You helped cover their crimes; you let those men die!"

A baby cried upstairs.

"Please, Jay—"

I balled my right hand into a fist, gathering force, and punched the table, inches from his head. I twisted my grip on his collar, lifting his face inches from mine, my wife and ex-mother-in-law pleading and pulling, begging me to leave.

I kept shaking him. "They were my family first!"

When Aiden came beside me and yelled, "Daddy, stop! Please stop, Daddy," I snapped out of it and let go. Stephen thudded to the table.

I pointed at the money on the table. "Every cent," I said to my wife, out of breath. "Every cent."

I stopped to look for my boy, to explain what had happened, apologize he'd had to see that. He was my child. He loved his father. But I couldn't find him. My son had disappeared.

CHAPTER TWENTY-ONE

THE POLICE LIGHTS came up behind me not long after I reentered Ashton town limits. I was on a secluded stretch, the name of the road escaping memory, though I must've driven it dozens of times. Jet streams whipped up ground cover, swirling old and new snow, conspiring to create an original storm, a world of infinite, imitation white.

In the rearview mirror, I watched the Ashton PD patrol car. I didn't recognize the cop behind the wheel. I could tell it wasn't Turley. Whoever the cop was, he wasn't getting out of the car, content to sit and wait, so I sat and waited, too.

Out of smokes, I sifted the longest butt from the ashtray and watched little snow tornados pirouette off the tarmac, gliding with grace. Reminded me of something, a particular time I couldn't put a finger on.

I hadn't had a drink since Jenny's. After body-slamming that sonofabitch Stephen, I'd sobered up. I was confident I'd pass a DUI. Still, every second counted. Thirty, sixty seconds ticked by, then another minute, which turned into ten, no one moving, an old-fashioned Texas standoff in a wicked New England nor'easter. If I had somewhere to be, I might've stepped out of the truck to see what was up, have a little fun, put the piss on. But I had nowhere to be. I smoked my dirty butts, blood alcohol level receding by the second. Morons.

Up the road, from the other direction, I saw another set of squad lights. The snow was really coming down now, slanting sideways through high beams as the car K-turned, pulling in front of me, blocking the road and boxing me in. If I'd wanted to leave I could've done so any time in the last twenty minutes.

From out of the car, here comes Turley, hitching up that giddy, shoulders curled, head down, positioning his big body to block out the storm. Hurricane winds couldn't bowl over that fat fuck. Instead of coming up to my window, he stopped passenger side, gesturing for me to unlock the door, and climbed inside.

He slapped his hat free of flurries. "Jesus, Jay," was all he said. He sounded as mournful as Adam Lombardi at the bar.

"What about it, Turley?"

"You stink like a brewery for one."

"I had a couple beers at the bar before."

"Before what?"

"Before you sicced Adam Lombardi on me?"

"No one sicced anyone on anyone. I told him I thought talking to you was a bad idea, but he's Adam Lombardi."

"And you're the town sheriff."

"Now that means something? I've always been a joke to you."

"Someone's feelings are hurt?"

"Jenny called me."

"I figured as much. Am I under arrest?"

"They live in Pittsfield. She didn't call the Pittsfield police, though I am guessing her husband wouldn't have minded." He shook his fat head, sad and slow. "You can't get out of your own way, can you." The admonishment didn't come with a question. "I'm here as a friend."

"Friend? Whose?"

"Jenny's. And I have a message for you. You can't go to her house again. Stephen's filed a restraining order. I'm also supposed to tell you not to bother calling. Any calls will be blocked, any attempts to reach her construed as 'harassment.' Her words."

"Gee, anything else?"

"Yeah. Jenny is contacting her lawyer regarding visitation rights. Yours are being revoked. Indefinitely. In addition to being wanted in connection to murder . . ."

"A charge I was cleared of—"

"The missing child support—"

"Which Jenny said she didn't want, and which I just paid her, in full."

A call came in on Turley's belt. He told me to hang on and took the call. Mr. Big Shot Sheriff had places to go, things to do that had nothing to do with me. My gaze drifted off, settling on the sea of colorless boundaries blending the mountainside, road, sky, all one big blur, heaven's descent or hell's rise indecipherable.

Turley ended the call, panning over. "Sorry about that. Holidays, y'know?"

I braced for the rest, and I was ready to fight back. Turley would have to call in the cavalry to save his ass. But he never raised his voice, relaying a message like he was calling in a lunch order to Giovanni's.

"Here's what's gonna happen, Jay. You're not going to have contact with Jenny or your son, that's what this all comes down to. Now if you want to pull some macho, head-case bullshit like you did back there, you're more than welcome. Not my jurisdiction. But I can promise, you *will* be arrested and charged and will have to spend whatever savings you got on lawyers to clean up the mess, and, frankly, Jenny and Stephen have more resources. They can wait you out. If you want my opinion—"

"I don't."

Turley pained a grin. "Have it your way. But this ride is over. Now come on."

"Where?"

"Do you want a breathalyzer? I'll get Scott to give you a ride home."

"Who's Scott?"

"My new deputy sitting in the car behind us. He can drop you at your place."

"And what am I supposed to do with my truck?"

I could see Turley champing to say "Not my problem." But, of course, he didn't.

"I'll get it towed back to Hank's." He waved me off like he was doing me a big favor, but I knew he couldn't leave a truck on the side of the road. "Town's dime. Happy Thanksgiving." He made for the handle. "I'm sorry it's come to this." He did not look at me when he said this.

He got out, trudging to his big-shot car, inching off the shoulder, making sure the lanes were clear. No one was driving in this shit except lunatics and lawmen.

All the times Turley had ridden me hard or busted my balls, he'd been trying to make me see the light, facilitate change. Tonight, he didn't bother with any speeches or even get mad. He'd given up on me, too.

I had the engine running, hot. I'd lost the right to see my boy. I entertained fantasies of slamming the truck in gear, peeling tires, making a run for it. Head back to that mutherfucker Stephen's house and not pull my punch this time. If I was going to suffer these indignities, I deserved the satisfaction. And if the moment could've frozen there, like old Paul Newman cracking the cue in a pool hall, or young Paul Newman kicking open the door in South America, some variation of Paul Newman, life preserved in the dying amber of living color, I'd have made my move. But nothing would freeze except the air and space outside. The scene would play out to its logical conclusion. Scott, Ashton's new deputy, would hit the lights and take off after me, and at some point, they'd arrest me. Turley was doing me a favor. I knew that. And I owed Jenny. Because as bad as today was shaping up to be, it could've been a whole lot worse. Because it can always be a whole lot worse. She could've let Stephen call Pittsfield PD, charge me with assault. Instead, she used the ordeal to make me go away. I couldn't get the look on my son's face out of my head. I turned the engine off.

* * *

An hour after Scott the deputy dropped me off, I heard the tow truck pull into the gas station lot downstairs. Unhitching the cargo, the driver dropped his load, before circling through mounting snows, back onto the unplowed road. Out the window, the winds and storm kicked up and continued on, obscuring anything beyond six inches in front of my face.

Life is simple in the abstract. Make better choices. Be a better person, more disciplined. Casting stones is easy. When Chris was alive and I was busting my ass, never missing a day of work despite hangovers, paying my bills on time, I couldn't understand why my brother couldn't get his shit together. To the town, Chris was a bad apple, the no-good kid who'd tampered with his dad's brakes and drowned his folks. (Right around Christmastime, too!) And in my brother's final drug-induced confession, he tried to make me believe he'd really done it, transferring the sexual abuse he suffered at the hands of Gerry Lombardi onto our dad. Like this would somehow free me. Problem was: it never happened. My father was a good man. Anything my brother said, a delusion. How does someone, no matter how good they are under a hood, manipulate a braking system so precisely that a car fails *at the exact moment* it's crossing a bridge? Impossible. The story was a folktale, another rural myth like that crane in the pond.

I used to think that the rumor haunted my brother, tormented him; that he did the drugs to escape the shame. I saw now, like so many other things, I'd been wrong about that, too. My brother wore that label with pride. It gave him license to do whatever the fuck he wanted, staying loyal to nothing and no one.

Without my boy, I didn't have anything left here. I didn't know where I'd go. Maybe Florida, see my old boss. Not the worst idea, get off the mountain for the winter.

At the closet at the end of the hall, I pulled down the tattered rucksack from the top shelf. When I fled the state last year, I hadn't had time to go through my things and select precious mementos, my brother's old backpack left collecting dust. I hadn't seen the thing since the day I called the cops on Chris seven years ago. Afterward I'd gone to my best friend Charlie's house, dumping the contents. I remembered being struck by the scarcity, the random- ness of my brother's existence. Coffee cards punched at the coffee shop, drug paraphernalia, dirty socks and tees, tabs of paper, ripped-off phone numbers advertising couches and DVD players. After Chris goaded the police into shooting him, I'd shoved the crap back, prepared to throw it in the dumpster. But I couldn't. This was all that remained of my brother. Fragments and garbage.

I didn't know why I wanted to relive the pain, why I ached to feel that hurt again, but I spilled the backpack onto my floor. The

Tupperware container with burnt spoon, expired driver's license with Chris looking better than I ever remembered, a hopeful spark in his eye, the promise of eighteen, sky's the limit, nothing's going to stop you.

That's when I saw the letter.

CHAPTER TWENTY-TWO

I DIDN'T BELIEVE in ghosts. I knew the voices in my head weren't real. I wasn't particularly spiritual. If anyone asked, I'd describe myself as a Springsteen Catholic. I believed in the love that you gave me, I believed in the faith that could save me. Didn't take it any further than that. I was skeptical of coincidence and conspiracy, even as I fell prey more and more to them. For as rocky as my mental state had grown, for as compromised as it could be, I didn't flat-out hallucinate anymore.

I'd been stressed that afternoon at Charlie's seven years ago. My brother was in trouble. We'd found those pictures of Gerry Lombardi; my stable foundation was crumbling. But I wouldn't have overlooked a sealed envelope with my name on the goddamn front, in my brother's unmistakable chicken-scratch handwriting. That note had not been there. Yet, here we were, years after his death, a message from beyond the grave.

Out of scotch, I brought my last beer with me to the couch. Popping the tab on the lukewarm can, I lit a cigarette and broke the seal.

Jay,

By now you've seen the pictures of Adam and Michael's father Gerry. I won't tell you about all the things he did to me when I was wrestling. In the shower, at his camp, at his house. I don't want you to think less of me than you already do. I can't say it was rape because I didn't fight him off as hard as I should have. I always needed to be loved and accepted. But I didn't want to do those things. I'd already started using drugs by that point and that stuff can make you do shit you normally wouldn't. But that's not why I am writing you this letter. I know I'm going away (yes, you really do know when your time is coming to an end), but I'm not scared to die. I'm scared I won't be able to talk to you again. I don't want you to feel bad or beat yourself up. I'm proud of you, Jay. I've always been proud of you. I know I drove you crazy and you'll never understand about the drugs but there's no one to blame but me. I'm just messed up, no good. I know when this is over, you might hate me more, but that's okay. If you need to hate me to move on, do it! Jenny loves you and you love her, and you have that wonderful boy. Do me this one small favor. I know I'm not in a position to ask for favors. But be a good dad, be a good husband. You were a good brother to me. I know after this is over you might think you weren't. Our relationship was everything I could've hoped for. Growing up, I hated watching how our father treated you. It was always about me and the wrestling team and the greatness he believed waited for me. It hurt to watch him ignore you. You always took my calls, Jay, you never turned me away. You didn't give me money for drugs because you cared about me and wanted to see me get better. That is what any good brother would do. I just couldn't get better. I had to do this my way. Please understand that. I love you, little brother.

Always your big brother,
Chris

PS I'll see you in your dreams.

When I finished, I couldn't breathe, sitting there, tears stinging my eyes. I ground my teeth, clamping harder than the jaws of life, legs shaking, hands shaking, heart clogging my esophagus; and if you've never had a panic attack, good for you. Because they are about the worst feeling on Earth. Every physical beating I'd taken—severing my saphenous nerve, the concussions and beat-downs, kidneys used as a football—a sunny-day picnic compared to this feeling.

Chris had to have written this letter before he'd found me that day at Jenny's—before he gave me a copy of the disk with the pictures, before I betrayed him and turned him over to the police, before he knew I was gutless. He knew he was going to die. And with what little time he had left, he tried to make sure I, his little brother, would be okay.

Be a good dad. Be a good husband. Forgive myself, move on. Hate him if I had to but don't hate myself.

And of all these humble requests, I had done not one.

We were past making amends. Even if Jenny didn't have a newborn with her new husband in her new home, I couldn't get a call through to apologize. And if I could, then what? Try to convince her to leave her rich, successful, stable husband for the psycho hillbilly drunk who'd just scared the shit out of her family the day before Thanksgiving? Who'd terrified his own son? My ex-wife had come to my apartment a week ago, after everything I'd fucked up, and shown me she was in love with me, that she was willing to give me a chance to prove everyone else wrong and rise above. This late in the game, with this many odds stacked against me, I'd had a fighting chance. The odds sucked. I'd probably lose. But I had a shot. One in a million is still a shot. And what had I done? Snuffed out any flicker of hope in glorious fashion, extinguished without sniffing deliverance.

I couldn't honor my brother's dying wish to just be.

But there was one thing I could do. Sifting through the wreckage of who I'd hurt, myself notwithstanding, I could throw good money after bad; I could keep moving forward. Like Rocky, I could stand on my two feet. I could face the onslaught, take my beating, and survive that final bell. What else did I have left?

In a way the choice had already been made. Too much time had passed for me to admit I'd been wrong about everything. I couldn't live in a world colored by Adam and Michael Lombardi's version of the truth. I'd live with what others saw in me, what they said about me when I wasn't around, how I was a bleak bastard, a dismal mutherfucker, a stark-raving lunatic, a bum in better clothes. But I couldn't live with that. I couldn't sit idle.

Adam and Michael had been hiring thugs to run Alison out of the rehab market. They had a hand in that fire. I knew it. I only had to prove it. So what if I didn't have evidence? Who cared that she didn't want my help? I didn't give a shit that her jealous, rummy husband was in town. If she was using me for leverage in their sick domestic games—if she wasn't paying me—so fucking what? If I could connect Adam and Michael to that fire, get them attached, somehow, someway, I could make them pay for what they'd done to my brother and me.

I could feel the clock winding down. It's funny. When your time is running out, you really do know the end is coming. Ain't that right, brother?

* * *

wounded_king1180: whats up?

I'd gone out for more beer and cigarettes. I was in no condition to drive, but the roads were such a mess, I'm not sure it mattered.

Ten miles an hour, turn the wheel left, turn the wheel right, seeing triple, pick the lane in the middle. I dropped the message for Fisher. Not sure why I didn't pick up the phone, text him now that I had his number again. I guessed I liked the distance, the separation of a screen. I was drunk.

> **jay_the_junkman:** i wanted to say im sorry

> **wounded_king1180:** what do u need?

> **jay_the_junkman:** nothing

> **wounded_king1180:** porter u r never nice unless u need something. lol. its cool ☺ seriously whats up?

> **jay_the_junkman:** just wanted to apologize. i havent been fair to you. im sorry

> **wounded_king1180:** were good

> **jay_the_junkman:** take care of yourself fisher

> **wounded_king1180:** when people get this melancholic it makes me worry. u r not going to do anything stupid are u? u can talk to me. i am ur friend. i know im not charlie but u r not alone either

I signed off.

Tugging my knit cap in place, securing it tight, I went to turn up the heater. This final mission shaped up to be a long night. Cranking the dial, it hit me. Oil. Heating oil to be precise. There's a distinct scent to kerosene. A lot of old-timey lamps used the stuff. The accelerant used a compound. Range oil, coal oil. I encountered combustible fuel in estate clearing all the time. I should've recognized that odor when I smelled it a couple days ago, except I'd been preoccupied by scornful ex-wives and a future life on the Turnpike. I knew that smell. It was the kind of mixture found at an oil processing plant. A heating company.

* * *

The Sunset Motor Inn didn't look any different at night. Same row of sad sacks camped in cheap lawn chairs, watching the Turnpike traffic zip past. What did a calendar or clock mean to men like this?

I walked past them without a hello this time, stopping at Number 7 and banging. No answer. Looked through the blinds. Nothing, cleaned out. I'd gotten the impression Bill had been a long-time resident of the Sunset Motor Inn. He decides to clear our right after I start asking questions about his friend? Larry had never returned my call. Had Bill relayed my message?

"Hey," I called out to the men on the lawn chairs. "What happened to Bill, the guy that lived in this room?"

"How we supposed to know?"

Another hand swatted in my general direction, the nuisance of a summer mosquito.

The third didn't move at all. He was younger than the other two, almost a kid. Twenty-seven, maybe twenty-eight. How bad do you have to fuck up your life that you're living at the Sunset Motor Inn before your thirtieth birthday?

I walked over and stood in front of all three. The worst of the blizzard over, a hint of moonshine poked through the clouds, a cold slice of heaven.

"I was here the other day," I said, "talking to the man in Number 7. Bill."

"Don't know no Bill."

"You're telling me you never met the guy? There're eight fucking rooms in this dump."

"Don't know nothing," the one said. "But if they shit ain't in there, then . . ." He threw up his hands, as if to say, "Well there's your answer."

The three men carried the same haggard look of the professional drunk, the leathered skin and rivered crevices, a deep mustard stain to the skin. Which made determining age tougher. The kid was a kid. But the other two? Fifty-six? Seventy? Forty-five? No clue.

When the first man, the talker of the bunch, brought the beer to his lips, I smacked it away.

"What the hell—" He made to stand, and I shoved him back in the seat.

"Whoa, buddy."

"Don't 'whoa buddy' me. You saw me go into Bill's room, asshole."

"I don't know nobody named Bill. Now why don't you piss off?"

He looked like he wanted to take a swing, eyes squinty mean. But he wasn't doing jack. The second guy held up a hand urging me to stay calm. The third one, the kid? Hadn't moved a muscle since I got here. Maybe someone ought to check for a pulse.

These fools had water on the brain. I wasn't getting anywhere with them. I made for the motel office. Lights and vacancy sign off, I cupped my hands and peered through the dark window. Empty chair, computer powered down, back door closed.

"Bill moved out."

I turned around. The third man, the young one who hadn't said a word, stood there sheepish, like someone had stolen his bicycle but he didn't want to say who for fear of getting his ass kicked, his voice thin, soft, airy.

"Why did you tell me you didn't know him?"

He shrugged. "He owes everyone money."

"So you lie for him?"

He nodded at the beer on the snowy, mud-sludged sidewalk. "Bought us a six-pack when he left the other day."

"Gave us a six-pack," the first man shouted over his shoulder. "What you got?"

"I got a fist ready for your mouth, how's that?"

He scoffed with a backhanded dismissal.

"How can I find him?" I asked the kid. "Where's he work?"

"Don't tell 'em nothin', Jimmy!"

"Shut the fuck up." I looked at the kid. "Tell me, and you make a quick twenty bucks."

"I don't know where he works, but I know where you might be able to find him. We drove out to this house once..." The kid stopped there.

"I'm not the cops."

"We drove out to this house to pick up ... stuff. And this guy, he seemed more than a dealer."

"You got an address?"

"Like a number? No. But it was in Davidson County. I remember the road. Payne Street. Wasn't a lot of houses."

"Payne Street. In Davidson County." What was I going to do with that? "Thanks." I turned to walk away.

"Wait," Jimmy said. "There was a big wagon wheel on a rock in the front yard."

"A wagon wheel?"

"Like decorative. Big. Propped against this boulder. And a little white fence around it. I remember because I teased him about how cheesy the place looked with that wagon wheel, like his dealer ate a lot at the Cracker Barrel."

"Hey," the first man hollered. "That's worth something."

I pulled a twenty.

"Here," I said, balling the bill in Jimmy's palm. "Have a party."

Why had Bill split? Did he know someone would come looking for him? If he bribed the three wise guys to say they didn't know him, he must not want to be found. Or was he protecting Larry? The way he'd answered the door the other day, like he'd been waiting for me. How much had I told him? I mentioned the fire. Was that what had him spooked? Covering for a friend? Or was there more to the man who reeked of kerosene and jet fuel?

CHAPTER TWENTY-THREE

I DROVE OUT to Davidson County and the house on Payne Street. Took me a little while to find it. Not many houses peppered the desolate country road, but they were spread out. Once I saw the wagon wheel and boulder, I knew I had the place. No cars in the driveway. Lights off. House falling down, planks peeling and boards weather-striped. I parked well off the road, in a culvert, safe from prying eyes. If this was a coke house, I wasn't pulling in the driveway and having Alfred Molina pop out in a kimono.

Treading lightly up the walkway, I soon realized the house was vacant. The blanket tacked to the window didn't cover it all. Hobo flotsam bobbed on a dirty sea, discarded cigarette packs, beer cans, Big Gulp cups. Squatters? This far out in Davidson County?

I tried the door and was surprised to find it unlocked. I poked around remains of the night. Coke dealers enjoyed far more opulence.

Walking around the old house, I checked the rooms, trying the lights. No power. I was freezing balls in there. Although it wasn't as cold as one might imagine, given the lack of a heater. The floor mattress was spongy, full of fungus, as if it had been dragged off the side of the road. No refrigerator, no running water. But as evidenced by the amount of refuse and human stink, someone had been living here, and recently.

The setup wasn't unlike the caretaker quarters at the farm. Whoever that man was, he hadn't been living there either. He'd been waiting for me.

He just had lousy aim.

In the corner, I spied glinting metal, something I didn't connect right away, its placement unexpected and unusual. A generator.

I touched it. The metal was warm. Panning around, I spotted the small floor heater. That was why the house wasn't as cold as it should be . . .

I heard footsteps crunch sticks outside the window, the scuttle of disturbed ground cover, twigs and ice. I stopped moving. Whoever was outside stopped as well.

Back to the wall, I slid, stealth as possible, navigating with boot tips to make sure a bullet didn't find me through the plaster. Or were those my footsteps I'd heard?

They started again. I did my best to determine how many of them there were. Like a drunk with blurred vision, I wondered if it was possible to be so wasted you heard double, too. Except I'd sobered up, relatively speaking.

I tried to gather bearings. Eyes adapting to the darkness, I mapped exit routes, slipping through what was once the kitchen, out the back door.

Outside was somehow darker than in. I could barely see my boots. I felt around the ground for a way to defend myself. A glass bottle would do. But I was in a backyard covered with snow, not much exposed. Toe-tapping blind, my foot kicked against a board. Not that big or sturdy, but when I peeled it up, I found a pair of convenient nails poking out the other side.

He was inside the house now. A split in the clouds shone on a small tool shed. Locked. But beyond that, a gutted car missing its hood and engine. The car clearly hadn't run in years, pocketed in rust, covered by a blue tarp. Sliding into the vacant cavity, I draped the tarp over my head, doing my best not to get jabbed by shards of corroded metal. I kept an eye peeled through the pockets of rust.

The back door pushed open. Some grumbling, cursing, footsteps scuffling. The night fell darker. He came my way. I felt the stock of a rifle set against the car and smelled a lit cigarette. I craned my neck to get a better look but couldn't see a face. I slipped and banged against the hollow body.

What happened next happened fast. The man reached for his gun. I popped out beneath the tarp, swinging my board, hammering down, nails going clean through feet. A blur of pale face, an errant blast into the sky, a howl. He let go the gun. I fell back inside the cavity, dropping to the ground, reaching underneath the chassis, feeling for the rifle, getting hold of the barrel, pulling the stock inside the car carcass with me. I'm not sure if I would've been able to get off a shot. But I couldn't try, trapped inside that gutted engine, imprisoned by the frame of rusted machinery. I heard the man hobble off, cursing and whimpering.

By the time I managed to climb out of the car, he was gone. I looked down at the board in the snow. Blood dripped from its nails.

* * *

I sat on a tree stump as the Davidson County Police canvassed the abandoned house, crisscrossing beams, searching for clues. I had no choice but to call it in. Explaining what I'd been doing there was rough, but this was the second time in the past week someone had tried to take a shot at me.

Turley ambled over.

I'd told Davidson County to call him. Turley was the closest thing to an advocate I could hope for in a situation like this. The first cop I'd talked to, a bushy, bearded bear of a man, didn't look too happy to be called out on this slushy, rotten Thanksgiving eve. When he started riding me hard, I said to call Sheriff Rob Turley in Ashton, that he would explain everything. Then I waited, hoping Turley would be in a better mood.

Turley motioned to the big, bearded cop. "Officer Stokes here says someone took a shot at you? Twice?"

I got to my feet. I'd had plenty of time to come up with a feasible backstory, but there weren't a lot of suitable reasons for my being in the middle of the woods, sniffing around an abandoned house, on the edge of Davidson County.

"I'm helping out a friend." I was careful not to use words like investigating or case or client.

Turley picked up on what I meant. He wasn't happy. Question was whether he'd throw me under the bus.

He took his time deciding, too. Maybe he was getting in the holiday spirit.

Turley turned to Stokes. "Jay does some investigating back in Ashton."

"Private? Why didn't you tell me that?"

"I forgot my license. And, let's face it, cops aren't always fans of guys like me." The line sounded lifted from a pulpy paperback I might've read in high school.

"Because guys like you muck up nights like this." Stokes stopped. "A P.I.?" He shook his head. "Didn't think there were many of you guys up in the mountains."

"There's not. I'm contracted primarily for insurance cases." I was ad-libbing, adapting on the fly, but that one felt right.

"What are you investigating?"

"The Pruitt Farm fire. Following up on a lead. Heard this place was a drug house."

"Drug house?" Stokes laughed. "You might want to check your sources better. No, this place belongs to Sally Jutras. Little old lady, the kind that bakes spinach pies and mothers several cats. Seventy-three. Unless Sally's unloading her extra calcium pills, she's not dealing drugs."

"You sure about that? The house—"

"I know everyone around here." Officer Stokes acted offended. "Sally's lived on Payne Street her whole life. Till last summer anyway." He motioned through the trees where not half an hour earlier I'd been hiding in the engine of an old parked car. "Relocated to the senior community in Calloway. Hasn't gotten around to selling this place yet. No money to fix it up. She works part-time for the county. You ain't saving cash that way."

"Someone's been sleeping here."

"Doubtful."

"Check for yourself. There's a generator inside."

Stokes' face contorted like he'd ben fed a gob of expired cream cheese. He called for a deputy. "What you get on the gun?"

"Unregistered," the deputy said.

"Of course." Stokes shook his head. "Live free or die," he muttered.

"What do you know about the Pruitt Farm fire?" I wasn't asking Turley for permission. Say anything with enough authority, folks tend to play along. I pulled my Marlboros, firing one up. I was speaking with a contemporary. Turley's eyes whittled mean. He'd backed my play to get me out of a jam, but in doing so, he'd also opened the door, validating my right to ask these questions. And I had a lot of them. "Arson, right?"

"Yup," said Stokes. "Owner of the farm. Whittaker Pruitt. Place was in foreclosure, bank swooping in. Last-ditch attempt to bail out. Didn't work so well. People died in that fire."

"I heard. Pruitt and a boy, Peter Pugh."

"Which side you working for?" Stokes asked.

"No side. Just need to piece together what happened."

I could feel Turley's contempt through the padded layers of his town browns.

"Your company is looking to deny the claim, I take it?" Stokes said.

"No one to deny it to. Pruitt had no family, no heirs." I was glad to have done my homework. "Belongs to the county now."

"Don't know what more I can tell you." Stokes scratched his big beard. "Except Pruitt must've had help. I have five boys who saw Whittaker Pruitt come running from far away, long after the fire started." He pointed down the valley, a ravine ravaged by flood ages ago. "Used an accelerant. Fire department ruled out a timer. The guys at the firehouse think he ran in to retrieve gas cans. Stupid risk with flames so high."

"Since when has your average criminal been accused of being smart?"

Stokes laughed. "You give us anything on the shooter tonight? Other than he was pale?"

"Who isn't pale up here?" Turley said.

"True," I agreed. "But he had an opaque complexion. Like when someone shaves for the first time in a long time." I knew that look well. When I got rid of the lumberjack beard after my year on the run, my skin bristled with its newfound nakedness.

"So two men," Stokes said, pensive. "One with a beard. One clean-shaven."

"Or," Turley said, "the same man shaved."

"You think it could've been the same man?" Stokes asked me.

"It was dark in there, and when people start shooting at you, you don't get a lot of time to study facial features."

"Fair enough," Stokes said. "We'll be in touch we find anything."

I thanked him for his time, shook his hand, and then slapped Turley on the shoulder, ready to bolt to my truck before he could read me the riot act. Instead I stopped. "One more question."

"Go for it."

Turley bristled.

"Richard Rodgers."

"Who's that?" Stokes asked.

"Davidson PD picked him up a few nights ago. Drunk and disorderly."

"Don't recall anyone by that name. Then again, it's possible one of my boys dumped him in the drunk tank, let him dry out, sober up. Why? He have something to do with this fire business?"

I thought back to the man hobbling into the wild, his foot impaled on a couple rusty nails. Something about him was familiar . . .

"Maybe," I said.

CHAPTER TWENTY-FOUR

I DIDN'T THINK Alison would be happy to see me. It was late. I didn't smell my best. And the last time I'd been here, she fired me. She knew I'd gone through her things. At the time, I thought she'd been leaving me alone so I *could* go through her things. As usual, my moral compass, so stringent and righteous, unwavering in its guidance, was way off.

"What are you doing here, Jay?" She pretended to sniff. "I don't have any money."

I wasn't a big material guy. I thought money was boring. Money didn't matter to me except that you needed it to stay alive, buy food, sustenance, and warmth. In that moment, though, I had all that cash on me. I extracted the wad from my wallet, holding it high for Alison to see, waving it for good measure.

"I don't need your money, Alison."

"Good to hear."

"I'm not a bum. And I don't need a handout. I told you it was a matter of time till I got back on my feet. I am a business owner. Just had to liquidate my merchandise." I tucked the money away. "But I appreciate the condescension." I waited for the invitation I wasn't getting. "Are you going to ask me in?"

Alison exhaled and made a grand show of stepping aside.

Two days ago, I was working for her, broke, struggling and sub-servient. Strange how a little change in your pocket can disrupt the power dynamic. I felt like I was standing straighter. A couple days' growth back on my face, some food in my belly, a little color, cuts on the mend, I was carrying a purpose again, a new man.

"What do you want to talk about?" Alison said, arms akimbo, the suburban wife's fighting stance.

"I'm trying to help you."

"Your way of helping always ends up being a sideways move at best."

"I need to know the truth about Richard. Is he in town?"

"For the last time. No! Not that I know of. Last I heard from my *ex*-husband was a drunken late-night phone call screaming at me."

"What about?"

"None of your business!" She stopped, reconsidering. "Okay, you want to know? I'll tell you. It was about you."

"Me?"

"Not you you."

"What's that mean?"

"Are you this obtuse?"

"I know what 'obtuse' means. I read. And, no, I'm not oblivious or thick or clueless or however else you define the word. I'm pretty goddamn lucid if you want to know the truth."

"Richard hasn't been sober since you came around three years ago. It opened up things."

"What things?"

"Marriage things. Why do you think I came to see you in the first place?"

"To fix up your house."

"I could've hired a hundred day laborers to do that! You were missing. For a year. Wanted in connection to a murder."

"I'd think that would make me a pretty lousy hire."

"Exactly!" Alison turned away from me, reaching for the sink, bracing as if a storm were coming.

I stood motionless, clueless, oblivious, thick. I had no idea what was going on.

"I had an affair. About six years ago." She kept her back to me.

"People cheat," I said. Not me. But people.

"I fell in love with him. Richard and I never recovered. When you came around searching for the missing Crowder boy, what was going on with us—"

"What was going on with us? I helped you find a missing boy."

She turned back around, coming closer. "You didn't help *me* do anything. That was all about Jay helping Jay."

"Yeah, I'm a selfish prick. I've heard."

"You remember that night at the bar. Where you invited me? For a date." She held up a hand stopping any half-assed protests. "Can we stop this now?"

"I don't know what 'this' is to stop it."

"Want me to explain it like we're in the seventh grade? Okay, I like you, Jay. Or to be more adult, if you're going to make me spell it out, I'm attracted to you. I thought that was clear."

I ran a hand down my face, squinting one bruised eye, as if there were a frayed wire inside my head and, maybe, if I cocked that space between my ears at the right angle, I could get the connection to spark again.

"So you came to my apartment," I said, "after not seeing me in two, three years, knowing I was wanted by the police, on the run—I looked like shit—about as far from fucking sober as a man gets, because . . . what? You wanted to start a relationship with me?"

"I wanted to get laid for one! I haven't had sex in two years! And I don't know, all right? It's fucked up. Being an addict is fucked up.

I've had twenty years in recovery—you think that changes any-thing?" Alison Rodgers, the most put-together person I thought I knew, threw back her head. "I'm as fucked up as you."

I took her hand. The one comforting thing I could think to say—"No, you're not. You're not as fucked as me; I'm a goddamn wreck"—didn't feel right.

Luckily, I didn't have to say anything because soon our hands were touching, caressing, soothing, bodies moving, pressing to-gether. We pulled one another tight and started kissing, slow turning fevered, desperate. Then we were backing up the stairs, hands fumbling, kissing some more, shirts unbuttoned, pants un-zipped, clothes peeled off and flung aside, fingers feeling for lights on the wall, flicking them off as quick, and then into her bedroom, falling onto the most comfortable mattress I'd ever felt.

Wasn't till we were finished and I lay there in the dark that I real-ized I hadn't had a thing to drink since Chris' unexpected letter. Maybe that's why it felt so good.

An hour later, as Alison lay asleep, I slipped away.

I'd been driving a good ten minutes and still couldn't convince myself of what happened back there. I checked my look in the mirror. I've always been a good-looking guy. Good looking enough. Not movie star or *GQ* handsome but I held my own. The cuts were healing. I had a few thousand dollars, money I could use to get back on my feet, a drop in the palatial bucket compared to a woman like Alison. What could I offer her? Or Jenny for that matter? Two women in the span of a week. I felt like the catch of Ashton. A low-hanging fruit, sure, but I'd endured yearlong droughts before. There were stretches when I couldn't score a sympathy handy from a hooker. And those were times when I was working steady, had consistent income, my drinking under control. Right now? I didn't give a shit if I lived or died. Maybe that was the appeal. I'd always thought that the whole "women want bad boys" thing was bullshit, a manufactured stereotype conjured by rejected, dull men. Maybe there was some truth to the asshole getting the girl.

Why did I feel so lousy? I should've been smiling, happy, feeling vindicated. But I wasn't a person to Alison. I'd been a thing, and while normally, as a man, I'd relish the idea of being objectified like that, tonight there was nothing in it for me except more loneliness, which I was already drowning in.

I'd gone there for answers. Which I didn't get. I couldn't help but wonder if Alison hadn't used sex to distract me.

Coming up on my place, I was ready to flip a U, go back and ask, when I caught Turley's squad car waiting in Hank Miller's lot.

The town sheriff clomped out, stubby finger raised, chest rising with a lungful as he prepared to let me have it for embarrassing him back there in Davidson County.

"If you want to do this," I said, jumping down and slamming my door, "come upstairs. I'm not freezing my ass off. I'll put on some coffee."

"Your coffee tastes like shit."

I headed up the well, leaving the door open, Turley on my heels. I was basking in the afterglow of sex, which added an extra level of smugness. I already seemed to have a particular talent for crawling up people's asses; acting conceited wasn't helping my cause.

I lit a smoke off the stove and waited. Turley's face burned beet-red, but he didn't say anything. I figured I'd get the conversation started, hurry the process along; I had shit to do.

"Sorry, man," I said. "I didn't know what else to do. Didn't need Davidson County running my name and having last year come up to bite me on the ass."

"Last year? You mean when you were wanted *for murder*?"

"A charge I was cleared of."

"While on the run."

"Hey, first I heard of that was when I came back to Ashton."

"Save it, Porter. You give me such a fucking headache."

"I love you, too, Turley."

"Why are you smirking?"

"I'm not smirking."

"You think this is funny? I lied to law enforcement. You aren't an investigator. I'd ask what mess you've gotten yourself into this time. But I honestly don't want to know. Please promise you're going to leave Adam and Michael alone? It's three days that they are in town. Three days. Can you promise me you'll *at least* do that?"

"I'll leave them alone."

"Like I can believe a word you say."

"Then why are you asking me?"

"Why did I help you tonight? Beats me. If you are so hell-bent on ruining your life, I should just let you. I watch you flail and thrash like a maniac, and I think I can help, try to be a pal, throw a line, but with you no good deed goes unpunished."

"What do you want me to say? That I'm an asshole? Fine, I'm an asshole. Ask anyone. This guy. That guy. Her over there. The fuck-face at the Gas 'n' Go, they all know: Jay Porter is an asshole." I threw up my hands. "Makes stupid decisions. Pushes away everyone who loves him. Blows every opportunity. His own worst enemy. Guess that's why everyone hates me."

"No one hates you, Jay. That's the problem. Everyone *likes* you. Or wants to. Everyone is rooting for you. We all *want* to see you do well, turn it around. And you keep on disappointing us."

I exhaled a ring of smoke. "Turley, at some point, that's on y'all." I didn't know why I used the southern dialect. But the moment felt right. So fuck 'em. "You don't like my choices? Don't like the way I live my life? Think my coffee sucks. Then why are you here?"

"Do you listen to yourself talk? One minute you're a strutting peacock preening, the only one who knows what's going on in this town full of the imbeciles, the next you're a worthless shit, undeserving of a kind word or good break."

"The piece of shit at the center of the universe."

"Huh?"

"It's an AA expression."

Turley glanced around my one-bedroom dump, at all the empty bottles and cans. "Maybe you should go back to those meetings."

"Tell you what." I gestured at his hefty frame. "You start hitting the gym, lay off the pork sandwiches, and I'll take it under advisement."

"What are you after? What the hell is it you want?"

"The truth!"

"About what?"

"All of it! You're right. I *am* the only person around here who sees what's really going on. Because I'm the only person in Ashton who doesn't have his nose shoved up the Lombardis' ass!" I swung an arm to encapsulate this entire rotten mountain town. "Maybe I'm not the nicest guy but at least I'm not full of shit. All these people walking around, judging me, waggling a finger, they've never worn my shoes, they haven't slept on my couch. This story isn't for them. I'm going to bed. I haven't broken any law."

That last one might've been a stretch but I didn't see Turley risking the extra paperwork. "So, yeah, great seeing you, Turley. Let's never do it again too soon. Fuck you very much. Now you can kindly show yourself the fuck out."

I hadn't had many victories of late. But having sex with a pretty woman and tossing the town sheriff out on his fat ass felt all right.

Watching Turley leave through the top turret, shoulders slumped, huffing, feet slogging through the cold and snow of the parking lot below, I would've felt a whole lot better if my phone hadn't buzzed right then.

And if I didn't answer it.

CHAPTER TWENTY-FOUR

"You're a dead man, Porter."

"That's how these things usually end."

"You think I'm fucking around?"

"I don't even know who you are."

"Stay away from my wife."

"Can you narrow it down?" I lit another smoke off the stove.

"That's your game, run around with other men's wives? Think that makes you some sort of big shot?"

I might've been overselling my prowess as lover man number one on Lamentation Mountain. I'd already figured out I wasn't talking to Stephen—he was too much of a pussy to make a physical threat—which left Richard Rodgers.

"How you doing, Rich? I heard you were back in town."

"Keep laughing. See where that gets you."

"An hour ago, it got me between your wife's legs."

"Fuck you, you fucking fuck! I'll fucking kill you!"

"Dude, I've seen you, remember? You're half my size, and you can't hold your liquor. You want to get together and talk about it, I'm easy to find." I caught myself. "Wait. How did you get this number?"

"I'm sure you'd love to know."

I'd just picked up this replacement phone. The only people who had the number were my lawyer Mickey Asal, Fisher, Alison, my ex-wife. And a man named Bill who was supposed to give it to Larry Pugh.

"I'm not as stupid as you think," Richard Rodgers said. "And when you least expect it, I'll be there. How do you think this ends? Me with nothing? You with my wife? My house? Business? My life?"

"Man, for one, Alison isn't your wife. You're divorced. She doesn't want anything to do with you."

"That's what you think. Keep the bed warm for me, Porter. I'm coming for you."

He clicked off.

I'd played it cool while I had him on the line but now I was fuming, heart banging inside my rib cage, head thrumming, throat dry. How did Richard Rodgers get my number? Was I worried he'd get the best of me? Not in a fair fight. I flashed on the gun Alison said she kept in her bedroom, which brought me back to something my ninth-grade English teacher, Mrs. Virostek, once said. She was talking about some playwright. If someone mentions a gun in the play's first act, it has to go off by the third, and I couldn't remember who the writer was—and why was I thinking about Mrs. Virostek, a woman I hadn't thought about in twenty years? Why was my hand shaking? Why did I feel like I might spin off the edge of the earth?

I was having a panic attack.

I hadn't suffered one this bad since I fled the state, running to Boston, living on the lam. I was out of pills, which meant I couldn't afford to panic. Panic attacks were a privilege, a luxury. So at my worst, the hardest time of my life, I'd been forced to steel my resolve. Hammer, nails, cerebral solder.

Now I was falling apart? Sweating some mealy-mouth milquetoast like Richard Rodgers?

Checked the fridge. Out of beer. Medicine cabinet, too, though I knew it, too, would be bare.

From feeling on top of the world to feeling like a bum.

Like that.

All I could do was hold onto the rails and ride this one out. *Use the energy.*

The fire.

That smell . . .

Countless heating and oil companies operated up here. Might've been the biggest industry next to tourism and sugarbushes. Larry had been let go, and I didn't have Bill's last name. I felt like I was overlooking a vital detail, a clue, like a song whose melody you can almost hear, taunting you with its inaccessible familiarity.

The union card. At the shack. When I thought Peter Pugh was a different man. Sixteen-year-old boys don't belong to the New England Utility Contractor's Association. But their dads might.

I fired off a quick text.

Clock closing in on midnight, I would've loved to sleep. But I couldn't rest now. I dropped in a chair to wait. My body had other ideas. I must've drifted off, waking twenty minutes later when Fisher called back.

"Everything okay, Jay?"

"I'm fine. What did you find out?"

There was a long exhale, followed by a longer pause on the other end.

"What?"

"I don't want to see you go off the deep end again."

"Never been thinking clearer." I lit a smoke, tapping my toes, using the mania, which restarted the second my eyes opened. "What did you find out?"

"Tyler Oil. Larry Pugh's worked there for about three months."

"Graveyard shift?"

"That I don't know."

"What about someone named Bill?"

"There's a couple Williams, one matching your general description, but it's hard to say. Five-ten, one-eighty. How many men fit that mold? But you said Larry Pugh had been fired?"

"That's what his buddy Bill told me."

"According to the temp agency records," Fisher said, "he's still there."

"You sure?"

"All I can go on is the tax stuff, but looks that way, yeah."

Made sense Bill would cover for his friend. Larry hadn't called me like I'd asked. Maybe he didn't want to talk. Maybe Bill never told him I'd stopped by, sparing his pal the added aggravation.

"What do you know about this Larry Pugh?" Fisher asked.

"Why?"

"Dude owes a lot of child support. Big-time. The government's docking his wages. You owe that much, I'm not sure it's worth working. Ex must've had a helluva lawyer to get that kind of settlement."

"He has a kid."

"Had."

"Right. How awful is that? The answer to all your problems . . ." I hard-stopped, the oxygen sucked from my lungs and the living room.

"What is it, Porter?"

I crushed my butt. "Nothing, man," I lied. "Thinking about my son."

"Sorry. That's gotta be rough."

I thanked him for the concern. Then asked for the address to the Tyler Oil plant.

After I ended the call with Fisher, I went to the sink and filled a glass with tap water, standing at the kitchen window, watching the latest storm encroach. The winter was mauling us faster, harder than usual, with no end in sight. The answer had been standing there in front of me, in the same room, three separate times.

CHAPTER TWENTY-FIVE

THE SNOWS STARTED piling up soon as I headed south. The fine, slanting kind that lets you know the tempest has only just begun. I thought about calling ahead, to see if he indeed worked the night shift, before realizing the flaw of that plan. If he paid three winos to lie for him, the guy was already on the lookout, wary of being exposed. If he learned that someone was calling his workplace and asking about him, he'd be in the wind—which he might be already—and I would've blown my best chance.

The Tyler Oil Company plant splayed far and wide. Workers milled across the tarmac, spread beyond boiling craters, suffering fumes in the shadows of the refinery. I'd done my best to look the part, skulking in my dirty jeans and heavy work coat, wool cap draped askew. Act eager, willing to please, not too uppity, as if I bought into the bullshit that one day the meek would inherit the earth.

Hot steam escaped from grates, hissing in the cold night. I almost forgot I wasn't back out there; almost didn't remember I had a place of my own to go back to; and that no matter how gnarly my life might get from here on out I would never be forced to seek shelter at the fucking Salvation Army again. Three or four large plows cleared space, reminiscent of those nights I spent searching for my brother at the old TC Truck Stop. I had a tough time shaking these glitches in the Matrix, these unmistakable parallels; finding excuses had become harder to excuse.

Alcoholics and addicts don't get jobs like regular people. With all the temp agencies closed, I pulled my cell and found the closest outfit on the Desmond Turnpike. Just needed a name. No one would be there to answer phones and refute claims at this hour.

I walked through the main doors. After midnight, no receptionist waited. Being a refinery, the layout wasn't like a standard office anyway, more an open space with a half circle desk and an artificial tree. I wandered till I found someone who looked like they enjoyed telling people where to go.

"Work Logic sent me." It was all I had to say. There's always some shit job no one wants, some menial, backbreaking assignment for the desperate. And grinders are only too happy to chew you to the bone; when they wear you out, they just call over for another body. Chimney sweepers are, by definition, expendable.

"A little late, no?" The big man with the meaty bits in his beard checked the clock on the wall. "Spillover from the vac pump?"

I nodded. Sounded good to me. I wasn't planning on actually working.

The man refitted his hard hat, expanding the band. "It's a fuckin' mess. You fill out all your paperwork?"

"Yup."

He led me down a loud concrete hall, the sounds of machines churning and gears burning, echoing, bouncing, booming. "You ready for seven hours of repetitive labor?" He snickered.

"You bet."

"Lockers are over there. Check in with Darnell after you suit up. Can't miss him. Tattoo on his skull."

"Great. Thanks. Hey, you seen Larry?"

"Larry?"

"Pugh. Larry Pugh. He's the one who referred me from the agency."

"Out in the yard. But you don't have time to socialize. We need to get moving." The man pointed at the changing room. "Get going. Or go home."

"Yes, sir." I saluted, fuck you, and slipped past the lockers, out to the back yard, a large snow-covered lot lit by high floodlight, revealing a fleet of heavy-duty machinery, tractor-trailers, tanks, extraction and processing expellers, lined up for on-site fueling.

About half a dozen men scrambled, hooking hoses to heating systems, coolant components, overworked, overtaxed, and frantic. I spotted the man I spoke with in Room 7 at the Sunset Motor Inn, the man who called himself Bill. By now, I'd figured out Bill and Larry Pugh were one in the same.

He stood on the opposite side, by stacked pallets and gasoline tanks, the coalescence and pyrolysis machines, distillation purifiers howling above the gates to hell. He looked like he was busting ass, sweating up a storm in the frigid winds. I hadn't pegged him for a hard worker. I clocked him, waited till he peeled off behind a truck alone, and then I slipped in behind him, following between conveyors and hulls. When we were far from prying eyes, I raced up behind him. "Hey, Larry."

"What the hell?"

When he jumped back, I noticed he was favoring one foot.

"You remember me?"

He didn't answer.

"I met you at the Sunset Motor Inn." When he didn't respond, I added, "You also took a shot at me out at the Pruitt Farm before you shaved. Then later at that old lady's abandoned house where you were squatting."

"You're nuts. I have to get back to work. I'm calling security. You can't be here—"

I stepped on his foot, the same one I'd impaled with nails the other night, twisting my heel and grinding my toe. He shrieked, wail masked by the thrum and thunder of big rigs sucking gasoline. I lifted my boot and he fell on his ass. He pulled off his boot and sock, wrapping the sock around his foot like a tourniquet. The wound bled fresh as new.

"My truck is in the parking lot," I said in between his whimpering. "I'll give you five minutes to tell your supervisor you're sick and need to go home. If your ass isn't in my truck in five minutes, I call the police and tell them you started the fire at the farm. There's still a way out of this for you." I had one hand. I had to play it right.

Larry Pugh nodded, head drooping, a dog with the fight whooped out of him.

I slipped along the chain link, out to the driveway and my truck, wondering if Larry would bite. I had no doubt he'd been the man at the caretaker's quarters, the darkness and beard throwing me off. Just like I knew the fire he'd helped start would trace back to the Lombardis. The fact that his son died in the explosion should work in my favor, the guilt he had to feel over such a tragic, unexpected consequence. The question was whether he would turn on them. How much could Lombardi have paid him if he was still working the graveyard at the refinery? Whatever it was, the payday was enough to commit murder. Had I made a mistake letting him talk to his boss first? I was trying to let him hold on to his job. Why was I such a bleeding heart?

I didn't get a chance to answer any of these questions, before I saw Larry Pugh slinking out, posture slagged, the walk of a condemned and very guilty man. I read a book a while ago about analyzing faces, dissecting the lack of symmetry; how one side carries your original, natural intentions, the other side what the world has done to you. I didn't know what the world had done to Larry Pugh. But it wasn't anything good. One half of his face was salvageable; the other looked like Brundle Fly. That eye betrayed every sin, every bad break, every dead dream. What remained wasn't human; it was an abomination.

He climbed into the passenger seat. I steered out of the lot, past the tall snowy pines and onto the main road. I was planning to go back to my place, have a nice sit-down chat, where I'd explain his options: rat out the Lombardis for the fire, or take the fall himself, eat the whole bullet. I had no interest in driving Larry Pugh further into the dirt. He was already down about as low as a man could go, screwed over by a vindictive ex-wife with significantly more means. Could've been me. Basically *was* me. Minus the ex-wife. At least the vindictive part. Whatever hot water I'd landed in with Jenny was my own doing.

He started sobbing. Softly at first. Then harder, getting so worked up he couldn't catch his breath, a toddler overstimulated, smearing snot across his face with the back of his hand. Which made me start the conversation sooner than I would've liked.

"Relax, Larry," I said. "I'm not interested in jamming you up. It's not you I'm after." I still had my eye on the prize, big game hunting.

Driving in my junker pickup through the wet snow on the highway, I didn't realize what I was really doing at the time: extracting the confession of a condemned man.

"I'm sorry!" he wailed. "Jesus forgive me for what I've done."

"Give me the names of the men who hired you," I said. "Stop covering for them. We can work something out." I wasn't a judge or jury, and I didn't know what the police would do to the guy—two people died, including his son. How much more of a price could a man pay? On the one hand justice wasn't up to me. On the other, well, we could play this a lot of ways. If Larry helped me out, maybe I could do *something* for him. By all accounts, Whittaker Pruitt had been a real asshole, not that he deserved his fate, but with Larry's own child dying in the fire, a sympathetic prosecutor might catch him a break.

Larry glanced over through tear-stained eyes. "My boy . . ."

"I know," I said. I resisted the urge to pat him on the back, instead pressing foot to throat. "Name, Larry. Give me a name."

Nothing.

"I know the fire you started traces back to the Lombardi Brothers. You can stop covering for them. You think they'll protect you? Right! They'll throw you to the dogs. The brothers wanted to buy Rewrite Interventions, at all cost, to corner a market and profit off sickness, which is why Peter was at that farm. So if you're looking for someone to blame for the death of your boy, it's those two. I don't care if you supplied the fuel or helped set the fire." I knew my reasoning was shaky. I realized I was willing to overlook Larry's hand in all this, but I was *so* close. Like the cops catching a low-level dealer and spinning him up the line to nab the bigger fish. Larry wanted absolution—and if forgiveness helped me nail those two pricks to the wall, I was happy to circumvent logic and give it to him. Except Larry wasn't responding like a man grateful for the opportunity. And he wasn't falling on any grenade out of chivalry or acts of altruism.

"Who put you up to this, Larry? Answer me. How much did they pay you? Talk, you sonofabitch!"

"Whoa, slow down, man." He meant my driving.

I glanced at the speedometer and saw I was pushing fifty on a road not designed to handle half that. I didn't give a shit. I didn't slow down, back tires slipping, sliding. Larry gripped the Jesus bar as I rode the pedal harder.

"Who were you working with?!" I screamed. "Tell me! Who told you to burn down that fucking barn?" Mouth dry, hands balled into fists as I raced on a collision course with the inevitable. I knew men were capable of selfishness and evil—I was no stranger to the dark heart of man—but I didn't want to find out how evil, how black. I asked the question. But I didn't want to hear the answer.

"Who were you working for?!"

"No one," he said.

The truth doesn't always come all at once or even in a linear, tangential fashion. It gets parceled out, piecemeal, left for you to reassemble. But when it comes together, the realization doesn't hit any softer.

Keeping my left hand on the wheel, I reached over with my right and punched Larry in the face, and I kept punching as he wailed and cried. I couldn't stop, five, six, seven shots. He didn't defend himself. Didn't lift a hand. He took the beating. And I didn't stop until I'd punched myself out.

He slumped in the passenger seat, body crumpled, caved in, all the composure of a boneless chicken. He didn't bother wiping off the blood, choosing to bathe in it.

"That was your kid, man, your flesh and blood."

"She was bleeding me dry," he cried. "She didn't need that money! I couldn't afford a lawyer. You seen where I was living. I had nothing!"

"How did you know they'd blame Whittaker Pruitt?"

"My mother. She works for the Davidson County tax offices. Told me the farm owed a lot of money."

"She . . . knew?" It made sense now. The old lady at the Davidson Town Hall. A phone call placed to her son that a man was asking questions about the Pruitt property. Get out there and take care of the problem. "That was her house in Davidson County, where you ambushed me the second time, wasn't it?"

He didn't answer, sobbing as he belted out his confessional. "I never got to see my son. I didn't know Peter. I wanted to! I tried!

Mary wouldn't let me near him. Oh, she'd take my money. That was all she wanted. Money!" No wonder he worked the graveyard and had so many jobs, surviving on so little sleep. His conscience wouldn't allow any rest.

"That's how you knew I'd be at the farm," I said, talking to myself, figuring out how all the twisted pieces fit. "How did Whittaker die?"

"He tried to save Peter."

I reached over and punched him again. I felt his jaw give. I was pretty sure I'd broken bone with that blow. Larry didn't let on either way. He spat a tooth into his hand. What kind of monster does that to his own son? For nothing more than money?

"Up at the caretaker's shack," I said, "when you were pulling that Uriah Heap bullshit, what was your plan? Shoot me and then what?"

"I was going to plant Peter's driver's license on you. Make it seem like you were the man helping Whittaker." He started whimpering again. "I didn't know what else to do. I didn't know why you was coming around."

"You got the accelerant from your work." I already had the answer. "What did you do with the cans?" A professional arsonist, a competent man, would've gotten rid of the evidence. Larry Pugh was neither professional nor competent.

"Shed out back at my mother's place." Larry stopped the histrionics, calmer now, resigned that his fate was in my hands. "That was my home. Until you showed up. Why couldn't you leave me alone? I can't go back there now. Police boarded up everything, driving by all hours. I been sleeping in my car last couple nights. I don't sleep so good."

I thought about slugging him again, but what was the point? His left eye was bruised and bloodied over, sealed shut, and his jaw slung unnatural.

"Shut the fuck up, Larry."

We drove in silence along the foothills of the Lamentation Mountain range, colder air descending from the western front. I had to think, and I didn't have a lot of time left.

It's over, man. Nothing is over!

"Who are you talking to?"

"I said keep your mouth shut."

"Where you taking me?"

Without realizing I'd made up my mind, half an hour later, I arrived at my destination.

This wasn't over.

CHAPTER TWENTY-SIX

I KNOCKED FAST and didn't wait for an answer. Testing the lock, I found it open. Despite the late hour, the lights were on in her house. I wasn't sure the response I'd get after we slept together the other night, if she'd greet me with a smile or reconsider her bad decisions. I figured it was win-win. Either I get a new girlfriend out of the deal or someone who could think straight and clean up this mess.

I was so focused on Alison's reaction to me, I'd glossed over the company I was keeping, the man whose face I bashed in after he confessed to killing his own son. Alison didn't know any of this. She just saw a kicked dog, faithful to his new master.

"Oh my God, Jay," Alison said. "What happened? Was there an accident?"

"Something like that." I pulled Larry along and shoved him inside her kitchen.

Her saintly instincts took over as she raced around, fishing washcloths from drawers, running icepacks under the tap, plucking antiseptics from the cupboard. I didn't have to correct her about a car accident or explain the situation, and Larry sure as hell wasn't saying anything, a guilty conscience and fear for the future rendering him mute. In the few moments we'd been there, everything so chaotic—Alison asking questions but not waiting for answers, Larry wincing as she dabbed the wounds I'd inflicted—I hadn't seen him walk downstairs, probably from the same room where I'd had sex with his ex-wife.

"What's he doing here?" Richard Rodgers said.

I turned to Alison. "What the hell?"

"And who's that?" he snapped at Larry.

"None of your fucking business. Dick."

"I wish you had called first, Jay," she said, before turning to Larry. "Can you tell me what happened? Did you hit your head? You might have a concussion. These cuts are bad. You need to go to the hospital."

"I didn't call the other night," I said, "and we seemed to have a good time."

"What's he talking about, Alison?" Then to me: "You're talking out your ass." Back to Alison: "Tell me you didn't really sleep with him."

"Richard, calm down."

"I'm sure you'd like to know."

"Fuck you, Porter."

I'd come here to tell Alison I found the man who started the fire, the reason she'd been forced to sell her practice to those two pricks, and then she and I could sit down together, talk about how best to move forward, spin it; how we could, for instance, use the opportunity to leverage maximum benefit for not only our future, hers and mine, but this town at large, this community, the whole region, New England, fuck, America, life. She'd have to see we were all better off without such evil in this world, right? But then *he* was there, fucking everything up.

Richard Rodgers wasn't an intimidating guy. Not that he was small. But he didn't strike fear the way a Bowman or Travis or a pair of dirty cops might. He was another of the sick and suffering, but there are different kinds of sick, and too many ways to suffer to count. A little liquid confidence goes a long way, and he'd had more than a few; I could smell the sour booze from ten feet away.

"Why don't you get out of here, Porter?" he said. "I was talking to my wife."

"Ex-wife," Alison corrected, which felt like a minor victory for me, until I realized I did the same with Jenny.

"He admit killing the coyote?" I said.

"Fuck you. I didn't kill anything. I love animals."

"As much as you love the bottle?" I pretended to sniff. "Must be five o'clock somewhere—"

Richard shoved aside the bloodied Larry, who had yet to say a word, rushing past Alison, and with a Viking battle cry tackled me. We slammed into the tall glass cabinet, china dishes spilling off shelves, crashing all around. Alison screamed for us to stop. Larry Pugh cowered, hands over head.

When I had my previous run-in with Richard Rodgers, he'd been shitfaced. Tonight he had a couple in him as well, but he wasn't as incapacitated. Back then I also hadn't slept with his wife. Not saying he kicked my ass—far from it—but he wasn't the target practice he'd been last time.

We grappled, twisting and turning, knocking into shit, Alison shrieking for us to grow up. Every so often someone would land a blow but nothing too punishing, space too tight, punches too measured. Mostly we kept calling each other "cocksucker" and threatening to do more damage than either of us could do.

We'd made our way around the kitchen table, a pair of demented synchronized swimmers, until we ended up back in the vestibule. In front of the island, Richard gained some leverage, enough to turn me around, driving his shoulder into my back blades.

"Get out of my house, mutherfucker!"

I had nothing to hold onto, no way to stop his momentum. At the front door, I flailed for the bannister, gaining traction. Closing my fist around a rail, I planted my feet and slipped his grip. Clutching the back of his collar, I tossed him out the door and down the steps, face-first into the hard ice and snow.

Taking air from the top step like Mickey Rourke at the end of *The Wrestler*, I aimed to finish him, but my aim was off. I clipped Richard's back, belly-flopping on the frozen walkway, knocking the wind out of me. We both lay in the snow, gasping for air. The truce didn't last long, and soon we were entangled in a bear hug, hooking punches to ribs and kidneys, trying to knee each other's balls.

Then the gun went off.

We both rolled over. I glanced up from my knees to see Alison hoisting higher the smoking gun she'd fired. Richard and I fell back on our butts.

I pushed myself to my feet, trying to kick him as I did so, but scored a grazing shot at best.

"Jay!" Alison screamed. She set the gun down on the top rail of the bannister, descending to our level. "What is wrong with you?"

"He started it!"

"What are you, twelve?"

"A gun, Alison?" Richard's eyes bugged wide. "Are you out of your mind? How long till the cops show up?"

We were in the middle of Middlesex, which was the middle of nowhere and the home to gun-toting zealots, but sure the cops might show up. So what? Then I started thinking about his arrest the other night for drunk and disorderly conduct in Davidson County. Addicts are always in trouble with the law.

"I'm out on bail," he said.

"And whose fault is that?" she said.

Her ex-husband shook his head, grousing, motioning my way. "This is what you want?" he whined. "Like he's any better than me."

"I don't know what I want," she said. "Except for you to go."

"The devil you know, Allie . . ." With a harried panic in his eye, Richard Rodgers retreated toward the road, stumbling, backpedal-turning to clumsy-run across the high, snowy field. I hadn't seen a car out there when I drove in. Then again, I hadn't been looking.

Richard Rodgers disappeared in the dense black night, leaving Alison and me, standing there, freezing.

We stared at one another a long time, searching for meaning. Or maybe I was projecting.

"Why are you here?" she said. The question carried more weight than she could've intended.

Like ogling the young waitresses at the Olympic Diner, I felt like I'd crossed a line. My face hurt. My knuckles were sore, back wrenched. I was too old for fistfights. What *was* I doing there?

Was I here for Alison? Was I here for justice? What did I have to offer her? Then, for the most fleeting of moments, I imagined another life, one in which I wasn't driven mad by a thirst for vengeance, one where I didn't push away everyone I loved or who, worse, had been cursed to care about me. I saw a man with a wife again, a job, a child he had the right to see; a man with a chance at true happiness. I wasn't lazy. I'd busted ass my whole life, never shied from a hard day's work. I could get back to that man, the one who dreamed and fought for the good things.

I didn't have the chance to answer any of these questions before I heard a gunshot for the second time tonight.

CHAPTER TWENTY-SEVEN

ALISON AND I rushed back into kitchen where Larry Pugh lay on the floor. Blood spilled from the hole in his head like fine wine at a party on the hill. I had a decision to make. With more time, maybe I make a different call. Maybe I sleep on options, weigh immediate gratification against a lifetime of living with deception, shouldering a burden I could never unload. But Larry couldn't pay any more for his awful crime; he was dead, and there were still wicked men roaming free.

The gun lay in Larry's guilty fingers, inches from the self-inflicted wound. A pool of shellacked red shimmered with the artificial light from multiple decorative lamps.

Alison took the hand off her mouth. "What . . . just happened?"

"This is the man who'd been vandalizing your property. His name is Larry Pugh. He started the fire at the Pruitt Farm that killed two people."

"Pugh?"

I could see the wheels turning.

"Peter's . . . father? Oh my God, Jay."

"I think that's how they got to him."

"How who got to him?"

I waited for her to say it.

"Adam and Michael?"

"He confessed it all to me, Alison. They used his son's addiction, took advantage of a desperate father and paid him to burn down the farm, to force you to sell Rewrite." I pointed at his bashed-up face, harder to discern with a quarter of it missing. "I think Lombardi had been sending reminders to keep his mouth shut."

"Are you telling me Adam and Michael hired men to do that to him? He looks like he's been tortured." She bent closer, studying what was left of his face. "Why didn't you tell me the truth?"

"I tried to. But Richard was here."

Alison started pacing, hand to forehead, forehead to lips, running through contingencies: How was this going to look to local law enforcement?

"Why on Earth would you bring him *here*?"

"Why do you think? A boy died in that fire. A child. I didn't know how you wanted to handle it. I was being considerate."

Alison didn't stop pacing. Her need for consistent movement reminded me of my panic attacks, when I'd walk in circles, ad nauseum.

She plucked a dishrag, dropping to her knees to sop up the blood, before I stopped her.

"I don't think you should do that."

She glanced up, comprehending the need to preserve a crime scene as blood pooled over cool tile, a Rorschach run wild.

"What are we going to do?"

I'd already told a lie. A small lie, a necessary lie, but a lie nevertheless, one that I hoped would serve a greater justice. But it was *my* lie. I was ready to live with it, win, lose, draw; I'd take it to the grave. But I couldn't win this fight alone. And I hated drawing Alison, someone I cared about, into my deception. What choice did I have? I convinced myself it wasn't a lie. More an omission. One small omission.

A shortcut to an inevitable conclusion that would most certainly be reached had we more time. I didn't know for sure that Adam and Michael didn't hire Larry to start that fire. He could've been covering up for them. Sure he could. That scenario still made the most sense. But then the coward blew his brains out before I could get him to confess. I was connecting the dots that anyone would connect.

"Jay?"

"You're going to wait till I leave and then you're going to call the police. Tell them that Larry came to you, admitted he started the fire. That Adam and Michael hired him to commit arson."

"I can't lie to the police."

"Are you going to tell them Richard was here?" I was gambling but it was a safe bet. The way Richard fled, Alison wasn't causing him more trouble. I never implied that, were I to remain here, I might let slip Richard Rodgers' involvement. If Alison inferred that, how was I to blame?

"I don't like being threatened."

"I'm not threatening you. Stating fact. Look at my face." Richard had gotten in a couple lucky licks. "Look at Larry's. The cops will think I did that. A fight. Between him and me. Before he died. With my past, what do you think happens next? You're not just covering Richard's ass, you're covering mine."

"Who did do that to his face?"

"Lombardi's thugs." I crossed myself, the desperation of a lapsed Catholic. "On everything I hold dear. That's why he was coming here. To come clean. He knew he wasn't safe. He needed protective custody. But none of that matters now, does it?"

By her expression, mouth muckling, lip nibbling, I could see Alison coming around, before better judgment got the better of her. "No," she said. "We tell the truth. Even if that means Richard being here. That explains your face as well."

And then I shredded any chance of a future with Alison, any hope of personal happiness. Every coffin requires a final nail.

"Alison, you want to get out of here, right? Move to Colorado to be with your sister and her family? Richard and me being here muddies that situation. There'll be an investigation, maybe a trial, shit you don't want to deal with, stresses to test your resolve." I stared down at Larry. "He *confessed* to me. He set that fire." I moved closer, appealing with all my charm, speaking softer. "He committed suicide. There'll be powder marks on Larry's hands."

"Mine, too. Remember? I fired the gun in the air to break up the fight between you and my ex-husband."

"Right," I answered, surprised by how fast I could think on my feet, the finish line so close. "Because a stranger was on your property and not answering your requests to identify himself. You fired a warning shot. If they test residue, and I doubt they will, they'll be able to tell the proximity of the shooter versus the size of the entry wound. Only one man could have shot Larry: Larry. He told you why he was here. You told him not to move while you went to call the police. You left the gun out. Your bad. Larry Pugh, besieged by guilt, took his own life—which is the fucking truth. He was addicted, poor, vulnerable. The Lombardis took advantage of a desperate man. This will all check out. You need to trust me."

The truth is always the truth, even if the picture isn't always clear to the unwashed masses; even if you have to rearrange the parts into a picture they can understand. The blood on the floor had stopped flowing, the wound gummed up with bits of brain, scalp, and hair.

"You know what Adam and Michael Lombardi are capable of." I moved in closer to finish her off with the hard sell. "You told me yourself. You found out they'd been vandalizing your property—"

"Not them personally—"

"No, just people they hired. Thugs and losers, down-and-out hoodlums who needed to make a quick buck, pressured into doing their dirty work for them. That is what they do, push people around, get people killed. People like my brother. The Lombardis have operated with impunity. For years. This is your chance—our chance— to see that they pay for what they've done. And all you have to do is tell the truth."

"And what do you think? The cops are going to take my word for it? Me, the bitter woman forced to sell her business? You think that's going to be enough to bring down two of the most powerful men in the state?"

"Let me worry about that part. The truth will come out, justice will prevail. All you have to do is repeat what Larry admitted. Of his own volition. The Lombardis paid him to burn down the farm. After that? That's up to the police to prove. But at the very least they should hear a dying man's confession. Right? And as soon as the police learn I was involved? Given my history with them? Forget it. No one will touch the case."

"They'll figure it out. The police aren't stupid."

"All you have to do is phone it in." I glanced down at Larry's body, growing stiff in the pale moonlight, increasingly confident my plan would work. "But you need to make up your mind. Fast. The coroner will be able to pinpoint the exact time of death. You've already waited too long. If you don't call it in soon, it's going to look suspicious. What's it going to be?"

CHAPTER TWENTY-EIGHT

As I FLED Middlesex via its one road, I passed the squad cars speeding to the crime scene. I didn't have a lot of time. But I had some of it, all the pieces fitting perfectly. So perfectly in fact I started worrying if I was getting too sure of myself, cocky, overlooking the obvious, walking into a trap. My whole life I'd had nothing but rotten luck. Get a little money saved, and my tranny drops. Like clockwork. Maybe God, the Universe, had taken notice, recognized the perpetual short change and was paying restitution. Someone was, like, "Hey, that Jay Porter guy. He's not so bad. He's got good intentions. I mean, he tries really hard. Let's lend him a hand." First the Hanratty money. Now this. Things were looking up for me. The plan didn't come without risks. But they were risks I was willing to take.

The cops might talk to someone at Tyler Oil, and maybe someone mentions seeing a man matching my general description asking questions, skipping out on a nonexistent assignment. But that worked in my favor, too. There was nothing so otherworldly unique about my physicality that I stood out; I was an everyman. And they wouldn't go to his job. Not if I redirected the search.

That was all I needed. A push, a nudge, a reason for authorities to poke around. After Alison repeated Larry's claims he'd set the fire and been beaten by Lombardi thugs, I didn't have to prove anything in a court of law. Adam and Michael were too goddamn slippery to convict anyway, but the court of public opinion? That was a different burden of proof.

I'd never tell a soul.

Passing the old house on Payne Street, I parked well down the block, steering my junker into the woods, under cover and out of sight. Sneaking around the edge of the property, I kept my eyes peeled for the swirling reds and blues, ears pricked for sirens signaling the end. All I saw was white. The only sound, my own labored breath and the rattle in my lungs.

At the tool shed, I smashed the tumbler with a rock, and grabbed what I'd come for. The snow kept falling, covering my tracks.

Back in Ashton, I found the old Lombardi homestead on Elton Drive. Hadn't changed since my brother's wrestling days. All the lights were off. I should've been nervous or worried, but I was strangely serene. I think part of it was because I didn't give a shit if I got caught.

Picking locks isn't like in the movies. You don't need two hairpins and a stethoscope. At least not for one of these old New England farmhouses, most of which were built in the 1700s. But I didn't need to get in the main house, which might have had an alarm anyway. I only had to find a reasonable hiding spot. If I couldn't get into the garage, I'd stash them in the back of a truck, by the garbage bins, hide them amidst old paint cans. Anywhere partially concealed would do. I spotted a stump and an ax, a place to chop firewood at the far end of the property. A wheelbarrow was flipped upside down.

Last thing I had to do was find a pay phone. Might've been the toughest part of the mission. The closet working pay phone I knew of was at a diner in Chevreport.

I placed an anonymous tip to the Davidson County Police and told them where to find the kerosene cans that started the Pruitt Farm fire.

Then I waited.

* * *

Thanksgiving came and went. I spent the holiday alone. I thought about going to the Price Chopper and picking up a Cornish game hen, making the saddest Thanksgiving dinner for one in the history of bachelorhood. Instead I grabbed prepackaged meats I could reheat in the microwave.

I considered calling Alison, to see what happened after I left, but that might make her suspicious, the last thing I wanted. Best if there were no phone records anyway.

The December snows arrived, and I began the slow process of putting my life back together while I waited for news from somewhere, the TV, Internet, newspaper. Nothing came. After a while I stopped worrying about it. The Bruins went on a winning streak.

The Hanratty money was more than enough to get me back on my feet. With a two-week onslaught of storms, I did most of my business from the comfort of my living room, contacting small warehouses to rent, storefronts that I knew sat vacant. I settled on the old Ashton Pharmacy building, a space half the size of my last place. Since the Walgreen's and CVS invasion, the onslaught of chain retail's stranglehold on pharmaceuticals, the Mom-and-Pop scene was dead; and I got the lease on Farmington Avenue for a song and dance. I reached out to old associates from the antiques game. A few guys acted surprised to hear from me, a couple brazen enough to ask about the legal shit. Most had the tact to get right down to brass tacks: the insider's scoop on upcoming auctions. I slated a full docket through the New Year. Next up: working with my ex-wife to see my boy again.

Being so busy, I didn't have much time for drinking. Not saying I went cold turkey or even tried to cut back. More like a great weight had been lifted, and I wasn't so geared up, aggravated, angry. I didn't have the time or desire. I was done. I'd played my part. The rest wasn't up to me.

When there were breaks in the storm, I hit a couple AA meetings. I hadn't been back to the rooms since my girlfriend overdosed last year. I thought returning would sting, make me miss her all over again. But I found a strange comfort in those rooms. I didn't consider myself an alcoholic—I drank beer, big deal; this is America, who doesn't?—but I enjoyed being around a community again, not feeling alone, not feeling like such a fuckup on a planet of one. I surrendered individuality. Sure, I was unique. Like everyone else. Plus, I figured, when my ex-wife and I began renegotiating visitation rights in earnest, having a record of regular attendance couldn't hurt.

Alison never called me. I never called her. I'd seen nothing in the paper about Larry Pugh's suicide or the Lombardis. When almost a month passed and the police still hadn't shown up at my door, I didn't feel disappointed; I felt relieved. I realized how shortsighted my plan had been to begin with. Didn't make a difference what Alison told the cops. As soon as those kerosene cans were discovered, Adam and Michael, state senator, would rail about a setup, and who was the most logical suspect? The guy who'd been harassing them for the past several years. Following this chain of thought, they'd press Alison, who wouldn't be able to hold out, and then they'd go to Turley; and with my working for Alison and poking around the Pruitt fire, the crusade ends in an unceremonious whimper, if not criminal charges against me. I stopped hoping to see the Lombardis go up in flames, content that my own ass wasn't getting burned. I was lucky that my impetuous, spur-of-the-moment decision hadn't blown up in my goddamn face.

* * *

Tuesday night, little before five, couple days before Christmas, I was boiling water for pasta. Add butter, salt, pepper, grated cheese, the dinner of champions. My phone buzzed. Fisher.

"You watching the news?"

"No, I'm cooking—"

"Turn on Channel 5. Now."

I flicked on the news. They were in the middle of the report.

". . . Lombardi lawyers denied on Monday all charges brought against Michael Lombardi and questioned the legitimacy of the indictment in a massive corruption scandal that has ensnared the state senator. According to unnamed sources, information on the confiscated computers trace to offshore Cayman Island accounts, providing a clear, uninterrupted line to the alleged bribery. With these charges, prosecutors have successfully unsealed court documents they say tie Lombardi Construction to the Disposal Solutions contract. As you'll recall, Adam Lombardi sold Lombardi Construction three years ago to join his older brother's campaign. The forty-nine-year-old state senator was arrested yesterday on charges of bribery and embezzlement following the raid on his Concord office last week. Michael Lombardi is represented by the law firm of Deal and Carlson. Both prosecutors and Lombardi have high stakes in the case. The court must issue its ruling by the end of December . . ."

"Damn," I said.

"I thought you'd be happier."

"I am happy. A little shocked is all."

"Why? We've known they were crooks for a long time."

"It's not what you know. It's what you can prove." I scratched my head. "What exactly are they charging him with?" I didn't recall hearing anything about a fire or the Rewrite Interventions sale, just a lot of mumbo jumbo crammed in between ten-cent words.

"Bribery, for the most part. Bidding collusion. They are contending Adam, with Michael's blessing, helped secure a state contract for a family friend's business."

"What business?"

"Waste management. Disposal Solutions. Rest stops off the highway."

"Wait. So nothing about the fire? The toxic soil?"

"I haven't read anything about the fire or soil. But the Feds confiscated every computer in Michael's office. Dude is *fucked*. I'm sure there'll be more charges. This is just the tip, bro." Fisher stopped. "You were right, Jay. You were right about all of it. Remember that reporter at the *Monitor*? During that kids-for-cash crap?"

"Jim Case."

"He has a scathing piece in today's online edition, tearing Michael Lombardi a new butthole for his role in the state's opioid crisis, how it's a conflict of interest to have a hand in the CCC and be taking that Century Cures Act money. I thought you'd have seen it by now. It's everywhere. Check the Internet. Their regime is crumpling. Adam is scrambling. He's lawyered up. And Michael, well . . ."

"Well what?"

"He's done. His political career is finished, bro. Never mind a run at governor. There are already calls for him to step down from the state senate. By the time this is over, Michael Lombardi will be lucky to be stacking shelves at Radio Shack." Fisher laughed. "You did it, Jay."

"I didn't do anything." This wasn't about the fire. This wasn't about toxic soil. This barely touched their rehab, any mention peripheral fallout. This had nothing to do with me. "All my efforts failed, man. This is . . . luck."

"You might not get the credit, but you were the one guy who believed. I lost faith. We all lost faith. But not you, Porter. And you were right, man." Fisher howled with joy. "You were right."

* * *

By Christmas Day, Michael Lombardi's campaign was reeling from the fallout and feeling the irrefutable effects. His approval ratings plummeted to the lowest they'd ever been. By week's end, he'd announced his resignation.

I scoured every news source, print, television, the web; there was nothing about the fire, nothing about the tainted soil. Far as I could tell, the stars had simply lined up. Lombardi was being wrung up over something totally different, a kickback case involving people I'd never heard of, a contract to handle garbage off the freeway. The timing, one, big coincidence. Which reminded me of the first rule I learned playing amateur detective: in the world of investigation, there's no such thing.

While I watched this unfold over those first few winter weeks, there were moments—not many, but a couple, here and there— where I'd wonder if what I'd done was wrong. According to Larry, he'd set the fire by himself. Sometimes I'd convince myself he'd lied to cover up for Adam and Michael—in fear for his life, to make more money—but I had no proof. I'd lied. I'd circumvented due process, committed one small crime to expose ones far worse. Surely the end justified the means?

After he stepped down from the state senate, Michael Lombardi held a press conference. All the local stations carried it live. Michael stood up there, alone. No family. No brother. No bodyguards or entourage flanking him. He looked smaller than I remembered, suit ill-fitting and falling off his frame, like sluiced meats dripping from slow-cooked bone. The man I'd known as arrogant, brash, cocky, smug, indefatigable cowered at the lectern, possessing none of those qualities. And as I listened to his voice quaver, watched the crocodile tears splat the speech someone else had written for him, I had a tough time not reveling in his misery.

I'll admit the suicide was shocking, but he knew the end was coming, and like all bullies, Michael Lombardi was a coward at heart. It was a matter of time, and by the time Michael Lombardi hooked up the garden hose to the tailpipe, more indictments were pouring in by the day, exposing years of corruption and malfeasance; prison time was no longer a question of if but when and for how long. Despite all this, the state mourned his death as a tragedy. Far as I was concerned, Michael Lombardi was no better than Larry Pugh, shit on the bottom of a boot, unworthy of being scraped off, save for the stink.

For his part, Adam didn't go so easily. He fought like a cornered, rabid 'coon, railing of a setup, and at one point I might've been an obvious suspect. But after the government confiscated those computers, every dirty deed dating back decades had been exposed, and I wasn't the only enemy Adam and Michael Lombardi had made over the years. We're talking price fixing, collusion, assault and battery, their years in the construction racket steeped in illegal dealings. I was but an insignificant gnat.

Still, I braced for a visit from Turley and the authorities, requests to turn over my computer. I'd already had Fisher scrub anything incriminating—why take the risk? But really, what was there? Chats. Searches. Long threads detailing what crooked douches Adam and Michael were, which, by the way, turned out to be true. I never said anything about Larry Pugh's confession, nothing about the evidence I planted. January came and went. Turley never did.

With the turning of the calendar, I lost any fear that Adam might retaliate. His entire world was crashing all around him; he didn't have time for petty payback. I read with great delight about his wife leaving him, the mounting legal bills. With his high-powered brother dead, Adam had lost impunity, his political safety net gone.

During this time, I lamented the loss of my own brother, regretting he couldn't be here to enjoy this. We'd started the fight together. I was ending it alone.

Michael got what he deserved. Adam was getting his, too. The Lombardi name was ruined.

My brother's death had been avenged.

So why did I feel so unsatisfied?

CHAPTER TWENTY-NINE

MICKEY ASAL CALLED a week later to tell me I could see my boy again. In another two weeks. Mickey cautioned me about what to expect. After my outburst, given my history, I'd be starting with supervised visits in a neutral location. Do that right for a few months, he said, no bumps in the road or unforeseen problems, show up when I was supposed to, stay calm, I could petition the courts for more. But it was going to take time. The best deal he could get. I wasn't in position to call shots.

All I had left was work.

I'd gotten a house to clear on Worthington Ridge, the best section of Ashton, many of the homes chock-full of hidden gems, Revolutionary War relics, mid-century artifacts, a New England treasure trove for a rag and bone man like me. The old gablefront yielded a veritable gold mine. Sheet music cabinet. Hooked rug and yo-yo quilt. Some old Harvard and Yale football programs. Dining chairs from the early 1900s. I crammed everything I could fit into the back of my truck, and then ducked inside the garage to see what else I could plunder and profit on.

On my way back through the kitchen, I tripped over the extension cord, smacking a wall. An old, rusty hook poked my thigh, tearing through my dirty jeans and long johns, catching enough skin to scratch blood. I went to the sink, hoping not to spend another night at the ER getting a retroactive tetanus shot. I'd unbuckled and was starting to drop my pants to inspect the damage when I heard footsteps creeping up the steps behind me.

I hadn't seen Alison Rodgers since the night Larry Pugh killed himself, the night we set in motion, via one little lie, the machinations to destroy an empire.

I didn't employ a secretary, was an outfit of one. I hadn't told anyone I'd be at the house on Worthington Ridge. Who would I tell? I didn't have any friends. I had no idea how Alison knew I'd be there. Maybe I'd mentioned it to Hank? I couldn't remember. What did I care how she found me? She had. And she looked beautiful. I let myself return to greener pastures, fleeting moments and different paths where happiness prevailed over baser instincts. Then, like an ember fanned by dangerous winds, hope drifted away, out of reach.

"Hello, Jay," she said, framed in the doorway of the old farmhouse. "Didn't mean to interrupt anything."

I buttoned back up. "Cut myself on a nail. Was about to wash the wound."

"Don't let me stop you." She forced a smile, a last playful attempt at flirtation. The effort felt perfunctory, a routine born of obligation.

"It's good to see you," I said. "I've wanted to call."

"I have, too." Alison glanced around the threadbare house I was scavenging. "I see you're back to doing what you do."

"I love junk. What can I say?"

"Giving up the exciting world of private investigation?"

I didn't answer.

"I guess it was never about that though, was it?"

She didn't need to spell it out. The last seven years of my life hadn't been about exposing old man creepers or freeing the innocent; never was about locating missing kids or protecting the abused. I wasn't on a mission for environmental justice, and I hadn't set out to solve the mystery of who started a fire and killed a teenage boy. I wanted to pay back the hurt.

"I came to say goodbye," Alison said, nodding over her shoulder. "Car's packed. Heading to my sister's in Colorado."

"I thought that was the spring." I stepped closer, near enough to smell the sweet creams she used to stay so young and beautiful.

"I don't need to be here to sell the house. That's what real estate agents are for."

"Well, stay in touch. Have a nice trip."

"I'm not an idiot, Jay."

"I never thought you were."

"Enough time and I could figure it out."

I started to say something, but she held up a hand.

"Please," she said. "At least don't insult me by lying more, okay?"

I pulled my cigarettes, struck a match, hands steady and cool.

"Maybe you were right," she said. "Maybe it's best to handle some things on your own. Some men the law can't touch." She paused, certain she had my eye. "I liked you."

"I like you, too."

"I hope it was worth it."

"Alison . . ."

"Take care of yourself, Jay Porter. I hope you get everything you deserve."

She exited through the swirling snows.

She didn't look back again.

* * *

I remained at the house long after dark, long after I was finished. I walked around the old, abandoned rooms, checking cracks and crevices I'd already scoured. Delaying. And I knew why. I couldn't head back to my place and face being alone. I couldn't stop thinking about Alison's visit and what I'd done. Like a parasite worming the gray. Drove me nuts. There I was, on the precipice of something good, maybe great—back on my feet, ready to build up Everything Under the Sun into one of the biggest liquidators in the state. Owen Eaton was dead, and with it my chief competition. Circumstances surrounding Eaton's death were tragic, but how was that my fault? The playing field was wide open. Yet, there I was, fighting that little fucker in my mind who kept telling me I didn't deserve any of these good things. What had I done that was so awful? Michael Lombardi didn't kill himself because I planted those fuel cans. The Feds had already been investigating him and his shitbag brother. For years. I had no reason to feel guilty. And if those cans *did* start the wheel rolling, so what? If my decision to take the law into my own hands was, technically, breaking the law, didn't the greater good warrant the circumvention? The government came after the brothers because the Lombardis were bad people. Bad things happen to good people. But bad things can happen to bad people, too.

Regardless of the pep talk I gave myself in that bone-chewing cold, I couldn't deal with the uncertainty. Had my little lie started all this? I had to know.

On a raw February eve, I drove to the Ashton PD, flurries lazing through streetlights, a picturesque snow globe disturbed. This was where it all began. One snowy night seven years ago when I was summoned by police to pick up my drug addict big brother because Chris had been arrested and was rambling about a townwide conspiracy. I didn't believe him until it was too late. Strange how our relationship improved after he died, the conversations in my head keeping me company. I hadn't heard his voice since the Lombardis were arrested. I missed it.

"How are you, Jay?" Claire, the receptionist, said, as I stepped in out of the cold. "How's Aiden?"

"Getting big."

"Almost what? Eight?"

"In April. Turley in?"

She thumbed behind her. "His office."

I waited for directions. All the times I'd been to the Ashton precinct, I'd never been in Turley's office. When I was picking up Chris, Pat Sumner was the sheriff. I'd never been in his office either. I always talked to the cops in Interrogation Room One. Then when I started being the fuckup, I was brought into that same room, only this time as the suspect. I wasn't wanted for anything now. No one wanted to talk to me. I was the one seeking answers.

"Down the hall," she said, "past the coffee machine."

Turley didn't seem surprised to see me. He didn't seem all that pleased, either. He had spectacles perched on the end of his nose. He looked so much older than I remembered from just a couple months ago. I noted the wisps of gray creeping in around the temples, the crow's feet scratching deeper.

"What can I do for you, Jay?" Turley set down the book he was reading. A procedural manual of some kind; I didn't catch the title.

"I've never seen your office."

"Yeah, well, this is it. Have a seat. What'd you want to talk about?"

"The Lombardis."

Turley pushed himself up and walked around me, closing the door.

On the drive over, I hadn't formulated any specific question. I wasn't confessing shit—just being here bordered on dumb. I'd been hoping the topic might come about organically, elephants in the room and all that. But Turley wasn't giving me anything. He'd exuded hostility since I walked in. On the one hand, I couldn't blame him. I'd caused him a lot of grief during my relentless war with the brothers. On the other hand, I'd been proven right. So fuck him.

"What do you know about the charges against Michael and Adam?" I said.

Turley shrugged, smearing a fat finger on the desk blotter, squashing a nonexistent bug. "You have access to the same TV stations and newspapers I do. Sure you've read about it. Feds raided Michael's office, had a warrant to confiscate computers. Then the charges came." He picked up a pencil, tapping it on his desk, big bounces off a bright pink pearl eraser. "Not sure what you're asking."

"You're a cop. I thought maybe you had information the press didn't."

Turley cracked a grin, well, more a sneer. "Careful what you wish for, eh?"

"Michael and Adam are bad people."

"Were. Michael sat in the garage with the car running and doors down."

"You want me to feel bad? Because I don't."

"I don't want you to feel anything."

"I don't care that Michael's guilty conscious got to him. He was an asshole. So's his brother. I've been saying it for years. No one in this fucking town believed me. Crooks, liars, weasels, murderers, kiddie fuckers. That whole family is poison. Father, sons, garbage. They are getting what they deserve."

"Is that why you came down here? To gloat?"

"I don't have an agenda."

"Then why are you in my office? Nobody sent for you." He laughed. "Most of the times I *did* send for you, a patrol car would have to chase you down to drag you in."

Neither of us said anything for a couple.

Then Turley's face broke into a wide grin. He slapped a palm on the table and leaned back in his big chair, relaxed and pleased with himself, a carnival barker minus the sloppy chewed cigar. "Want to hear a story, Jay?"

"Sure, Turley."

"While you were gone, I was out on patrol, driving around. Summertime. Those couple glorious months where shit actually grows around here and you can cruise in a short-sleeved shirt and shades, enjoy a refreshing breeze, an ice cream cone from the Dairy Queen on Main. I get a call from a tractor-trailer driver. Just passed this dipshit smoking crack in the front seat of his car on the Turnpike. Two girls with him. Blazing the pipe. Middle of the day. Truck driver can see everything they're doing 'cause the cab is so much higher."

"What's this got to do with me?"

"Hold on. So I head out to the Turnpike. Have the description of the car. Maroon rust bucket. I slip behind them, follow." He nodded through the wall. "Not far. Out past the crane in Duncan Pond."

"I know the spot—"

"Now the thing with being a police officer, I can't just pull over a car. Need something called probable cause."

"You have a truck driver who saw them smoking crack. Driving under the influence. Reckless endangerment."

"And a public defender has that tossed as hearsay. This asshole is jeopardizing families' safety on the freeway, running the risk of killing someone. But I have rules I have to play by. That's what the law is, Jay: a set of rules that we all have to follow. Even if we think we know better. Even if we feel—we *know*—that taking a shortcut, breaking the rules, playing by our own might speed up the process, help in the long run, be a *good* thing, we still have to play by the rules. Otherwise we are no better than the criminals we chase." Turley leaned back, a cat satisfied with a bucketload of fried canary.

I fit my knit cap and stood up. "Thanks for the story." Asshole. I thumbed out the door. "I better get going. Got to get up for work tomorrow."

"You do that."

At the door, I turned over my shoulder. "What happened with the crackhead driving the car? You pull him over for having an air freshener hanging from the mirror and obstructing his view? Or was a taillight out?"

"Didn't have to pull him over. Once I got behind him, he steered to the shoulder before I got a chance to turn on the lights." Turley picked up his book again. "Guilty conscience, I guess." He slipped the glasses back on, nose in the book. "You have a nice night."

CHAPTER THIRTY

THE VISITATION TOOK place on a cold, late February day. So
many calls back and forth, lines drawn in the sand, negotiations,
rules of engagement, it made me sick. Aiden was *my* son. And here
I was having to work out the details for the right to be in the same
room with him, overseen by some state worker who didn't know
shit about me, my freedoms surrendered without a say. There were
things I wasn't allowed to talk about, subjects I wasn't allowed to
broach, like anything to do with Jenny's husband or my
mother-in-law, and like a rube I agreed. I hadn't seen my boy in almost three months. Last year had been three times that long; this
felt so much worse. Like certain stretches of road can make a trip
seem longer because they are so dull, so lifeless, these months
spanned a lifetime.

Half an hour. Timed, supervised, graded, evaluated. Rules and
regulations.

"Sorry," Mickey Asal said, "this is where you start. You're in the
system now, and there is only one way to deal with a bureaucracy."

"What's that?"

"Find out what the rules are and follow them."

I arrived at the Chuck E. Cheese in Pittsfield an hour early, sitting in a booth and observing the craziness. Screeching five-year-olds

ran wild, harried dads and frazzled moms trying to reel them in. I sat with envy. These parents didn't know how good they had it.

The weekend crowd frenzied, noise level on overload, freaky animatronics banging on drums, the swirls and whirls of assorted games hitting jackpots. I wondered if I should've suggested a better meeting place, a quieter spot, but I'd brought Aiden here so many times over the years, Chuck E. Cheese was our special hangout, our "boy time" as Aiden called it. We'd get a large pepperoni pizza and pitcher of Coke, and I'd let him play games until he won whatever he wanted, and I'd look down at him and think, "There it is, Jay. Irrefutable proof you've done something good with your life." No matter how awful this life got, I had my boy; they couldn't take that away from me.

I watched that front door as if it contained the secrets to the universe. Soon Aiden would see me. He'd burst through with squeals of "Daddy! Daddy!" And when he jumped in my arms and I could smell his hair and touch his skin again, all would be right with the world and me.

Jenny arrived with my son. She saw me but didn't come in, choosing instead to wait on the ice-slicked walkway in the cold. Aiden clung to his mother's side and wouldn't meet my eye, no matter how big I smiled or frantic I waved. I made to get up and go to them but something told me to stay put. I stopped trying to catch their attention and studied my family encased behind glass.

A few moments later, the social worker, a big lady with the bemused look of an overworked cashier, showed up. She said something to my wife, and Jenny nodded. She and Aiden still wouldn't look at me. The social worker barged in, bulling my way. She toted a big brown satchel.

"Mr. Porter," she said, but didn't offer a hand.

"Yeah, nice to meet you, too. Can I see my son?"

"First we have to establish a few ground rules."

"I know. The stuff I can't talk about, Jenny's husband and all that."

"You have a history of violence, Mr. Porter, which is why I am here. There are guidelines, rules of conduct. Failure to comply with these rules will result in the termination of this meeting."

"Excuse me? Who the hell are you?"

"I am the only way you see your child. And I suggest you watch your language and keep your temper in check because as soon as I say this visitation is over, we are done here. Think of today as a trial and me the judge. Listen to my instructions. Obey them. Do not get on my bad side." She patted her satchel. "I am here to observe the interaction, report back on what I see and whether or not I believe the exchange to be healthy. My only concern is the welfare of Aiden. I am not here on your behalf. Are we clear?"

A part of me—a huge part of me—prepared to rage, my anxiety levels through the roof. This was *my* son, *my* flesh and blood. Who the fuck did this woman, with her dumpy blazer, frizzy hair, and hangdog face, think she was? Instead I took a deep breath and held my hands in a truce. "Sorry," I said. "Whatever you need."

The social worker, Ms. Johnson, laid out what would happen next. In a couple minutes, Jenny would bring in my boy. I was not to engage my wife. We'd sit at a booth. I'd get one half hour with my son. If at any point my son showed signs of distress or feeling unsafe, Ms. Johnson would terminate the meeting. There were other stipulations, but I stopped listening, staring past her shoulder until her mouth stopped moving.

As I stood there listening to her squawk, wondering how it had come to this, I reminded myself this was penance, and the lapsed Catholic in me understood. Like my lawyer said: find out what the rules are and follow them. I didn't have to believe in the sanctity of the Division of Children, Youth and Families. I had to play the game. Any moment now, I'd see my boy, hold him close, and all this hurt and anger and bullshit would go away.

When she was finished, Ms. Johnson waved my family in, and Jenny brought Aiden over. I tried to catch my ex-wife's eye—nobody was going to tell me I couldn't say hello to Jenny Price—but she gave me nothing, not even a phony smile.

"It's good to see you, Jenny—"

"You are here to see Aiden," Ms. Johnson reminded me. I backed off. I'd have plenty of time to mend fences with Jenny later.

"I'll be back in half an hour," Jenny said to Ms. Johnson.

Then my ex-wife made for the exit without so much as a head bob in my general direction.

Fine. Whatever. Be that way. I had my boy back. A half hour was a half hour, supervised or not. Thirty minutes was heaven.

Except when Jenny left, Aiden didn't squeal "Daddy! Daddy!" and he didn't jump in my arms. He refused to meet my eye, sticking close to Ms. Johnson's side, as if I were the stranger.

We sat in the booth and I ordered a pepperoni pizza and pitcher of Coke.

Waiting for the pizza to come, I tried to talk to my son. I told him how much I'd missed him and how hard these past few months had been without him. I assured him everything was going to be all right now, I was back, I was his dad, and nothing would keep us apart again. I asked him about school and friends but he didn't answer with more than a quiet yes or no, uninterested in any subject. So I told him about my job, how I was back to estate clearing and going to make some real money this time, and maybe I could take him on a vacation, camping or something, just the two of us. Maybe even Disney World. Aiden nodded but his expression said he'd rather be anywhere else. Jenny swore she'd never turn my boy against me. I didn't know what was being said about me at home, if anybody was bothering with my side of the story, but one thing was clear: they'd turned my boy against me.

Ms. Johnson's presence didn't help, her sitting there, silent, jotting notes in her little book, passing judgment. How was my son supposed to feel comfortable in that situation? Either way, Aiden wouldn't talk. Not about friends, not about drawings he'd made or cartoons he'd watched or new toys he got from Santa.

"I have your Christmas present in my truck." Being banned from having any contact included sending a Christmas gift. I'd bought him a brand-new robot dinosaur. Remote controlled, like a hundred bucks. "Want to guess what it is?" I asked.

Aiden shrugged.

"Come on," I said, "guess."

"Mr. Porter, please don't antagonize him."

I wanted to scream, drive my fist through a wall, tell this asshole lady to fuck off, but of course I didn't.

"Okay," I said to my son. "I'll give you a hint." I leaned in, whispering, "It's a dinosaur."

"I'm not into dinosaurs anymore."

Ms. Johnson looked at her fancy iPhone. "Your half hour is up, Mr. Porter."

"But the pizza hasn't come yet." I could see the clock on the wall. I still had a few minutes left. "At least let me get the Christmas present from my truck."

"Next time," Ms. Johnson said, ushering Aiden out of the booth.

I saw Jenny standing at the entrance.

When they got to the door, Jenny whispered something in Aiden's ear. He broke free and ran back to give me a quick hug around my waist, turning his head when he did so, before returning to his mother.

I watched the three of them leave the restaurant, walking through the snowy parking lot, as the server arrived with the pizza.

* * *

On my way back to my town, I stopped at the grocery store for beer and cigarettes. I also picked up a copy of the *Ashton Herald*. The whole of the valley spread before me, one long open road. I considered driving up to Echo Lake, park by the bridge, crack a tall boy and listen to some music. Maybe Springsteen. Felt like a Springsteen day. Most of them were. But it was getting late and dark clouds threatened the horizon. My one-bedroom above a filling station hardly filled me with hope. But I couldn't get up for sitting in a dirty cab, waiting for roads to close.

The apartment was cold and dim. I popped the top on a beer, put the rest in the fridge, and lit a cigarette off the stove. The short days of winter swallowed the sun. Heavy cloud cover blotted the towering rocky peaks. I didn't bother turning on the lights. Bringing the paper with me into the living room, I sat by the window. There was enough natural gray to read the headline. Which was the only part I cared about.

Adam Lombardi Pleads Guilty, Faces Up To 25 Years In Prison

Details, a bunch of words that didn't mean shit to me, splayed below. Fraudulent intent. Mechanic liens. Larceny. Money laundering. I knew the definition of these words and terms, I wasn't stupid, but I didn't care about particulars or specific charges. All that mattered: Adam Lombardi was going to prison for a long, long time. He'd lost everything he loved and held dear, his money, his family, his reputation. Now they were taking away the only thing he had left: time.

Sinking in my chair, I kicked up my feet and watched shadows dance on the wall. Day surrendered to night. The room went dark. A shrill, hollow wind rustled bare branches on the trees outside my window, and with the loss of light, Lamentation seemed to rise, creep closer, asphyxiation by degrees.

I raised a toast to old ghosts.

"I win," I said to no one.